$\mathscr{L}$UCY

Books by Vicky Adin

The Cornish Knot
Portrait of a Man

Brigid The Girl from County Clare
Gwenna The Welsh Confectioner
The Costumier's Gift

The Disenchanted Soldier

The Art of Secrets
Elinor
Lucy

THE ART OF SECRETS Book 3

LUCY

VICKY ADIN

Also available for Kindle.

A catalogue record for this book is available from the National Library of New Zealand.

Produced for Vicky Adin by AM Publishing New Zealand
www.ampublishingnz.com

Cover Background Image: Bev Robitai

To order copies of Vicky Adin's print books:
www.vickyadin.co.nz, www.amazon.com

Ebooks available from www.amazon.com

For the generations of women who fought
for what they believed in

Organisations & Acronyms

The Women's Christian Temperance Union, WCTU and
WCTU NZ (1885–present)

The Women's Franchise League of New Zealand, WFLNZ
(1892–1894) with branches referred to simply as Auckland,
AWFL or Dunedin, DWFL.
It reformed as **The Auckland Women's Political League**,
AWPL (1894–1925) until it became part of the Labour
Party.

The National Council of Women, NCW (now NCWNZ)
(1896–present)

The National Organisation of Women, NOW (1972–1999)

**The Women's International League for Peace and
Freedo**m, WILPF (now WILPF Aotearoa) (1915–present)

The Society for the Protection of Women and Children,
SPWC (1893–1955) renamed **New Zealand Federation of
Home and Family Societies,** and still going strong.

Characters

1892–93

Lucy Young – 21 years old, ardent suffragist and humanitarian
Aloysius Young – Importer, widower, father of Lucy
Mrs Adams – Lucy's confidante
Mrs Bush – The Youngs' housekeeper
Richard Harris – Lucy's fiancé
Harry Harris – His father, a retailer (Mrs Harris and Grandma Stone)

Milly – Lucy's best friend
Hope Willoughby – Another friend

Amey Daldy – Historic figure, president of WCTU and Auckland
　　　　　Women's Franchise League

2022

Emma Grainger – Genealogist and story-writer
Luke – Her husband, a publisher
Rose – Their 10-year-old daughter
Jess – Emma's best friend, a florist
Olivia – Livvy, Jess's daughter and Rose's best friend

Paige Frazer – 19-year-old student and climate activist
David Frazer – Her businessman father
Cameron – Her brother, works in their father's business
Ryan – Paige's surfie-looking boyfriend, an environmental scientist

1

A new client

Auckland
March 2022

"To conclude, throughout history women have suffered from gender inequality, enforced poverty and bigotry. Many still do. But by studying our past, we can better understand how the imbalance of power created such prejudices, and how our women ancestors fought for their rights. Rights *we* should never take for granted and should continue to fight for, even today. Thank you for listening."

Emma stepped down from the podium to lively applause and slipped her mask back on, still fearful of the virus that had left her feeling washed out nearly six weeks on.

Her blonde bob tossed back and forth as she accepted the words of congratulations for her presentation on family history research, hoping something she'd said would resonate with these young sociology students.

From the corner of her eye, she spotted her husband Luke at the back of the lecture theatre. *What's he doing here?*

"Excuse me, Mrs Grainger," said a tentative voice beside her as she collected her things. "Could I ask you something?"

"Of course, but please call me Emma." She turned her pale blue eyes towards the young woman.

Keen eyes peeped over a colourful orange face mask. "What you said just now about women's stories being an essential part of family history. Why do you think they matter so much?"

Emma studied the dark-haired girl, of similar height to her, seeing both scepticism and optimism. "Because I believe women have always been the silent power behind the scenes, shaping the world for the better. They're the ones who show courage in the face of adversity, standing up to right the wrongs directed at them."

The girl hitched one shoulder, looking unconvinced. "I wouldn't know anything about that. My mum died when I was little, and my dad … well, he's a businessman 'focused on the future' he said when I asked him. But he did say once my mum came from a long line of troublemakers."

Emma wasn't certain how to interpret that comment but felt ill at ease at the underlying ridicule. Was it meant in jest, as a term of respect and admiration, or implying something far more hurtful? It sounded insensitive to say the least. "Personally, I love strong women who stand up for themselves," she said, pushing aside negative thoughts of someone she didn't know. "They're the backbone of society."

"D'you think so? Dad always said …" Clearly bothered, the girl's thought drifted.

Emma smiled. "What's your name?"

"Paige. Paige Frazer."

"How can I help?"

The girl looked downcast. "Um … I'm told not to ask so many questions, but I'd like to know more about my mum."

With growing curiosity, Emma asked, "Where's your mother's family?"

Paige dropped her eyes towards her sneakered feet. "I don't know. They …"

"Sorry to interrupt," said Luke. "Everyone else has gone. Are you nearly ready? Or shall I come back?"

Emma looked between Luke and Paige, hesitating.

Paige solved her problem. "I won't hold you up. I've got another class anyway."

"Listen …" Emma rummaged in her handbag for her card. "Give me a call and we'll talk."

The girl took the card, shrugged one shoulder again and left without another word.

Emma watched her walk away, her ponytail swinging, convinced something was troubling her but she had no idea how she could help.

Luke picked up her bag. "Ready?"

"Yes. This is a lovely surprise. I wasn't expecting you?"

His eyes were warm and loving as he looked down at her over the top of his mask. "I wanted to take my clever wife to lunch to celebrate."

Emma grinned as a sense of happiness filled her. She sometimes pinched herself at her good fortune. Life wasn't always this good. "Where's your car?"

"I caught the bus, so I could chauffeur you home in yours."

Emma's eyes glistened in gratitude as their footsteps echoed in the long university corridors leading to the car park. Since her Covid infection, sudden waves of exhaustion came over her at unexpected times. Too often, if she was honest. Luke had seen how it wiped her out, but then he'd always looked out for her well-being. He was the most caring and gentle soul she'd ever met.

"Now, lunch. Italian or Thai?" he asked, cutting in on her thoughts.

She shook her head. "I couldn't eat that much. How about that little tapas place?"

Settled at their table a short while later, Emma turned the conversation back to Paige. "I don't know anything about her other than she's a second-year student, which hardly counts after last year's string of lockdowns. But she struck me as vulnerable and wanting reassurance about something, but I have no idea what."

"Isn't that typical of students?" asked Luke. "It's a big new world, being in university. Don't you remember?"

Emma studied her husband of twelve years. Now in his late forties, a few sandy hairs showed at the temples of his thick brown hair. Matching, intelligent eyes missed nothing, and he'd kept his slim, long-legged frame, thanks to all the cycling he did. To her he was as handsome as he'd ever been.

As the tapas came out, Emma and Luke tasted each dish. She pulled a face. Her taste buds still hadn't returned to normal.

"How did your lecture go?" he asked.

"Remarkably well." She drained her water glass and poured another. "And the lecturer confirmed she'd had permission to purchase some copies of my new book for the library."

Emma hoped her latest book, encouraging people to begin their search for their family history, may save some of them from losing their identity, like she once had. She'd grown up not knowing any extended family until, by chance, she'd met her grandmother Charlotte, well over a decade ago now, only to lose her again to cancer far too soon.

Emma remembered how Charli had coaxed her to investigate her family tree, and she got hooked. She was still hooked, and wanted to help others discover their roots, their history, the way she had. It had made such a difference to her sense of belonging.

"That's great news about the book," said Luke reaching for another tapas. "Students have had a lot of challenges to overcome in the last couple of years."

Emma pushed her plate away. She couldn't eat another bite. "I suspect some have struggled a lot. I've been reading about all the mis- and disinformation on social media, and how life's become far more confrontational. People are showing signs of having lost their bearings and feeling displaced. And they are much quicker to anger, and more worried about what the future holds. Like that girl I was just talking to."

Emma, too, had lost her bearings once. She knew what it was like to feel displaced. She'd come a long way in the years since she'd met her grandmother. Charli had taught her the art of writing, the joy of discovery, and the gift of compassion. *And the art of keeping secrets*, Emma chuckled to herself, remembering how slowly Charli had revealed all the secrets she'd held, which set Emma's life back on course. Without her, Emma dreaded to think where she might have ended up.

Without Luke, that's for certain. Charli had pushed them together.

"What about her?" asked Luke.

"I don't know exactly, but she told me her father had said she came from a long line of troublemakers. I hope it's not the put-down I think it is, but something's bothering me about her."

"Why? She's not your problem, Ems. You gave her your card. If she wants you to research her tree, she'll be in touch. Shall we go?"

Emma nodded but couldn't put aside her doubts. Luke had never felt displaced.

* * * * *

"Who's on the school run today?" she asked before they went to their separate workspace for the rest of the day. Working from home had made such a difference to their lives, allowing them to share the chores and look after their ten-year-old daughter Rose Charlotte, named after her great-grandmother who'd had a great love of roses. They had much to be grateful for, even though the lingering global virus was still too prevalent to ignore.

Emma enjoyed working from the room she called the library, filled with her favourite mementos and antiques. French doors led out to the rose garden and the path for clients to use. Luke was equally at home in the purpose-built office in their garden he'd used since the Covid lockdowns prevented him going to the city.

From there, he ran his successful editing and publishing business inherited from his father, which included managing all of her famous grandmother's stable of books under various pseudonyms. Not that she'd known anything about Charlotte's other names until much later.

"There's no school run today," said Luke. "Rosie is going to Livvy's. Jess will drop her off later."

Emma smiled. "She's a marvel." Jess and she had attended antenatal classes together and now their daughters, Rose and Olivia, were also the best of friends. She gave Luke a quick kiss. "I've got some notes to write up about today, and a chapter to finish in the other family history I've been researching. The one where I'd found a unionist from the 1890s. Talk later."

Under one of Charli's pen names, she'd continued creating the romance novels her grandmother had taught her to write and had even branched out into a series of family-history-inspired novels under her own pen name, but she'd retired both a couple of years ago to focus on her genealogy sleuthing and ghostwriting career. She loved discovering people's pasts for them and then writing their story. It felt far more real to her than fiction.

Luke looked at her sternly. "Shouldn't you lie down for a while first? You look tired."

Emma knew he meant well, but she didn't want him fussing. "I'm okay. Honestly. And I'm wanting to get on with this."

"I know you don't always feel rested after a lie-down, but I think you should try," he implored.

How could she rest when her brain was so busy? "I'll be fine." Her tone held a note of defiance.

"Okay. If you insist." He didn't sound convinced. "Just don't say I didn't warn you."

Sometimes he was just too much. She left without another word and shut herself in her library.

It didn't matter how many family trees she'd worked on for clients over the years, every time she found a new titbit the family didn't know, she felt the thrill of discovery. And a great sense of satisfaction telling them something special about their ancestors. Writing their story was a bonus. To bring the past alive, turning the bare facts into an emotive tale she believed would be handed down the generations, was a treat she revelled in.

She turned to her client's story, clearly imagining the scene in her mind, and let her fingers do the talking, portraying the movie rolling inside her head …

Ruby Marshall sat in the congregation of St Andrew's Church in the September of 1888, spellbound by the resounding voice of the Reverend Rutherford Waddell. He railed against the 'sin of cheapness', the lust for low-priced goods that forced wages down below subsistence level – to the point 'where women earned a miserable fourpence a day, if they were lucky'.

As one of the many seamstresses and tailors working in Dunedin at the time, she understood such hardship, but Ruby would never have expected a highly regarded man of the cloth to protest against the leading citizens of the city on her behalf. She'd hung on every word that echoed from the beams as he decried the owners using 'sweated labour' in badly ventilated 'sweatshops' and beseeched them to change their ways.

"We must 'fight against this evil,'" he'd shouted. "We must bring about a society based on the 'supreme law of love.'"

Some days, Emma could easily conjure up such an occasion and often wished she could have been there. The newspaper reports were so graphic she only needed to personalise it to bring the words alive. Sadly reflecting there were many women throughout the world today who still suffered such conditions, she double-checked her facts and wrote on.

Little known to Ruby, Mr Silas Spragg, senior reporter from *The Otago Daily Times* was also in the congregation that day. He became an ardent supporter of the voluble reverend and reported on the sermon. Within days, other newspapers had picked up the charge, and from then on, the matter gathered momentum.

Within three years, Reverend Waddell's sermon had 'triggered a royal commission and galvanised public opinion to support the newly formed Liberal Party, resulting in a suite of social and labour reforms'. But more importantly to Ruby, Waddell founded the Dunedin Tailoresses' Union. As its first president in 1889, aided by Miss Harriet Morison, he helped negotiate shorter hours and better pay for the women. Ruby Marshall was one of its first members.

Emma put parts of the section in quote marks and would cite *The Otago Daily Times* as her source in the bibliography. She was about to start another section on

Ruby's involvement with Miss Harriet Morison and the Tailoresses' Union, when her mobile rang.

"Mrs Grainger … um … Emma … It's Paige. Can I ask a favour?"

Emma listened as Paige hummed and hawed, and asked questions in the silences, trying to pinpoint what the girl wanted from her. Scribbling notes as she went, she discovered Paige's father David Frazer worked in finance. Private equity investments or suchlike, he'd never bothered to explain the details. *Or she never asked*, thought Emma.

Paige had one brother, five years older than her, who worked in their father's company, learning the ropes. They'd both attended boarding schools while their father built his business. Her paternal grandparents lived overseas six months of the year, and she wasn't close to them. She didn't know anything about her maternal grandparents.

In short, thought Emma, *the girl's lonely for female company*.

"Dad has no interest in the past and gets annoyed if I ask him," said Paige, "but … I dunno, since I've started uni, I think … well … I've realised I want to know more about … about who I am. Why do I think so differently? Why do I like history and care about the environment and people. No one else does? Sorry, I'm babbling …"

So, Emma wrote, Paige was a humanitarian, and, going by what his daughter said, the father was egocentric.

"Not at all," reassured Emma. "It's nice to know you're passionate about these things. But I'm still not sure what you'd like me to do."

"You inspired me. All that history and women's stories and …"

"And?" Emma encouraged, feeling she was pulling teeth.

"Will you … can you …?"

Emma heard the catch in the girls' voice, which dropped to a whisper.

"I'm nothing like my father and brother. I don't share their viewpoint, and I'm beginning to feel I'm adopted or something. I'd like to find out who I am, but I don't know where to start. I, um, I can pay you later."

The penny dropped. The girl was asking for free advice, something Emma rarely considered.

"How old are you, Paige?"

"Nineteen. Coming up twenty. Dad threw me this stupid 'coming of age' party. It was supposed to be for my eighteenth but got delayed twice because of Covid. I hoped he'd forgotten, but no such luck. He invited all his business friends and colleagues, and I was the showpiece. It was supposed to be the social event of the year."

"I gather it wasn't what you wanted?"

"Nope. But I didn't have any say, and my stupid boyfriend said I was being selfish and ungrateful for objecting."

Against her better judgement, something about the girl drew Emma. A gut feeling that she needed someone on her side, and it didn't sound like she had anyone. Emma relented. "Sort out a day when you don't have lectures and we'll meet up. Let's talk about what you do know, and we'll go from there."

Looks like I have another family story coming my way, she thought happily. *I wonder what this one will reveal.*

2

Where it all began

Auckland
1 June 1892

Lucy Young sat in the social hall of Auckland's YMCA on a cold Wednesday afternoon, keen to play her part in the next phase of the women's franchise movement. She felt honoured to be included in the select group of about thirty stalwarts.

Lucy had not understood social inequality before she'd met Milly's step-grandmother, Amey Daldy, a strong-minded Christian woman who lived up to her unshakeable egalitarian beliefs. Now Lucy wanted to be just like her, unafraid to stand up for what was right in life.

"Isn't this wonderful?" she said, using her usual catchphrase, turning her head right and left between Hope and Milly. The three girls had been fast friends since schooldays. Neither as dark-haired and dark-eyed as Hope, nor as fair and green-eyed as Milly, Lucy was more pragmatic, and smart, and the most committed to the cause. She knew they were too young to stand amongst the women leaders, but they could sign petitions now that all three had reached their majority.

"I hope something can be gained from this meeting," she added as she waited on tenterhooks for Mrs Daldy to speak. What she lacked in experience, she made up for with fervour.

After her mother died when she was quite young, Lucy's father had freely discussed politics and business and other matters with her, and she'd never thought there was anything unusual about it. She'd been shocked by the stories of brutality against women, the poverty and hardship they endured, and slowly began to grasp the widespread imbalance between genders.

"We must do something to bring about a fairer society," she mumbled, quoting a phrase she knew by heart.

Lucy could never fathom how the law allowed such unfairness. She struggled to believe that women didn't even have rights over their own children. The older she got, the more she empathised, the more she considered it grossly unjust and the more she wanted to change the situation. The vote would be one way to gain equity.

"I am here today," announced Amey Daldy, "prepared to stand up and state that we are determined that the women of this colony receive enfranchisement."

Lucy's heart soared. Perched on the edge of her seat, muttering under her breath, she could almost recite Mrs Daldy's words, she'd heard them so often. Lucy couldn't fathom why Hope wasn't as eager, but before she could say anything, Milly put her finger to her lips to quieten Lucy's constant commentary.

With the help of a housekeeper and a separate household next door to home her husband's orphaned grandchildren, Mrs Daldy had been responsible for much of their upbringing. Lucy had spent a great deal of time in the Daldy household over the years, listening to the tiny firebrand and her friends plan for the day when women's franchise would be a reality, and was a full-hearted convert.

She greatly admired the sexagenarian who had recently stepped aside as the founding President of the Auckland branch of the Women's Christian Temperance Union, the WCTU, to launch this new campaign.

"After the successes of the Dunedin branch of the Women's Franchise League," continued Mrs Daldy, "formed a few months ago by Miss Helen Nicol and Miss Harriet Morison, who we are fortunate to have with us today, we believe that Auckland needs a similar organisation."

Lucy was eternally grateful her father had allowed her to voice her opinion and debate issues with her as if she were an equal. He treated his staff, both at home and at the importing company he owned, the same. Certainly Mrs Bush, their housekeeper, had never had reason to complain.

Listening intently, Lucy sat forward, jiggling and fidgeting, nodding and agreeing with the phrases she knew so well.

Lucy jumped as Milly put a restraining hand on her arm. "Sit still, Lucy, and listen."

"It is imperative that we make the franchise movement more public, more accessible. There is much confusion around the prohibition standpoint of the WCTU, and the right …" Mrs Daldy paused, emphasising the word, and raised her voice, "… and it is the right, for women to have the power to vote." Mrs Daldy waved to acknowledge the polite gloved-hand applause encouraging her to continue.

After the failures of the 1891 petition, Lucy found today's presence of several prominent names, both male and female, reassuring. They were not alone. Maybe this year, they would win and put an end to the constant setbacks women had known throughout her life.

"Don't you just want to stand up and shout out loud?" she asked Hope, as she and Milly stood to join in with the clapping. "To say yes, it is time. Yes, it is our right. Even those men who gave their apologies sent notes stating their full support."

Hope shrugged, muttering. "It'd be more than my life was worth. Mother would not approve."

Hope's mother, Mrs Willoughby, knew Mrs Daldy well. Both had been staunch members of the Temperance Union since Mary Clement Leavitt had visited from America in 1885. The pair had been a force to contend with, but now Mrs W wanted prohibition above all else, while Mrs D wanted the vote. Both wanted more say in the way the laws affected them.

The two women hadn't fallen out completely, but there had been a change in priorities. Lucy could see Hope would obey her mother, while Milly would do whatever Grandma Amey wanted. She sensed a growing rift she hoped wouldn't break up their friendship.

Mrs Daldy's voice continued in the background as Lucy thought about her friends. Of the three, Hope was the most fashionable and liked to be seen wearing the best money could buy, attending all the right occasions and being at the centre. She revelled in the attention her striking dark looks attracted. In contrast, Milly conveyed an air of delicacy that belied her stubborn yet caring nature.

"Would you please expand upon the confusion you refer to, madam," asked Sir George Grey.

Lucy knew of the former Governor of the Colony and as the Member for Newton, and was delighted he had accepted the invitation to attend, despite his frail health.

"Isn't it wonderful he is here," said Lucy. "He'll be a great help in the House." Much of life was wonderful to Lucy, optimism was her strongest trait.

"Shush." Milly, the peacemaker, who, while encouraging Hope to be less sulky, could be relied on to temper Lucy's more enthusiastic outbursts.

"I will, sir," said Mrs Daldy, rising to the cause. "One of our main stumbling blocks, I regret to say, is the WCTU's firmly held position against liquor. Those who are the most vociferous in their opposition to women's franchise are so because they disagree with the Temperance Union. They believe granting women the right to vote will also result in prohibition. We must separate the arguments if Parliament is to favour our petitions."

Murmurs and mutterings could be heard in the hall as the listeners whispered to their neighbours, including Lucy. "Like Mrs Willoughby," she said to Milly in an undertone, casting an eye towards Hope whose thoughts seemed anywhere but in the room.

Calling order, Reverend Berry invited Sir George to comment.

The MP rose to his feet. "Thank you, Mr Chairman. Mrs Daldy, I believe today's meeting will be most enlightening." He nodded to the lady before addressing the audience. "Let me assure you, as far as Parliament is concerned, I believe the majority of its members are in favour of women voting. No, more than that, I would say determined upon passing some measures towards that outcome."

The meekness of the polite claps following his words frustrated Lucy, but she sensed increased hopefulness in the hall. "Isn't it wonderful?" she repeated. "We are sitting here, right now, in the middle of such a momentous occasion."

"Goodness, Lucy. Will you sit still and listen," hushed Milly once again.

"In fact," continued Sir George, "there is an marked awakening of the 'quasi' slavery situation many women are in and who have no voice in the matter. I fully support any Association that will bring an end to the situation, but I would go further still. I believe there should be a Chamber of women to whom all legislation is submitted for approval."

Mrs Daldy interjected. "I fear such an idea would frighten the public too much, sir, and any progress toward enfranchisement would be lost. Our aim is to be granted the freedom to vote. The ability to elect the good and true men whom we believe will make laws that consider the rights of both sexes."

A chuckle. "You may be right, dear lady, but I am satisfied within my own mind that female suffrage will come and that it will come very soon. Such an outcome would bring incalculable advantages to mankind."

For as long as she could remember, Lucy had learnt about the rights for women – or rather the lack of them – through the words of Polly Plum and Mary Ann Müller, and the writings of the British philosopher, John Stuart Mill, penned before she was born. She'd heard more about the franchise since the first WCTU branch was established some six or seven years ago, but there'd been as many failures as successes over the intervening years. But today, Lucy believed, offered promise.

"Continue, Mrs Daldy," said Reverend Berry.

"As a Christian woman, I believe in temperance. Too many women are the victims of violence and poverty due to intoxication to be ignored. I deplore drunkenness and licentiousness. It is an abomination, but, I repeat, we must separate prohibition and women's right in the minds of men if we are to win the vote."

Chairs scraped against the wooden floors as women stood to applaud her words.

"Yes!" shouted Lucy, standing and clapping loudly until Milly pulled at her jacket when a signal from the chairman indicated silence and people retook their seats. There was still much debate to be had and she hung on to every word. She frowned at Hope sitting sullenly.

"Sir, if I may," said Harriet Morison, remaining on her feet. "I am a stranger to Auckland but from my experience in Dunedin, I believe the time has come."

Lucy fixed her eyes on the woman, nodding as Miss Morison outlined her reasons.

"The laws of the land have been framed almost solely in the interest of property and trade. Men make all the decisions, men have all the power, and the law reduces women to little more than chattels."

Undertones of agreement rippled through the audience.

"It is on the grounds of humanity that women claim the right to vote. To have a voice in the making of laws that govern their lives. I hereby propose this meeting immediately forms the Auckland branch of the Women's Franchise League of New Zealand."

Cries of "Hear! Hear!" and "Yes, indeed," echoed throughout the room, decorum suddenly absent.

At last, thought Lucy, adding her voice to the throng thinking she must write about it in her journal. A few minutes later she was once more disheartened as amendments and counter-amendments were put forward. She frowned. "Why all the quibbling? Can't we just get on with it?"

"Patience, Lucy," said Milly. "Grandma Amey has done this so many times, she knows what she's doing. You know that. They need to agree now to be as one moving forward."

Meanwhile, the women at the front table conceded one point to gain another, especially Mrs Daldy.

"I believe both men and women should form the League as working members. It is my belief that women alone will not achieve as much without men's help, however much we desire it."

"If we can do without them in the bedroom, we can do without them all the time," suggested a lone voice, shattering the protocol of the room.

"Speak for yourself," answered another, drawing a few cackles.

"My man will support us, he's lazy enough to do what I tell him."

"Remember, ladies, the bedroom is a good place to persuade your man around to our way of thinking."

Roars of laughter followed, despite the obvious discomfort of the men in the audience. Lucy blushed at the intimate comments but hoped the women were right.

"Ladies, please!" The gavel banged loudly on the block until order was restored.

Lucy leant across and whispered to Hope, "I think it's going to happen. We will have a new League to help fight the battle."

"So what if you do? I guarantee Mother won't like it."

Lucy began to wonder why Hope was even there. At least Milly was a fellow champion for the cause.

Finally, the wording was agreed upon.

"The Resolution is unanimously passed," stated the chairman with a single tap of the gavel. "I hereby state that on the first day of June 1892, the Auckland Branch of the Women's Franchise League of New Zealand is officially inaugurated."

Much cheering and applause followed while Lucy and Milly, amongst many, raised their hands to commit to the sub of one shilling for ladies, and five shillings for men.

Amid the commotion, Lucy felt the odd one out in many ways.

Mrs Willoughby, despite her staunch views, and Mrs Daldy especially had welcomed her to their homes. Indeed, Lucy was often included whenever Mrs D went out and about in her buggy on her many visits around town to drum up support for the idea of women's enfranchisement. But Lucy's father was totally against the temperance women, calling them all sorts of bad names. At times, she felt trapped between duty to her father and her loyalty to the franchise.

"And to start the funds off in a healthy manner, I will donate the sum of five guineas," said Sir George, whose announcement brought further noisy acclaim.

"I encourage you all," challenged Reverend Berry in his sonorous voice, once order was restored, "to do as Mrs Daldy and her other ladies have done, and that is, write letters. Write to your Parliamentary representatives, to the newspapers, to every women's organisation, and to the churches. Write about your belief in women's enfranchisement and exhort everyone to bring about this change. Will you do that?"

"Yes, yes!" shouted Lucy. "I will."

God, and her father willing, she'd found her calling.

3

Revelations

Over the rim of her coffee cup, Emma caught sight of Paige pausing at the café door. The girl's eyes were downcast, and it was hard to gauge her mood behind the black face mask.

Something had bothered Emma about the young woman from the start. On the surface, Paige was smart, well educated, from a well-to-do background, and had ideas about what her future would look like. But at their first brief meeting, and again during the short phone call, Emma sensed … anxiety was too strong a word. More like lack of direction, and now she saw doubt.

Emma stood and waved, catching Paige's attention. After two years of Covid restrictions – from vaccine passes to gain entry to cafés and gatherings, and everyone keeping two metres apart, to sanitising hands and wearing masks – life was beginning to return to a semblance of normal. People had become complacent and less compliant since restrictions had eased, despite the virus having morphed into something more contagious if less deadly.

"I'm sorry if I'm late," said Paige, eyeing the empty coffee cup and removing her mask as she sat down.

"Not at all. I came early. People watching is one of my favourite pastimes."

Emma enjoyed observing people, often picking up ideas she could use in her writing. Even behind the compulsory mask wearing, body language provided insight into behaviour patterns that differed greatly with age, and gave a hint of their emotional state.

Today, she'd been practising her skills for when Paige arrived, hoping she could interpret the girl's state of mind. Although what she expected, even Emma couldn't pinpoint. "Order whatever you like. My shout. I know students never eat properly." Emma knew the young woman still lived at home and eating well probably wasn't an issue, but it would be worth it to keep her talking.

They ordered lunch, chatting briefly about the food, the weather and university life until Emma tired of Paige's prevarication. "So, tell me. Why did you want to see me, exactly? You're clever. You could work out how to do a basic search on your family and find much of what you're seeking. I could give you some websites and hints to get you started, if you'd like, but I suspect there's more to it."

The girl's eyes unexpectedly pooled and she took a deep breath. "I'm not sure how to explain. While I was listening to you talk about the importance of family and their stories, I felt this sense of … loss. Having no one to talk to about my family made me seem … I dunno, unimportant, I guess. It relegated my mum, and all the mums before her, to insignificance. That nothing they did or said made any difference because nobody was listening. Does that make sense?"

"It does to me. We all need to feel valued." Emma paused, assessing the girl in front of her. "Don't you?"

Paige shook her head. "My father is so wrapped up in his reputation that he tends to ignore my opinions. My brother is as bad. Neither of them understand my views on the environment. For them it's all about making money. The more, the better. And being seen in the right circles, with the right people. I hate it."

Emma heard Paige's bitter tone. "Silly question, but have you tried talking to your father about how you feel?"

She laughed. A dismissive laugh that said it all. "I've tried. Believe me, I've tried, but he won't listen. I'm a girl. I don't understand. Just look after 'my pretty head'." She mimed the quote marks.

Emma had no experience of father–daughter relationships and no advice to give, but she could tell Paige was getting worked up. The issue had obviously been an ongoing bone of contention. "What about friends? Your boyfriend?"

"Ex boyfriend," she stated fiercely. "I ditched him after that stupid party. He was never on my wavelength anyway. Thought I was too soft. I think he used me to find a way into my father's good books."

Emma inwardly cheered. Any boyfriend who could call his girlfriend selfish for *not* wanting something deserved what he got.

"Don't get too despondent. Believe me when I say, that over a long period of time, women have done a lot to change this world for the better, and will continue to do so. I'm sure you'll be one of them."

Emma watched the girl's face light up.

"Do you really think so?"

"I'm absolutely convinced," Emma reassured, her heart melting that such little praise and affirmation could mean so much. A gut feeling kicked in. "You will be a force to reckon with. Choose your purpose in life and go for it."

"I already know what I want to do – I just don't know what to call it in simple terms. The descriptions are all so boring and pedantic. And overly complex. They put people off. But … I want to be an advocate for climate justice and work towards a more sustainable future … to do what's best for the planet."

"Sounds like a good plan," Emma murmured, finding herself on shaky ground. She didn't disagree about climate change, something needed to be done, but apart from a bit of recycling, she'd left the big picture questions and the state of the planet to others.

Paige became animated. "Natural or man-made, the arguments don't matter any more. The science speaks for itself. Weather extremes are creating havoc throughout the world, and our emissions are at an all-time high. The human cost is heartbreaking. We have to reset the balance somehow. We're clever enough to adapt, to find solutions. I want to be one of those people."

Impressed by her passion and intentions but thinking her a little naïve, Emma was about to suggest she temper her goals when Paige shook her head.

"I know I've got a lot to learn. It'll be ages before – *if* – I'll ever get to become a voice for the future, but it's imperative we change how we do things. To stop it getting worse. It's not just a climate issue any more, it's a social and human rights issue. That's why I'm studying sociology, looking at it from a different angle. I'm much better with people and words than science and analysis."

By the end of her spirited outpouring, her eyes glowed with possibility. Emma decided she couldn't argue with Paige's goals, however idealistic. "I think you have your work cut out."

As if reading her mind, Paige continued. "I know. And it's so frustrating. So many businesses who could make a difference are so entrenched in their ways they don't want to change – or don't want to spend the money. I wish they'd stop. There's far too much wastage and air pollution. We've got to find better ways to do just about everything."

Emma almost laughed at her passionate indignation but didn't know enough to comment. "Didn't I just say you'd be a force to reckon with?" she said, hoping to encourage Paige. "That's very forward thinking. I wish you well. Now, back to my original question, how can I help?"

Paige's face immediately dropped and that look of doubt crept back into place. "Remember I told you my dad said I come from a long line of troublemakers? It's why he tries to keep a lid on what I do. But there's lots he doesn't know."

"I rather like the idea of generations of rebels in the family," smiled Emma.

Paige took a deep breath. "I think I'm about to become one of those so-called troublemakers. I'd like to know who *were* these women in my past. What was their cause, and how did they defy the norms? Were they agitators who achieved something, or just women who argued the toss at home?"

Emma considered how to answer as she poured more water into their glasses, and thanked the masked-up waitress for clearing their table. "Would it change your ambitions for the future if you found out your ancestors were simply harridans, bossy and overbearing in the home, instead of political movers and shakers who achieved something?"

"I don't know," she answered honestly, looking puzzled. "I don't want to cause anger and division – there's enough of that as it is. I want to find ways that will get people to pull together. But I'm at the point where I don't trust my own judgement. My dad doesn't agree with me on anything. I'm told to leave it to others, to wiser heads, to not worry about things I can't do anything about. Except I have this feeling I should try."

Emma decided she liked this young woman. "So do I. And, I believe, knowing about our past helps us make decisions about the future. History teaches us a lot if we're prepared to listen and not make the same costly, arrogant mistakes. I think it's time for you to learn about your past."

"Are you saying you'll help me find my family?" Paige looked at her with expectation.

"I am, but I need some information from you to get started."

"Such as?" asked Paige, eager to tell Emma anything she wanted to know.

Emma ordered another coffee for herself and a smoothie for Paige and pulled out her notepad.

Spirited voices from a group of three young men arriving at the café, none of whom wore masks, attracted their attention. Paige turned around to see what the noise was about, and Emma saw her jaw tighten and her shoulders tense. The girl bowed her head, but one of the men had spotted her.

"Paige? Fancy bumping into you. I wouldn't have thought this place was one of your haunts."

Emma didn't like his scornful tone, even if his smart jacket over a white T-shirt and dress jeans gave him an air of casual control.

Paige clenched her fists but kept her head down.

"What? Still not talking to me," continued the young man, with a smirk. "Don't worry, your brother's taken me under his wing. I don't need you any more."

Emma felt her blood boil at his disdain. She glared at the young man. "Unless you have something more pertinent to add, you're interrupting a private conversation. Please leave."

He smiled smugly and plunged a hand into his jeans pocket. "I've got better things to do with my time anyway." The other two men were signalling him to the counter as he sauntered off in their direction.

Emma had barely drawn breath when a second man butted in.

"Excuse me, lady. I don't know who you are, but I want to talk to my sister. In private." He grabbed Paige's elbow, pulling her to a half-rise trying to get her to go with him.

"Let go of me." Off balance, she tugged her arm away, turning an angry face towards him.

Exactly how it happened Emma wasn't sure, but the next thing she knew, the table went flying. Crockery crashed on the floor, shattering to pieces on the polished concrete, and Paige ended up tangled in the table legs.

The brother reached down to pull her up, but she lashed out, kicking him in the shins. "Get away from me." She scrabbled to her feet, breathing hard, staring him in the eye, daring him to try again. "Don't touch me. Do you hear?"

"Stupid cow! Whatcha do that for?" he demanded, his face now a shade of puce. "I only want to talk."

"Well, I don't want to talk to you."

"I think you'd better. I could always tell your daddy what you've been up to and get your allowance stopped."

The fury on Paige's face set off alarm bells. With the whole café now staring at the ruckus, and his two friends gathering behind him, Emma decided to withdraw. She stood quickly and faced Paige's brother.

"I'd suggest you do as she says and leave her alone, whoever you are. Before someone accuses you of assault."

Emma gathered their belongings, put her arm firmly around Paige and guided her out the door. She'd phone later to apologise and offer to pay for the damage, even if wasn't her doing. "Come on, get in the car."

Paige had gone silent but obediently climbed in.

As Emma drove off, a glance in the mirror told her nobody was following. She turned on the radio to let music fill the silence while she drove along Tamaki Drive. Paige would explain if she wanted to. If not, it wasn't her place to ask.

Throughout the journey, Paige's mobile rang several times, but she shut it off without answering. Then Emma heard the text dings start. Paige furiously tapped out some responses. From the tension infusing Paige's body, Emma suspected harsh words were being exchanged. Neither spoke.

A few minutes later, Emma pulled up at Okahu Bay. "Let's walk."

Paige nodded and got out of the car. Emma noticed she left her phone behind. After taking a deep breath of fresh sea air, Paige meandered towards the beach, hands shoved deep in her pockets, her sneakers making squeaking sounds in the sand. Emma followed, prepared to wait for her to speak. They wandered along the water's edge, towards the boardwalk at the end of the beach and the wharf at the point beyond. Part way, Paige began to say how sorry she was.

Emma stopped her before she could complete her sentence. "You don't need to apologise. You did nothing wrong. Those two were the instigators. The darker one of the two I assume is your brother, and the other?"

"My ex," mumbled Paige. "Useless snake."

They reached the end of the wharf.

Emma gazed out to sea, listening to the sound of the waves lapping below as she leaned on the railings. "If it's any help, I think you did the right thing in making him an ex if that's the way he treats you."

Paige winced as she inspected the graze on her forearm and eased her shoulder.

"Are you hurt?" asked Emma.

"It's nothing. Must have banged it when I fell. It'll come right." Another moment of silence until Paige said, "I've not seen Cam like that before. He's never violent. Something's up."

"Are you sure it wasn't bravado, showing off in front of mates?"

"Who, Simon or Cam?"

"You tell me." Since Emma had no idea which name

belonged to which man she could add little more.

"Cameron. My brother. He usually ignores me unless he wants me to do something. He's certainly never grabbed me like that before. As for my ex, Simon has always loved to show off. I think that's what attracted him to me in the first place. He thought there was money or glamour or something in being attached to the daughter of a big shot." She hitched one shoulder. "His loss. I'd hoped never to see him again."

Emma didn't know how to advise Paige about that situation. Raised as an only child of a single mother, she had no experience of family dynamics. Paige would have to figure that one out on her own. "Shall we head back?"

By the time they reached the car, Emma could see the tension had gone from Paige's shoulders and her face had lost the disgruntled look. "Feeling better?"

"Yes. Thank you. And thanks for rescuing me. The walk helped."

"Do you still want to investigate your family tree?"

"More than ever. If Dad stops my allowance because of something Cameron says, then he will. There's nothing I can do to change that, but I won't be treated like a nonentity by Cam or anyone. They'll soon find out what sort of troublemaker I can be if they try that sort of nonsense again."

Emma smiled. She suspected that final 'they' was targeted at her father.

"Do you want to tell me what you've been up to that your brother hinted your father might like to know?"

Paige grinned, but defiance flared in her eyes. "I wagged school a couple of times to join a School

Strike 4 Climate protest. Dad found out and grounded me for ages. What he doesn't know is I now volunteer for a climate change group. It's mostly low-level social media stuff, although we've done a couple of sit-ins, and written submissions on public policy and debate. I guess Cameron saw my name on a Twitter post or something. Like I said, he thinks I'm soft. I think he's greedy. We don't agree on much."

"Okay then. Let's see what sort of firebrand you can be and who you came from."

4

That first meeting

Auckland
15 June 1892

A fortnight later, Lucy still couldn't contain her enthusiasm. "I am so excited. I'm going to attend every meeting."

"I wonder what your father will think of that," said Hope, who was looking to see if her fiancé was waiting for her as they left the YMCA hall. "And since you're not on the committee, why bother?"

Lucy pulled back her shoulders and lifted her chin. "I might be able to help somehow. They said the fortnightly meetings would be open to members, and I'm sure Father won't complain about me going to talks with Christian women," winked Lucy. "Mrs Daldy is planning several public meetings."

Hope pulled a face. "I can't see anything interesting in those endless meetings saying the same thing over and over. It's so tiresome."

Lucy didn't understand Hope's indifference. She enjoyed the fortnightly meetings. Especially after

Mrs Daldy had explained how it was the best way to encourage unity and create a sense of joint purpose. And it saved her a lot of talking. 'When everyone is in the same room, I only have to explain myself the once.'

"I doubt I'll have much choice. I'll do what Grandma Amey tells me to do," said Milly, watching Hope. "Are you expecting a certain Mr Michael Fernley to be here waiting patiently for you?" she teased as she nudged the other girl with her elbow.

Hope appeared chastened. "Maybe. He said he might. What if I am? Just because you've decided to be a spinster, don't expect me to follow suit."

Milly grinned and linked her arm through Hope's. "Don't get all cross and bothered. After everything I've seen, there's no way I want to be saddled with a man telling me what to do and babies at my feet. I've had enough of that with my younger siblings. Come on, let's have tea."

Lucy, wearing a navy wool gored skirt and matching jacket over a white blouse, and a bonnet framing her pert face, linked arms on the other side of Hope, and the three young women laughingly made their way along the street towards the tearooms. Hope looked the epitome of fashion and outshone her companions in her mauve dress worn under a stylish dark-purple cape coat with slits for her arms and a muffler for warmth. Even her hat was designed to attract attention, with a wide brim and overlarge trimmings. Milly's princess-style dress flattered her slim, almost childlike figure, but the warm-beige hue under her sturdy brown coat and bonnet did nothing to enhance her features and kind-hearted nature.

Once seated in the tasteful surroundings with just the right amount of feminine touches in the lace cloths and floaty window dressings, Lucy poured the tea from the elegant teapot into matching cups.

"What will you say in these letters Reverend Berry wants us to write?" asked Hope.

"Something about society having matured, and the time is now ripe. You heard the speeches and the responses put forward to counter the arguments," replied Lucy.

They placed napkins over their laps as they'd been taught, and one by one, picked up their cake fork and delicately placed a morsel of Victoria sponge into their mouths, carefully wiping away any stray dusting of icing sugar.

"What, like how women shouldn't be lumped in with children, criminals and lunatics as the only ones not allowed to vote? Or the one about women having smaller brains than men, but what we lack in quantity we make up for in quality?" pouted Milly. "I can outwit my brothers any day of the week." The three of them burst into giggles.

"Those may not be the most persuasive defences, but yes. Proving that better-educated, better-informed women will be a stabilising influence on society and will bring about humanitarian laws for the betterment of all. But we mustn't be strident," said Lucy, realising she was sounding rather schoolmarmish, but like so many women she'd listened to over the years, she truly believed they were the power behind the scenes. Having the vote would prove that. "Our arguments must be logical and win people over with eloquence."

"And you still say your father is going to be happy with all this?" said Hope, raising an eyebrow as she looked scornfully at Lucy.

"I believe so. I'm sure I can persuade him with sensible arguments and get him away from the idea that people like your mother are out to ruin his life."

Hope frowned, clearly displeased. "It's not my mother who is the problem, nor any woman who believes drink is the root of all evil, but your father who insists on imbibing."

Lucy wiped her mouth on her napkin as she sought to rethink the retort on her lips. She and Hope had fallen out before over her family's teetotalism and she didn't want it to happen again.

"I am not suggesting your mother is at fault. But there is little I can do to stop my father enjoying a glass of port or a brandy on occasion, especially when he has friends to dinner. It's part of doing business. Unlike the many women who suffer cruelly from drunkenness, I've never seen my father drunk. He has never been violent towards me and pays me an allowance to spend as I choose. He also treats our housekeeper, Mrs Bush, with respect. I don't see the harm in him. He is not against women's rights. He is against prohibition. That's why I like the idea of this Franchise League being independent of the WCTU. It takes the argument for women's franchise away from the demand for temperance. The two are separate in my mind, as they are in Mrs Daldy's." Lucy smiled inwardly. She believed she just put forward a counterargument that was both logical and eloquent, and one she could use many times over.

"Ooh … aren't we being righteous," smirked Hope.

"You are right, Lucy," said Milly cutting in before Lucy could respond. "Grandma Amey has said this for ages. Tackle one issue at a time. Engage with the men. Win the right to vote first. Once women are allowed to vote and can choose who they want to represent them, then they can push for laws around temperance, or any other issue affecting them, as they wish."

"When Mr Fernley and I are married," said Hope, pulling on her gloves, smoothing each finger into place, "I won't be allowing a single drop of liquor in our house. The motto 'lips that touch wine will not touch mine' is my motto too."

Lucy thought her friend was being too imperious. She would only marry someone who treated her as an equal, with a mind and thoughts of her own. A partner who would listen to her ideas as she would listen to his, and together they'd come to an agreement. In return, she would respect his wishes. If the occasional wine in social surroundings was his choice, then so be it.

First, she had to find that man. A man like Mr Richard Harris perhaps.

In the meantime, she had letters to write.

* * * * *

The pair had met several months earlier at her home, of all places. Her father had invited Richard's father, Mr Harry Harris, a business acquaintance, to supper. She'd had no idea his son would be present, but while their fathers talked business at the other end of the table, she and Richard had held a somewhat stilted conversation about their interests.

"And what is your role in the business, Mr Harris?"

He smiled a little sheepishly. "Mostly to do as my father tells me, at this stage, but I have ideas for the future."

To her left, she could hear her father mention something about a joint venture to which Mr Harris senior, loudly enthusiastic, concurred. Lucy wondered what was being set up.

She returned Richard's smile. He was certainly a handsome man, tall and slender, with brown hair and honey-brown eyes, and well dressed but not a fop. She liked what she saw. "And does your father listen to your ideas?"

He took a sip of his wine to choke off a chortle. "Not often, I'm afraid to say. But I'm a patient man, Miss Young. I will bide my time. What about you?"

"My father has raised me to have opinions, Mr Harris. I hope that doesn't offend you."

His eyes sparkled across the table. "Not at all. I would be interested to hear your opinion."

Did he actually wink? Self-conscious, Lucy shifted in her chair.

"If you don't mind me asking," he continued, "what is your opinion of the latest fashions?"

Lucy stared at him, confused. "I give very little thought to fashion. I have a dressmaker who provides me clothes I consider comfortable and she considers becoming. That is all I require. I need much more than frippery to occupy my mind."

His face lit up. "Do you indeed. Such as?"

Mr Harris senior's voice became more voluble with each glass of brandy. Lucy decided they were exploring how the Harris emporium could benefit the Young importing charter.

"I beg your pardon?" She pulled her attention back to Richard.

He dabbed his mouth with his serviette as he finished eating, neatly placing his knife and fork together on the plate. "I was asking what interests you have."

"I enjoy my church activities, and helping at the charity stalls. Bicycling when the weather is fine. Most of all, I enjoy talking with Father about the business and politics."

Richard tilted his head to one side and raised an eyebrow, but his expression was one of surprise rather than censure. "How interesting. Go on." He leant forward to listen more intently.

Encouraged, Lucy took a deep breath. If any arrangement was to develop between their fathers, and by extension, the two of them, then he had to know how passionate she was about securing the vote. "My time is mostly consumed by the campaign for Women's Franchise." She crossed her fingers under the table and hoped he wouldn't take against her.

"Since there is wine at the table, I am presuming you are not a prohibitionist. Either that, or you have no influence over your father at all, which would surprise me greatly."

Was that all he was interested in? Drinking? Surely not, although his portly father, whose waistcoat stretched tightly across his belly, did seem keen on more than a drop to accompany his copious dinner. But more than the liquor he consumed, she deplored the smell of his cigar. She was unused to the odour at such close quarters, since her father had never indulged. She opened her fan to waft the smoke away from her, while she watched her father refill the man's glass but left his empty. He'd always said it was better to do business with a clear head. Richard, too, declined the offer of brandy.

"No. I am not a prohibitionist," Lucy answered, drawing her attention back to the young man across the table. "Although I do believe in moderation and propriety. But I also believe it is time women had the vote. And I am doing everything in my power to achieve the franchise."

"Such as what, precisely?" Was he seriously interested in what she did, or was he probing so he could belittle her efforts?

Lucy raised her chin slightly. "Mostly, I write letters. To as many individuals and organisations as possible to encourage their support. I attend meetings, and listen to the speakers and follow their suggestions, and I have been known to accompany Mrs Daldy, the League's President, to collect signatures for a petition. But enough about me, Mr Harris. What is it you do on a daily basis?" Two could play at that game.

"Nothing as important as you, I assure you," he replied. "I seem to spend my days doing paperwork, utterly boring paperwork. Our accountant does the figures, our storeman balances the stock, my father charms the clients, and I am left …" he turned his head to look glumly at his father, "… with little."

He sounded if not resentful, certainly exasperated as he continued to look across at the two men at the other end of the table with longing.

"Tell me about your company," she said, endeavouring

to draw his attention away from his father's disregard.

He shook his head slightly, as if to bring his mind back to the conversation at hand. He looked sad and his voice was flat. He fiddled, spinning a spoon around against the tablecloth. "Our outlet is barely more than a warehouse with a glass frontage. Goods are displayed haphazardly. Boxes and crates take up most of the space. In general, customers carry goods away with them, although we do deliver if requested, and we deliver the larger pieces, of course. In my opinion, it's inferior to other stores selling similar goods, but it's no good talking to Papa about it."

Lucy did not hide her surprise. "Why ever not? I always tell my father what I think would benefit the business. He sometimes needs a female perspective on what to bring in."

Richard attempted a smile. "You are fortunate. Papa says when he wants my opinion, he'll ask for it."

"Well, I'm asking. What are your aspirations?"

For the next fifteen minutes, he regaled her with his vision of a modern general merchant with electric light, glass counters, display shelves and uniformed staff offering an array of goods to vie with any other similar emporium.

"I congratulate you. They are indeed great objectives. I hope they may come to fruition."

"What's that, my dear?" asked her father rising from the table.

"We were just sharing our thoughts on the future, Father."

"Glad to hear it. Harry and I have concluded our business. Say goodnight, dear."

They, too, stood, and she bade Mr Harris senior farewell.

Richard took her hand and bowed. "I would be honoured if we could continue our conversation at some other time, Miss Young. I believe you and I have many ideals in common."

"Thank you." Her heart leapt. "I shall look forward to the opportunity, should one arise." There was still so much to discuss but, given his father's manner, she hadn't expected Richard to be so liberal and accept her role in winning the vote so easily.

Could he be the perfect soulmate?

5
The first clues

Wanting to avoid another run-in with her brother, Paige had suggested they meet for coffee well away from busy Newmarket. "I've got a top-of-the-range electric bike to get around. I refused to drive the smelly fossil-fuel car Dad wanted to buy me."

Admirable, and in keeping with the girl's values, but Emma wondered if the car was offered as a safety measure by a devoted father or as a status symbol by a boastful businessman. She'd need to be careful not to start judging this man she didn't know by his daughter's pique.

As usual, Emma was already seated when the girl arrived.

"Is this any good?" asked Paige, as she sat down. She handed Emma a wooden trinket box with a brass inlay that was clearly old, giving Emma an adrenaline rush.

"I went hunting for something of Mum's and found this hidden in my father's wardrobe," Paige continued, running her finger over the 'L' engraved into the central brass diamond. "I don't know what half of it is …" She hesitated, suddenly deep in thought. "I guess he must

43

have kept it for a reason. Was he going to give it to me someday? Or maybe I'm hoping for too much."

Despite herself, a feeling of pity for the girl surfaced, and Emma was glad she'd agreed to help discover something about Paige's past. She knew she was getting too involved too quickly with the young woman, but justified herself with the argument that she'd wished she'd had a 'someone' to talk to at the same age. "Whatever his reasons, when, or if, he intended to tell you about it, at least you have something that belonged to your mum, now." She paused wondering whether to express her concern. "Have you told him you've taken it?"

The girl shook her head.

"I think you should. Otherwise he might think there's been an intruder." Emma left the rest unsaid.

Paige shrugged that one-shoulder hitch that was a regular gesture of hers. Emma couldn't decide if it was indifference or a barricade against hurt, but it was beginning to irritate.

"Can you tell me anything about it?" asked Emma as Paige lifted a gold locket on a heavy rope chain from the box.

"Nope. But I love this locket. There's a photo inside. See?" She opened the locket to show Emma the tiny black-and-white image of a Victorian woman.

"Do you have any idea who she might be?"

"Nope."

Paige shut the locket and held it tightly in her palm while Emma fingered through a collection of pins, badges and crests, and other bits of antique jewellery. She'd have to try to do a reverse image search to find out what some of the badges were. One or two had letters on them that might help. At the bottom was a newspaper cutting. Feeling her pulse quicken, Emma took a glance at the date and the length, and reluctantly left it to read later.

"That's quite a gold mine of information," she said. "It'll take a while to decipher it all. May I take it home with me? I promise to look after everything. But you must tell your father. All right? I don't want to be accused of stealing."

"He won't care."

"But I do. Promise me you'll tell him."

Another one-shoulder shrug.

"Paige?" Emma admonished, glaring at her.

"Okay, okay. I'll tell him. But I want to keep this." The gold locket was still clutched in her hand, the chain wrapped around her thumb.

"Of course. Can I take a few photos of it?"

Emma got out her phone and took several snaps front and back, and of the chain and the clasp, looking for a maker's mark but didn't find anything helpful. "Have you got any photos of your mother or grandmother? They might help."

Paige shook her head again. "One of my mum, but it's not very good. Dad's not into photos much. He never bothers. I'll see if there's any old ones packed away."

Again, Emma sensed the sadness of Paige's life. She was missing out on so much. Now she had Luke and Rose to love, Emma knew how important family was.

She picked up a more modern enamel pin and held it up for Paige to see. "Look at this." The creamy-white background showed the words Women's Suffrage on the top curve and Whakatū Wāhine on the lower curve. In the middle was a purple and gold loop with the dates 1893–1993.

"Wow. That's cool."

"Going by the dates, it was made for the Suffrage Centennial. I wonder if your mother had anything do with the celebrations? She'd have been a little older than you are now, I think. Were your parents married at that time?"

"Dunno. Cam was born in '98."

Emma made a note to investigate and continued to rummage through the box.

Full of beans now, Paige asked, "Do you think my mum was a suffragette? Or an activist of some kind. Is that what Dad meant?"

"I don't know. Maybe. And *our* women were called suffragists, women who peacefully lobbied for universal suffrage – the right to vote – through petitions and writing letters. Unlike the British suffragettes who were far more militant and often ended up in gaol after acts of civil disobedience."

"I didn't know that." Paige started to look through the jewellery more keenly, picking up the odd badge. One with a dove and some leaves, another with a female gender symbol. "Are these women's activist groups?"

"I suspect so, but let me do some research and try to date them before we jump to conclusions."

"It'd be cool if they were." Her eyes sparkled. "I'd like to think my mum was a protester."

Again, Emma's empathy for the girl rose. She so desperately needed something to give her life purpose. "I'd better get started then. Let me know if you find anything, and send me a copy of any photos of your mum. I'll see what I can discover and we'll meet again in a few days." She gathered her bag and carefully held the trinket box. "By the way, what was your mother's name?"

"Lucy."

Buzzing to begin, Emma raced home to read the article.

* * * * *

Awed by its age and fearing the ancient newspaper clipping would disintegrate if she handled it too much, Emma searched the Papers Past website until she found the detailed account from the *Auckland Star*, dated Tuesday, 5 July 1892.

Headlined 'Eloquent Female Advocates', the lengthy article covered details of the well-supported meeting of the Auckland Women's Franchise League held the previous evening at the Opera House, on what must have been a cold winter's night. What a momentous occasion that meeting must have been.

She pressed her hands to her face and rubbed her eyes before getting up to stretch and pace the room, trying to shake off the sudden wave of lethargy.

The article was a gem of information, full of names and who said what, which gave her a lot to work on. She suspected few people would know anything about those women who fought for what they believed in, other than Kate Sheppard, the most famous of the suffragists. Emma felt a great sense of pride reading about the many unsung women who had coordinated the movement elsewhere in the country.

She sat down again and wrote a list of the names to work on later, and began searching for information about the Opera House. From one description, a picture of the theatre decked out with plush seating, dark colours and heavy proscenium curtains formed in Emma's mind. She could even imagine the whirl of sounds, filling the multilevel auditorium. Built in 1882 in Wellesley Street, it had been considered one of the finest in its day. "Oh, what a pity," she mumbled as she read it had burned to the ground in December 1926.

Soon after, Smith & Caughey expanded its original Queen Street store to incorporate the area where the Opera House had once stood, to give them additional street access from Wellesley Street. Fascinating as she found it, none of it, so far, helped her with Paige's family.

She turned her attention back to the trinket box and was busy writing down names and organisations, trying to decipher how the badges fitted, when her mobile rang. "Hi, Jess."

"Hey, Ems, are you around? I've got something to show you."

"Sure, pop on over. I've got a few things to show you too."

While she waited for Jess to arrive, Emma started on a rough guesstimate of the generations of women leading to Paige. Allowing a span of twenty-five years for each generation, she took a stab that Paige was probably Gen 6. Her mother, Gen 5, and her grandmother Gen 4.

Emma's mind buzzed. Maybe two or possibly three leaps more would take her back to a suffrage connection. What was her grandmother's name again?

Emma checked the original notes she taken. She'd written to check Amelia as a possibility. She smiled. Of course! If one of Paige's names was Amelia and her mother was called Lucy, she'd take a bet on the naming pattern being continued in some form.

Emma looked up at a tap on the French doors. All she could see was an enormous bunch of flowers and a pair of leggings and sneakers. She scrambled around her desk to open the door. "Who are they for? They're gorgeous."

"This delivery is for you." Jess manoeuvred her way inside.

"Me? Who from?" Emma sniffed at the heads of roses, lisianthus and iris surrounded by greenery.

"Someone who loves you." Jess put the florist's water box on the wine table in the corner. She'd never looked back since getting into the floristry business after her divorce.

"Luke sent them?" Emma puzzled. On the occasions he had bought flowers, he brought them home himself. But she felt he was too cross with her at present to be buying flowers.

"No, silly, they're my way of saying *take care of yourself.*"

"Not you too." Emma reached out to hug her friend before they sat in the wingback chairs to chat. "Thank you, they're lovely. You spoil me."

"You're welcome, and yes. Me, too. Luke tells me you're still feeling exhausted. I worry about you."

"I'm much better than I was," argued Emma, but the raised eyebrow and the don't-give-me-that-nonsense look from Jess defeated her. "But, okay. There are still times when I feel tired for no reason. But I can't give in to it. I'm in my forties not my nineties." Emma was sick of people fussing. "I've got work to do."

"I remember what you told me when I was going through divorce hell. Breathe deeply and take one day at a time. There's no point in killing yourself. Will you at least take your own advice?"

"Maybe."

Jess waggled a finger towards her. "You'd better. Now what're you working on that's so important?"

Emma immediately perked up at the chance of talking about what she'd discovered. "One client is proving relatively simple. They had quite a bit of information about their ancestor, Ruby, all the way back to the Tailoresses' Union in 1890. I just need to flesh out what I know about the history and put her in the mix. I'm quite enjoying that, but the other one is a bit more complicated."

"In what way?"

"I met this girl when I gave a presentation to a group of uni students. She approached me when I'd finished and asked about how she could find the women in her past. I felt sorry for her and offered to help. Her mother died young, her father's too busy for her, so's her brother, and there doesn't seem to be any extended family. By the sound of it, she's the odd one out in a male-dominated household."

"That's not so unusual. What's the problem?" asked Jess.

"I'm not sure. Her father seems to think she's a 'troublemaker' because she has ideas about climate action, and she thinks he's a money-grubber."

"None of that sounds like something you want to get involved with," warned Jess, knowing how compassionate Emma could be.

"Normally, no, but she brought me this box." Emma reached across to her desk and handed it to Jess. "It's full of badges and pins belonging to activist groups as far back as the suffragists. She thinks they belong to her mother." Watching Jess finger the various items, Emma had a thought. "Have you ever visited the Centennial Memorial in the city?"

"The one by those steps below the Art Gallery?"

"Yes. Do you want to visit it with me?"

"Good grief. Why?"

Emma slumped in her chair. "No reason, I suppose. It's all online. I just thought I might get a feeling about things if I went there."

"Looking at you at the moment, I'd say stick to the online version. But I'm guessing you've already done that."

"I have." Emma rested her head against the wing of her chair, curled one leg under the other and yawned. "Did you know they used over 2,000 handmade tiles to portray nine of the women leaders, the bicycle women and the emblems? It's huge. It lines the walls on both sides, and covers two sets of steps." Emma tried, and failed, to stifle another yawn.

"Wasn't there a big fuss about whether it should be moved or redeveloped or something. I read some women got together to save it."

"They did."

"So what's the story with it now?"

"It's a heritage site."

"That's good, but what has it got to do with what you're working on?"

"I have no idea. But there's got to be a connection somewhere."

Emma let her eyes close.

"I'll make us a cup of tea while you take a moment," said Jess. "Won't be long."

As Emma drifted off to sleep, she imagined the scene at the Opera House she'd read about.

6

A step forward

Auckland
4 July 1892

At 8 pm on the dot, Mrs Amey Daldy rose from her place as chairwoman behind the official table and walked to the centre of the stage. Banners of white, purple and gold hung behind her, and baskets of white camellias decorated the sparseness. Silence descended on the animated crowd filling every cranny of the Opera House from the gallery to the pit, with many more standing in the corridors.

Lucy, sitting in the front of the dress circle with her two friends, drew a deep breath to settle her nerves. The tiny lady, with her distinctive lace cap, was wearing a camellia corsage pinned to her high-collared grey dress, which still sported a bustle from last decade, but no one cared. She exuded such zeal for the cause, Lucy was once again held in thrall.

"Isn't it wonderful," she whispered to Milly. "I wrote so many letters inviting people to attend and look how many are here."

Lucy never tired of the so-called interminable meetings Hope complained of, or became bored by the repetitive nature of the message being delivered. If anything, they inspired her to think of new ways to ensure the message was heard. She felt a sense of oneness, a unity of purpose in being together. She was sure that was why Mrs Daldy held so many meetings. To unite people. Even so, Lucy had never taken part in a gathering as large as this before. She turned her head to survey the audience and take in all the details. To say she was impressed was saying the least.

Lucy counted herself as one of the stalwarts, even if she considered her involvement with the movement small scale, and was determined to do more. For the time being, she followed Mrs Daldy's instructions and spent her time writing letters, handing out pamphlets and listening to a handful of well-dressed, reputable women discuss the points to debate.

The audience was restless as people began to arrive and take their seats.

"Shut that baby up!" yelled a male voice as one particularly loud squalling infant was carried into the auditorium.

Lucy had never expected to find so many working women present, still dressed in their work clothes. Some carried infants and babies strapped to them in well-worn shawls, and many had not washed recently. She held her handkerchief to her nose wondering what such women would add to the meeting.

She immediately scolded herself for her uncharitable thoughts, as she patted her swept up hairstyle with her new ribbon-and-feather bedecked bonnet placed jauntily to one side. The whole point of the franchise case was equality for all women, regardless of their situation. She should not judge people by their clothing but by the values. Women deserved better. No one was above another.

"This meeting," announced Mrs Daldy, her voice filling the auditorium, "has been called by the Women's Franchise League. Its aim is to give the women of Auckland the opportunity to proclaim … To the Government. The Legislature. And to the world – that they claim the right – equally with men – to choose the representatives who make the laws by which they live."

The polite clapping from gloved hands following her opening statement became swamped by shouts of ayes from amongst the workers, and far too many nays for Lucy's comfort. Mrs Daldy raised her hand for quiet and continued explaining how and why the League had been formed and the involvement of Miss Helen Nicol and Miss Harriet Morison.

Appearing more confident as her speech progressed, Lucy watched as Amey Daldy paced to and fro, cleverly engaging people on both sides of the auditorium. Lucy's eyes followed her, and she spied none other than Richard Harris leaning nonchalantly against the wall at the end of her row, watching her. Arms folded, he held his bowler hat in his hand but touched his forelock as a grin spread across his face. Lucy blushed and quickly turned her attention back to Mrs Daldy.

"I am pleased to see so many young women here tonight. And encouraged. The duty of exercising your right, honestly and intelligently, will fall to you in the future."

Letting the words she'd heard before fade into the background, Lucy surreptitiously turned her head to look towards Mr Harris again. He was still watching her. She gasped quietly. His hat was now perched on the back of his head. She thought he looked so handsome and was gladdened to see him there. This time she smiled back as they added their applause to what had been said.

Encouraged, Mrs Daldy continued, her voice reverberating. "I invite, nay, I exhort, every woman to enrol as a member of the League, that we may obtain the franchise without delay. Let us make New Zealand the brightest gem in our Sovereign's possessions, by leading the van in this grand crusade."

Cheers, foot stamping, hand waving and rapturous applause concluded Mrs Daldy's speech. A few male voices heckled, but whatever they were trying to say was drowned out by supporters demanding the franchise.

Lucy stared around her in wonder, overcome by a deep conviction that she was a part of history-making that would be talked about for a long time to come. Her eyes met Richard's again, and she felt certain he, too, shared the same sense of destiny. In that long gaze, they were of one mind and one heart until she forced herself to tear her eyes away from his.

Mrs Daldy called for order and the next speaker rose to put forward the formal motion demanding franchise to be voted on.

"Hear, hear!" came the almost unanimous response as Lizzie Rattray explained the purpose of the motion.

"Since women are subjected to the same laws as men we should be entitled to have a say on who makes those laws. Yet we do not. We are expected to pay the same taxes. To pay the same fare on the railway and aboard the steamers as men …"

"But we don't eat as much," shouted a woman from the crowd, drawing laughter from those around her.

Lucy could see men, whom she assumed were reporters, scribbling furiously in their notebooks, recording all that was said. A thrill shivered through her, followed by a moment of doubt. Would they faithfully report the words spoken, and the sense of oneness she felt? Or would those words be twisted and used against them?

She knew of men opposed to the idea of prohibition, but how could any rational person dispute the logical entreaties for women's franchise? She shot a quick look towards Richard again, who seemed intent on the speaker. She studied him for a moment longer, luxuriating in the opportunity to admire him without him knowing before she pulled her attention back to Mrs Rattray, who was still putting forward arguments in favour of her motion.

"Why should wage-earning women be treated any differently to wage-earning men?" she demanded.

Lucy could not agree more and added her voice to the acclaim. She wanted to throw off the propriety that smothered so many women beneath unwritten codes of behaviour. But she couldn't quite bring herself to speak out more loudly. Not yet. Not with Richard there, in case he disapproved. That topic was yet to be broached, but his being at the meeting was a good sign.

Boos and catcalls filled her ears. "How dare they deny women the franchise!"

By now the impassioned audience were calling out and jostling each other. Wanting to wave, to be heard, to see better, to be seen. Others clapping loudly muffled the few dissenters who had dared express a contrary opinion. She lost sight of Richard as people moved across her line of vision. Was he still there?

More speakers took the floor to reiterate their sentiments about equal rights and freedoms.

Mrs Ellis shouted, "Taxation without representation is tyranny! We have carried the 'Eve' burden long enough. Franchise must be ours."

The ovation continued long after Mrs Ellis sat, until Mrs Daldy was forced to call for order. Lucy's ears rang as silence once again descended and the more formal part of the evening began. She knew the routine inside out.

"We are glad to have with us tonight men of influence, who support our cause," announced the chairwoman. "We will need such men, so I hereby call on Bishop Cowie to say a few words."

Mr Bell, a regular agitator, called out from the audience. "Excuse me, but I understood no gentlemen were to speak tonight."

"Not so," replied Mrs Daldy. "We make no distinction between men and women who wish to help the movement."

Lucy had met the Bishop Dr Cowie and was thankful of his support. He often made sense of things.

"After the eloquent speakers we have heard so far tonight," he began, "I fear my input is of lesser value. But I wish, however, to suggest …" He put his fist to his mouth to clear his throat. "Clearly, it would be absurd to suggest that women would be as good as men as soldiers, or stokers on a man-of-war. Or that men could be as good at nurturing a child or nursing the sick in hospitals. It is equally absurd to think that the gentleness, forbearance and unselfishness that are women's strengths would deteriorate should they be given the franchise. If men and women are alike in the eyes of God, they should be alike in the eye of the law."

Like the others, his speech was peppered with applause and shouts of 'hear, hear'. Lucy sat on the edge of her seat, alongside the hundreds filling the house listening, interjecting and bolstering every word. But there were also dissenters.

"Rubbish! You don't know that? What if …" Mr Bell's attempts to question Bishop Cowie were shouted down with booing and jeers.

"Sit down."

"Put him out."

"He's not welcome."

For a moment, a frisson of fear at the sudden animosity sent goosebumps up Lucy's arms. She prayed the crowd would not get out of hand. A glance to her left reassured her that Richard was still there. Looking at her. Smiling at her. She returned his smile, feeling safer knowing he was nearby.

"Order. Order," called Mrs Daldy, the echo of the gavel resounding off the walls. The arrival of a constable who took the man aside at that point restored control.

Lucy relaxed. "Isn't this wonderful?" she whispered to her companions.

Hope looked at her witheringly. "I wish they'd keep

the hoi polloi quiet. Though I admit the likelihood of succeeding is now more viable."

"Hope!" interjected Milly. "That's so patronising. Don't let Grandma Amey hear you. Women are all in this together, regardless of class."

Hope shrugged indifferently as the girls listened to more speakers, each of them emphasising the points of justice, equality and intellectual ability that every other speaker had addressed.

The motion was passed without further ado and a second motion was put forward by Mrs Kerr Taylor. By now, the audience was shouting and clapping after nearly every sentence. A few hecklers continued to try to out-shout the women but were soon put in their place.

"Be quiet!"

Was that Richard's voice? Her eyes sought him out. He stood near the guard rail of the balcony with his hands cupped around his mouth. "Quiet, I say."

Reverend Barry was next to try and quieten the electric crowd. "I can only say how sorry I am that the Bill passed by the Lower House last year was thrown out by the Upper House. And by a mere two votes. But this year, I believe the Act will become law, and before many more weeks shall pass, as it justly should," he shouted above the clamour.

"What about women's brain size then?" yelled another man. "We all know their heads are smaller."

"My dear man, if people were to be denied a vote based on the size of their head, then the brilliant Sir Walter Scott would have been one of those. He had perhaps the smallest head of his generation," rebutted the Reverend, to much hilarity.

"My 'ead's bigger than your balls. Bet I put it to better use." A women's voice echoed from the gallery followed by a babel of vulgar comments.

"At least women'll use what's up there for thinking, not what's down there for mating."

Lucy blushed at the coarse language. Her father would not like it at all, if he'd known, but she couldn't restrain an internal giggle. Richard, meanwhile, did not hold back. She could see him guffaw quite openly, his head tilted back and his mouth wide. A warm feeling swept over her that he should find such frankness amusing, and acceptable.

Mrs Daldy banged the gavel several more times calling for further order. "Quiet, ladies and gentlemen. Quiet, I beg you. We must conduct ourselves in a dignified manner. We have important business to conclude."

Once the rustling and murmuring had settled, Mrs Daldy indicated Mrs Schnackenberg should take the floor to put forward a third resolution, one that expressed gratitude to the wonderful Sir John Hall for his support and influence.

The motion was seconded as the auditorium once again burst into applause. Whoops and cheers echoed around the theatre at each of the following speakers. People stood to add their voice and second motions so fast Lucy couldn't keep up with who said what.

"I move that the Secretary be empowered to send copies of the resolutions passed at this meeting to the Honourable Mr John Ballance the Premier, Sir John Hall, Sir George Grey, and the Auckland members of Parliament," Mrs Williams stated solemnly. "I sincerely pray the two Māori members who voted against the motion last time will not do so again."

Their names were engraved on Lucy's memory; Hori Taiaroa and Major Rōpata Wahawaha.

Last, but not least, Mrs Caradus. "I move that the hearty thanks of this meeting be accorded to the press for the generous support given to this movement."

Lucy was glad to hear someone say it out loud, feeling guilty for thinking otherwise earlier in the evening. "There's so many on our side, surely it will pass this year," she whispered to Milly.

The entire auditorium was on its feet. Voices seconded the motion and supported its adoption.

"Thank you one and all," said Mrs Daldy after calling for silence. "I believe that brings us to the conclusion of the evening. I am gratified by such large and enthusiastic support for our cause. May we succeed."

Still on her feet, Lucy added her gloved hands to the tumultuous clapping. She grinned broadly, her flushed cheeks and bright eyes spoke of her enthusiasm. "I must remind Mrs Daldy I am willing to collect signatures for the petition," she told Milly.

As she exited the row, Mr Harris was waiting. She looked up at his tall frame. Warm eyes returned her gaze, and in that moment, she knew he was the one for her.

"May I escort you, Miss Young?" He proffered his arm as she gazed once more into his eyes and folded her arm inside his.

7

Fretful moments

Emma was rushing by the time she reached the café. She'd become so engrossed in her latest search she'd lost track of time. Paige was already seated at a outdoor table in the corner. To Emma's surprise, she had a blond, surfie-looking, young man with her.

"Sorry I'm late," she puffed.

"That's okay. I'd like you to meet Ryan. He's um, well we're working on a climate change project together."

Emma saw the way Paige looked at him and thought there was more to it than Paige was telling her. "Shall we order first, then we can chat," she suggested, wondering how she could talk to Paige about her family with a stranger listening.

"I'm just leaving," he said, getting up from the table. "Nice to meet you." He turned to Paige. "Catch up later, babe."

Emma held her tongue at the label, hoping he wasn't going to be added to the list of arrogant young men who thought women lesser beings.

"Isn't he gorgeous," said Paige as soon as Ryan was out of earshot.

"He seems nice enough," hedged Emma. "But I thought you were single after getting rid of that Simon boy."

Paige shrugged. "I was, but I met Ryan at the beginning of last year. He thinks along the same lines as me. Then when Si turned into such an idiot, I thought, why not? I asked Ryan if he'd like to go for a bike ride." She grinned mischievously. "It's only been a few months, but he's so much nicer than any other boy I've met."

Their drinks and food arrived, and Paige continued to tell her about Ryan's interest in climate and the environment. "I know he doesn't look it, but he's actually Cam's age and is doing his postgrad in enviro science."

Emma filed away that piece of information, thinking the girl had a lot of common sense hidden beneath her inexperience. "I wish you luck, then. Now, I've found out a few things about those pins. There were dozens of them."

Paige pushed aside her empty plate, and leaned forward with arms folded on the table, eager to hear more.

Emma opened her notebook. "A couple marked 'For God, Home and Humanity' with a ribbon bow in the centre are Women's Christian Temperance Union badges. The WCTU was once a powerful force and nearly achieved prohibition in 1918 until votes from the returning soldiers were counted."

"Wowser! Truly?"

Emma laughed. "Where did you hear that term? It came from the Temperance Union."

"Did it?" She hitched her shoulder. "To me it's just a longer way of saying wow. As in, that's 'cool' or that's 'lame'." Paige mimed inverted commas around the words.

"Interesting, but not quite. A wowser was someone – especially a woman – who wanted to stop men drinking alcohol."

"Huh! That makes sense. What about the other stuff you found?"

"There's quite a few variations of the WCTU badge. And several iterations of the pins for NCW – the National Council of Women, which formed a few years after winning the vote in 1893 – and NOW, the National Organisation for Women, which was a different group and came decades later."

"Never heard of them. What did they all do?"

"Basically, they were all forms of feminist groups where women could meet away from the home, to discuss anything from domesticity and cooking to politics and activism. Some still exist, because they changed their focus to suit issues affecting women's lives over time."

"Something like the action groups I go to?" queried Paige.

"Pretty much."

"Cool. I like that idea. What else?"

"Let me see," said Emma, reading from a list. "There's a Quaker one, a few anti-war, a nurse's pin, and a feminist badge from the 1970s. A couple of Women's International League for Peace and Freedom badges, which seem a bit out of place to me, as it's more European based. That's the dove and laurel branch one. They date from World War One, so later than the others. The WILPF were … are," Emma corrected, "mostly anti-war protesters."

"You mean they're still around today? Wow. I don't agree with war either. Look what's happening in Ukraine right now. It's awful. Nobody should be allowed to kill people." Paige made that harrumph sound again. "Tell me more."

"Which, about the badges or the peace league?"

"Both, but the peace league first."

"Look them up on their website if you're interested. But like I said, anti-war since World War One, and briefly a branch of the Labour Party. Still anti-war, anti-nuclear and had quaker connections. Aha! That might be where the Quaker badge fits in." Emma scribbled a note in her journal to follow up and try to discover which generation would fit. She didn't mention the SPWC badge she'd found. There was little point until she could identify the initials.

Paige stared at her in disbelief. "You really get into this stuff, don't you."

Emma momentarily looked taken aback. "I do. And I make no apology for it. And isn't this what you asked me to do?"

Paige's one-shoulder hitch annoyed Emma this time. She was too tired to be bothered with bad manners.

"Look, if you want to know about the past, I'm willing to help you discover it, but don't waste my time if you'd rather be somewhere else, or with someone else."

"What're you getting huffy about? I didn't say anything."

"No, but that dismissive shrug you give says a lot."

"What? This?" She demonstrated. "Is that what's got you all snarky? It's nothing. Means okay. I get the drift."

"Well, it's a funny way to say it. Most people would think it rude."

Anger flickered and Paige's eyes turned golden. "If that's what you think, I'm done." She gathered her bag and strode out of the café.

Emma watched her unlock her bike, put her helmet on and ride off at a surprising speed, wondering why Paige had suddenly got so angry. There had to be something more behind it. She'd apologise next time for misunderstanding – assuming Paige wanted to meet again. Emma hadn't meant to be so snappy, she was just so tired, and she still had the trinket box. She'd need to return it but meantime, she wanted to do more research. Those badges had her intrigued.

* * * * *

Days had gone by and Emma still hadn't heard from Paige.

"I wouldn't fret," said Luke when she sought his advice. "If she wants you to continue she'll ask. You can't do anything if a client doesn't want you to."

"Yes, but … she's not exactly a client, is she? She's not paying me."

Luke never interfered with her business decisions. If she wanted to do pro bono work, that was her choice, but he didn't like her getting too deeply involved. "Don't get caught up, Ems. A touchy teenager isn't your problem. You don't need her angst on top of everything else you're coping with."

She gritted her teeth at his constant reference to the fatigue she was suffering, but refused to bite back. "I can't help worrying, though. Something's not right. And I still have the trinket box. I'll have to give that back, at least."

"When she wants it, she'll make contact. Let her stew for a while. I'm more concerned about you."

"I'm fine. I keep telling you. It's you who keeps blowing it up to be something bigger."

"One of us has to take care of you, since you don't seem interested."

"I don't need looking after!"

"Tell that to the doctor. Then if she says there's nothing wrong, I'll let it be."

"I don't need to go to a doctor. I'm fine. Do you hear me, I'm fine."

Furious, Luke stormed off without another word. Emma watched him stride along the corridor, their usual harmony shattered.

With a thumping headache and close to tears, she made her way to her office. She hated fighting with Luke, but she couldn't seem to get through to him any more. Determined to take her mind off their argument, she switched on her computer and turned her thoughts to Jean, her other client. She found it uncanny that she should be researching one story only to find that Paige had presented her with a number of pins and badges from the same women's groups.

Never one to simply do the basics of her job, she wanted to know more about the girl's father. She suspected he had a lot to do with the young woman's brittleness.

She put David Frazer's name in a Google search and saw the smiling face of a man in his late fifties, and checked her notes. *He's older than I expected. Paige's mother was a good decade or more younger.*

Returning to the screen, Emma read about his rapid rise in the business world. Sole shareholder of his own corporation, operating as the umbrella for several subsidiaries. Newspaper reports of his business dealings ran from charming and charitable to high-handed and intractable, depending on who had the larger sphere of influence.

From what she could fathom, he was a hard-nosed businessman, who thought highly of himself and his ability, and liked to show off. All of which fitted the little asides Paige had mentioned. Emma'd had a bad feeling about him and nothing she had read made him appear any more congenial, but he wasn't her problem.

She shut the search down and opened up the page on Ancestry she'd set up. She added the known details to Paige's profile and guessed at some others. As she was writing down the naming pattern and trying to fit dates, she let out a groan at the stabbing pain slicing her head, and screwed up her eyes.

Headaches – and tears – were becoming a more regular and frustrating feature of her working day. She stretched her shoulders back, easing the ache that had developed and made a note to book an appointment with an optometrist. Maybe she needed glasses. Some days, she felt so tired she struggled to concentrate. Falling asleep in the chair the other day while Jess was making them a cuppa was embarrassing enough, but at least it hadn't been a client.

Thinking about clients, Emma checked the time. Jean was booked for three o'clock – she had just enough time to take a stroll around the garden and clear her head. Out amongst the roses, Emma felt fresher, but swallowed a couple of paracetamol to be sure. By the time Jean arrived, she felt much better.

"Hello, Jean. Come in and take a seat," she said, indicating one of the wingback chairs she loved.

"What information do you have for me today," asked her client, a down-to-earth woman in her late sixties.

"Something quite significant."

"Ooh. Don't keep me in suspense," said Jean, breathlessly, her hand on her chest.

"I believe your ancestor Ruby was a suffragist."

Jean's eyes lit up. "Oh my, that's a surprise. I didn't think we had anyone important in our family." She suddenly frowned. "I'm sorry to say I'm rather ignorant of what went on in those days. You'll have to tell me about it. We learnt more about the suffragettes in Britain."

"We did," agreed Emma. "And they were forced to become much more militant and violent to get heard."

Jean brightened. "That's right. There's been a movie about it all, hasn't there. One of them died, didn't she."

"Yes. Emily Davison was killed by King George V's horse when she ran onto the racetrack."

Jean looked up and put her forefinger to her lip before pointing at her. "I remember now. They went on hunger strikes to protest at their treatment and were force-fed. Must have been ghastly."

Emma sat up straighter in her chair and stretched her neck. It wouldn't do to fall asleep. "Even after all that, British women didn't get the full franchise for more than three decades after us. Thankfully, none of that happened here."

"My goodness. I hadn't thought about it like that. So, our Ruby was a suffragette. How marvellous."

Emma picked up some papers from the desk and handed them to Jean. "It's all in there, but briefly, from the foundation of the Women's Christian Temperance Union, the WCTU, in 1885, the idea of the franchise and temperance went hand in hand."

Jean pulled a face. "I'm glad we didn't get prohibition. I like a good G&T myself, and my Charlie loves his beer. You're not old enough to remember the six o'clock swill, are you? It wasn't good. Men would rush into the bars after work and drink as much beer as they could before 6 pm closing. Disgusting, noisy places they were too. No woman would be seen in them."

"No, I wasn't born then, however ..." said Emma, attempting to turn the conversation back, but Jean was in full stride.

"They didn't extend the hours to 10 pm until the late 1960s. What a change that was! You could get a drink with your meal at restaurants, and at the club after the footy. We had some good times in those days." Jean sighed. "We even had wine at our wedding. Don't remember what it was now. Probably something sweet, but we felt so sophisticated back then."

Emma listened politely. Of course she didn't personally remember, but she did know the history of the time. Early closing was first introduced in 1917. She just hadn't thought it relevant.

"How does Kate Sheppard fit in then?" Jean asked suddenly, taking Emma by surprise.

"Oh, um ... she was based in Christchurch and the WCTU's driving force responsible for promoting women's rights. She wasn't the only one, by any means, which is where your Ruby comes in a few years after that."

"Well I never! A real-life suffragette." Jean put her hand to her heart again and let out a long sigh, giving Emma space to continue.

"I was looking for Harriet Morison, of the Tailoresses' Union. You remember, Ruby was a seamstress."

"Yes, I do. But I hadn't realised she was a crusader. Wasn't the union about getting better conditions and wages?"

"That too, but more importantly, Harriet became a campaigner for women's suffrage."

"And our Ruby knew her?"

"Without a doubt. Harriet Morison was a radical for her day, and helped establish union and franchise branches throughout the country. I believe Ruby was a member of several of those fledgling organisations seeking a better deal for women."

Jean nodded. "Wouldn't you just love to talk to Ruby right now about what she did and the people she knew?"

"Indeed I would. Fortunately, many women left letters and journals telling us about their lives. They're gems to any historian, and I don't know what I'd do without the newspaper archives."

"I don't think I've ever felt the need to write to a newspaper in my life," said Jean. "Oh, I've got old copies of *The Weekly News* at home. I wonder if she's in them? I must look. We're so fortunate today that we have equal rights."

Wealthy Western women might have them, thought Emma, *but not all women*. Many aspects of women's rights still needed rectifying, in her view, especially for those who were neither white nor wealthy.

"You said on the phone you had something to show me," said Emma.

"That's right. I almost forgot what with all your news and everything." Jean rummaged around in her handbag and pulled out a small mesh bag. "I thought you might know what this was." She handed Emma a faded scrap of fabric.

Emma recognised the colours instantly. "That's part of a suffrage ribbon. It stands for Give Women the Vote – Gold, White, Violet. Did this belong to Ruby?" Emma was eagerly wondering how she could tie all these women's movements together.

"I wish I knew."

8

On the campaign trail

August 1892

In the weeks since that triumphant meeting in early July, word had spread, hundreds of letters had been written and dozens more meetings held. Lucy had attended every one and had written so many letters her fingers were stained with ink. Some days her hand ached with the strain. To ease the tedium, Milly would join Lucy at the dining table in the Young household.

"I'm so tired of writing the same thing over and over," moaned Lucy. "It's all so stuffy and been said before. I wish we could come up with a new approach."

"I know! But we have to write what we're told, and explain it clearly so everyone can understand," answered Milly, tucking another letter inside its envelope and adding it to the stack.

"Everyone knows why by now, surely? It's been talked about enough."

"Have you heard from the delightful Mr Richard Harris lately?" asked Milly with a look of such innocent enquiry that Lucy almost laughed, but instead put her hand to her mouth to cover a pretend cough and lowered her head to hide the blush.

"Once or twice," Lucy said offhandedly.

"Ooh. Do tell," said Milly, eyes almost popping from her head with excitement.

"Nothing to tell yet." Which was the truth, but she certainly hoped she would have something to tell Milly soon.

Lucy chewed on the end of her pen, thinking, writing a few words and crossing them out. "What do you think of this: Ladies, imagine the thrill of casting a vote that could change the way our lives are governed. You can be one of thousands of women who will change the world as we know it …" She paused, reread what she'd written and continued to write, reading out loud. "It is with great pride I ask you to welcome the canvassers who will be collecting signatures in your area soon. If you should miss them, do hurry along to your nearest church hall or women's group and sign the petition there. Demand women receive the vote! Together we can succeed. Do not delay."

"That's wonderful, Lucy. Clever you."

Alongside many hundreds of other women throughout the country, Lucy set about collecting signatures to reinforce their claim. Armed with posters and wearing camellias they were instantly recognisable wherever they went.

Every week, paired with one of the married women with whom she had little in common, other than wanting the vote, Lucy faithfully trod the path from house to house collecting as many signatures as they could. "She's got the charm of a stick of wood," complained Lucy next time she saw Milly. "No wonder no one stops to listen to her. Or sign the petitions. I usually manage to leave a sheet behind, hoping they might sign it, but I'm not sure many will."

On a number of occasions, Lucy met animosity. Few men gave them the time of day. She was often told, 'Get away with you,' or 'Stop harassing my wife,' and 'Don't you go asking around the back either'."

These were common phrases among the men of means, while 'I don't want nuffin' to do with any of you wowsers. Bitter old hags the lot of you,' was a refrain she heard time and again from wage-earning men.

But she was not deterred.

Lucy decided Saturday half-day was not the best day to visit. "I think you and I should go together," she told Milly, "and begin our rounds shortly after nine o'clock on weekday mornings when the men are away at work."

"Sounds like a good suggestion, but I should ask Grandma Amey first."

After consultation, the girls were given permission to change their routine as long as they went together. "And don't go any near public houses or workplaces without an escort," directed Mrs Daldy.

Lucy and Milly developed a plan, and three days a week, as the women of the house, from the mistress to the maid, began their daily tasks, the two girls would stand smiling at the door.

"Good morning, mistress. We are here to help you gain freedom of choice," said Lucy, followed by Milly.

"A voice in what happens to you, and a say in the laws that govern this land."

Finishing with Lucy declaring, "Sign here and the future is ours."

They quickly found favour amongst the younger women who were eager to have some influence over their lives, however little that might be.

"But I dunno 'ow to sign me name," whispered one young woman, shamefaced.

"That's all right," said Lucy, surprised by how many she met who had such little education. "I can write your name for you, and you can make a mark."

On their travels, Lucy began to better understand the call of the temperance union for prohibition as a means to fight against poverty. She was appalled at the women's stories of violence and hunger and desperation.

As she and Milly trudged along, Lucy said, "I'm ashamed to say I never realised how many people don't have the basics of warmth and comfort in their homes like we do."

"I've seen some of it before," replied Milly sagely, "while doing charitable work with Grandma. Work-worn women, overrun with children and endless chores, and worried how they would put food on the table. It's a terrible situation. And another reason I don't want to marry."

"But Milly, being a spinster isn't the answer, is it? It can be a lonely life with few options. How will you manage?"

"I've options enough. Grandfather, Captain Daldy, will see me with enough funds to support myself, and he's promised me the house as long as I look after my siblings until they don't need me any more. And I will not want for company, as I will continue to do charity work."

Lucy hoped Milly was right. But to not have someone to love and who loved you seemed an empty life to Lucy. She'd seen what it did to her father.

As the pair made their way around, they discovered older, wealthier women, keen to have a say in the laws of the land, and the poor and dispossessed signed the petition more readily than some of the more-contented married women. But it was the poor who affected her the most. "I'm so glad to be doing this work, Milly. I feel I am truly helping those who are so much worse off than I'll ever be."

Each week they gathered at Mrs Daldy's home with a few of her closest allies to catch up with the latest news and prepare for the fortnightly meetings.

"Congratulations, ladies, we've done it. Six petitions, with over 20,000 signatures in total from all over the country, have been sent to our patron, Sir John Hall," she said, praising the man who had vociferously advocated on their behalf for over two years. But she warned they faced yet another setback. "I find it unconscionable that a man of Mr Fish's standing, as the Member for Dunedin, should stoop to such low standards," explaining to the group about an opposing petition he'd contrived to deceive women. "He had the audacity to send canvassers out pretending to collect genuine signatures for the franchise, whereas in truth, his forms were opposed to the vote."

Gasps of dismay and abhorrence filled the room as Milly and Lucy poured tea and served slices of fruit loaf. "Nasty man. May he get his comeuppance soon."

"How could he do that?" asked Lucy, taking her seat beside Milly, noting that neither Mrs Willoughby nor Hope were present, which seemed odd to her. She would try to find out later why that was the case. "It's so unfair."

"I know, Lucy, my dear, but there are men like that. Underhand and scheming. Fortunately, he has been called out by Sir John Hall, in Parliament no less – he presented a fresh petition signed by the women of Dunedin requesting their names be reassigned to the genuine petition."

For weeks after the petitions had been sent off, Lucy and Milly followed every newspaper report concerning the franchise and Electoral Bill, summarising the arguments and counterarguments between the House of Representatives and the Legislative Council. Each fortnight, the leaders of the League reported on what they knew with increasing consternation.

"I can't bear it," Lucy told Milly after yet another disagreement. "It's so unfair. We sent 9,000 signatures last year, and we've garnered more than twice as many this time. Surely we can't fail again."

In a surprising turn of events, one that helped offset the disappointments, was the presence of Mr Richard Harris. He'd been waiting for her after a meeting. He raised his hat with a small bow, and smiled shyly. "Miss Young. It is indeed a pleasure to see you."

"And you, Mr Harris. And you." She could barely contain the grin craving to break free.

He extended his arm. "Will you walk with me?"

She took his arm and they began to make their way up the hill towards Karangahape Road and along to Symonds Street and home.

"What brings you to town, Mr Harris?"

"You," he stated seriously. "If you will permit it, I wanted to say …" He cleared his throat nervously and in one gushing breath continued. "I've asked your father if we may walk together and if I may call on you on occasions when he is also at home, and he has given his permission, if you are willing."

Lucy was more than willing. She was delighted, if rather surprised. Her father had not mentioned any desire for her to marry. He seemed content to keep her at home to act as the mistress of the house, with Mrs Bush coming in daily as general factotum and housekeeper.

"That would be welcomed, Mr Harris. I would enjoy the opportunity of conversing with you." She didn't mean to sound so formal, but she had little experience with young men and was unsure of the proprieties.

"Then I will be happy to escort you, Miss Young, whenever I can get away from Father's business, and we will discuss the topics that interest you along the way."

From then on, she and Richard walked to and from any number of meetings and church services, or strolled through the park together, getting to know one another better. She avidly listened to his aspirations for the future design of a grand department store, and he willingly encouraged her to talk about her experiences gathering signatures and how well her latest letter writing was going. Only her commitment to the League kept them from meeting more often.

"I was horrified by their tales," she said to Richard on one of their excursions. "It seems so unfair that women are living such reduced lives because of their menfolk spending all the money on drink before there is food on the table."

"Don't get too involved, Miss Young. The franchise won't immediately relieve their situation, never mind what happens. Poverty is a curse, but when faced with feelings of hopelessness, people do turn to whatever gives them joy. For a man, a drink at the pub with their mates is one of them. It gives them a sense of freedom."

Lucy wasn't so sure. The women had no such freedoms. They had nothing that made them feel happier about themselves or their lives. They and their children were the ones who suffered the consequences. "What can be done then? When the wages are so poor they can't afford to have proper housing and feed their families?"

"Nothing for you to worry your pretty little head about."

Lucy instantly removed her arm from his and turned towards him. "Do not patronise me, Mr Harris," she glared, indignation oozing from every pore. "If we are to remain friends, you have to understand and accept how important this is to me. It's only right women should have a say over what happens to them. And it is most unfair that men should decide every aspect of our lives. I want to be treated as an equal, to have my opinions respected and not belittled. I want …"

"I apologise," he interrupted, holding his hands up in supplication, but wearing a happy grin. "I didn't mean to condescend. Some matters are too great even for me to comprehend. I'm sorry if you considered me offhand. I am not a politician and I don't wish to be, but I am on your side. Am I forgiven?" He took her hand and raised it to his lips. The eyes that beseeched hers over the top won through and she smiled.

"Yes. I forgive you."

* * * * *

Lucy was having trouble controlling her temper as she sat next to Milly and Hope, who had recently returned to the fold, listening to the other women of the group discuss the machinations revolving around the Electoral Bill.

"I cannot be certain which way the House will vote," said Mrs Daldy. "Our opponents continue to try to defeat us in a most nefarious manner."

"Again," muttered Lucy, wishing she could say what she really thought about the plots designed to cloud the issue. She wished she was older, and had more money at her disposal, and could … Could what? she asked herself. She was doing everything possible as it was.

"They are now attempting to prove women would soon take over Parliament, to the detriment of that hallowed institution …"

"But that is not our plan," interrupted Hope's mother. "Our aim is prohibition."

"I beg to correct you, Mrs Willoughby. It is not. The aim of this League is the franchise. Nothing can be achieved without it."

Lucy saw the disgruntled look on Mrs Willoughby's face at the rebuke and wondered if she would try to undermine them too.

"Shame on them," spoke Mrs Caradus, their Treasurer.

"Yes, but they go even further. Our nemesis, Mr Henry Fish of Dunedin – after all he has done to attack us – is now trying another approach to deny us our rights."

"It is my ardent wish that Mr Fish will lose his seat," said Mrs Rattray, receiving calls of agreement.

"Regretfully, that is not within our power as yet," Mrs Daldy reminded her. "But I'm sure Miss Morison and Miss Nicol will find ways to make life uncomfortable for the man." Light-hearted laughter followed her words before she announced, "Fortunately, the amendments were rejected outright."

Sighs of relief.

"That is good news," said Mrs Rattray. "But what news from our British friends?"

Mrs Daldy shook her head. "Some progress is being made. A Bill was recently presented to the House of Commons to confer the vote on spinsters and widows. Not a perfect outcome, but a step forward. Sadly, Mr Gladstone changed his stance once too often and the Bill was defeated. However, they say there is hope for the future. Meanwhile, we must continue to gather more signatures. With the Legislative Council stacked against us, we have an uphill battle."

After the meeting broke up, Milly asked, "Shall we take tea? Let's go to that place that does those delicious cakes."

"I can't today," said Hope. "My fiancé is waiting for me. We have plans to discuss."

Lucy had considered declining too, hoping to meet up with Mr Harris, but she changed her mind when she saw Milly's disappointment. "Tea would be delightful."

Moments later, the two girls stood at the door farewelling Mrs Daldy's visitors. "I don't think we'll be able to count on her friendship for much longer," said Milly, watching Hope walk away. "Mr Fernley seems to command a lot of her attention."

"I think Hope is also greatly under her mother's thumb on the matter of prohibition, which pits her against Mrs Daldy."

"Good luck to them on that," laughed Milly.

9

A step backwards

"I can't believe he'd do this to me!" Paige screeched over the phone.

It took Emma a couple of attempts to calm her down so Paige could explain clearly what had upset her so much and Emma could grasp what the girl was saying.

"He invests in oil! I hate him. I absolutely hate him! How could he!"

Emma took a deep breath and rapidly thought how she could respond without sounding patronising or approving. "I'm sorry, Paige. I know it goes against everything you believe in, but I have to say it's not uncommon in business. Oil makes money, and didn't you tell me your father was all about making money?"

She heard a dismissive grunt, which she interpreted to include Paige's signature shrug. "That's what he said. But why oil? Why not new technology or solar …?" The girl drifted into silence.

As sympathetically as she could, Emma tried to soften the snub. "I suspect it's a long-standing arrangement. Something he got into years ago when oil wasn't the issue it is today."

"That's not the point. The point is, he doesn't care. He's anti everything I believe in. That's what hurts. He really doesn't care about me or what I think."

Emma thought that unlikely but couldn't come up with anything off the cuff to counter that suggestion so said nothing.

"I asked him to stop," Paige continued, unabated. "I begged him to sell out, and all I got was to be told not to worry my pretty head about matters I didn't understand. I can't stand it. He thinks he's so superior."

She let Paige finish her expletive-laden rant, hoping it would be a long time before Rose began using such words, but the bubble of anger burst almost as quickly as it began. Emma heard the deep intake of breath and next time she spoke, Paige sounded more composed.

"Maybe I should leave home. Set out on my own path. What d'ya think?"

Here I go again, thought Emma, answering an in loco parentis question. It was none of her business; Luke wouldn't like it one bit, but she couldn't let the girl do anything rash either. "I wouldn't rush into that decision just yet. Think about it. Your father is paying for everything right now. Your home, uni fees, transport … Would he do that if he didn't care? Would he still pay for everything if you left home? It'd be a struggle if he didn't, and there'd be less time, and money, for your activism."

Emma heard the sigh, but couldn't decide if it was relief or disappointment.

"Okay. Makes sense, I suppose. I'm just so mad. But then, if I'm not there to go off at him all the time, it would probably make life easier for him, and I have no intention of doing that!"

Pushing her advantage, Emma added, "Staying home means you can focus on making your mark on the world, instead of worrying how to pay the rent and buy your next meal."

Paige chuckled. "Yeah. That too. There's another protest next week. One day, I intend to do a lot more."

"Meanwhile, finish your education."

"Not you too," she sighed again, as if the world rested on her shoulders. "But, yeah. That too. Nobody listens if you can't prove your point."

"Talking about proving a point, I'm sorry about our misunderstanding the other day. I wasn't …"

"That's okay. It was my fault," interrupted Paige. "I'm so used to put-downs I overreacted."

Nonplussed, Emma asked, "So, do you want to carry on searching your family tree? What're you hoping to find?"

"Yes. Pleeeease? I don't know what to expect, exactly, until I find it. But I'm certain there's something. Dad's so cagey about Mum and the past, it's almost a joke. Cam's as bad. They're hiding something. I'm sure they are. Although Cam says he doesn't know anything. Maybe he's as much in the dark as I am."

"Speaking of Cameron. Is your ex-boyfriend still hanging around?"

"Don't think so. If he is, he's keeping well clear of me."

"Wise man," Emma grinned. "Did you find any photos?" she asked, wanting to change the subject.

"Oh, yeah, hang on a tick."

Emma could hear sounds in the background and next thing a 'ting' announced the arrival of a message.

"There's one of Mum on the beach when she's young. It's not very good. Her face is in shadow, but when I took it out of the frame to take a better photo of it, I found a little black-and-white one in the back."

Emma opened up the attachments and looked at the two photos. As Paige had said, the photo of her mother could have been any bikini-clad young woman on the beach wearing a bucket hat, a ponytail and laughter. The black-and-white one looked to be an old-style 2 x 3-inch print, darkened with age. She dragged it into Photoshop and zoomed in on it. Two things struck her straight away: the seated woman holding an infant on her knee bore a striking resemblance to Paige; and she wore a white camellia – the symbol of the suffragists. Emma guessed it was taken around the 1900s but she'd have to get an expert to confirm it. "Is there anything written on the back?" she asked eagerly.

"Nah. Nothing," said Paige. "I looked, but isn't the brooch she's wearing at her throat in amongst the stuff in the box?"

"Wow, you've got sharp eyes," Emma said, already reaching for the trinket box. She rummaged around and pulled out a simple gold bar with a central ruby mounted in a gold circle. "You're right. I've got it. Now all we have to do is work out who it belongs to."

The more she searched for clues, the more confused she became. There were so many women's organisations she'd never heard of. Some morphed into similar groups with different names; others faded away never to be heard of again.

Deep in thought, Emma jumped at the unexpected ring of her phone.

Jess's voice echoed down the line. "Hey, hermit. What you doing?"

Emma glanced at the clock. A little after one. "Working. Why?" She glanced through the French doors seeing a beautiful blue sky.

"Have you paid any attention to what's going on in the world today?"

Emma's pulse edged up a notch. "Why? What's happened? Have I missed something?"

"Yes. Coffee. With me. Remember?"

Emma swallowed a spasm of guilt. "Sorry. I completely forgot."

"Thanks a lot, friend." Jess laughed to take the sting out of her words. "Now, will you get your butt down to the beach café right now."

Twenty minutes later, clutching takeaway coffees, the two women strolled along the beach, soaking up the sounds and smells of the ocean. A lack of energy had forced Emma to give up her regular morning runs since having Covid, and she missed the stimulus, resenting the feeling of lethargy that plagued her most days.

"So tell me," said Jess, a worried frown etching her features, "what has you so engrossed you forget to go out?"

Emma shrugged inside her jacket at the unexpected gust of cool autumn air. "Nothing special, now I've managed to whittle my workload down to two projects."

"That sounds more reasonable. You're too kind for your own good sometimes and take on too much."

"Yeah, I know. I was a bit overloaded with clients for a while after I was sick. Still, their histories are done now and they're happy. I've still got one older client who wants her family history written that's okay; the other one is a bit more challenging."

"Oh yes. The girl you met after your talk at the university?"

Emma nodded. "She's itching to become a fully fledged climate change advocate to save the environment, but her father not only objects to her activity, but is downright hostile to it, from what I can gather. Her brother sides with her father. She's diving in all sorts of directions trying to find her way forward."

"Sounds like a normal teenager then."

"Yes and no. She's fickle, I'll give you that, but well intentioned. Her father keeps telling her she's from a long line of troublemakers and she wants to know what sort. Delinquents or activists? Or somewhere boringly in between?"

"Ooh, that sounds rather intriguing. What've you discovered so far?"

Emma stared out at the ocean, deep in thought. "Not much. I showed you the trinket box she found, didn't I, with its dozen or so badges from women's groups over the decades? Remember the suffrage pin from the 1993 centennial – long before either she or her brother were born. And a lovely brooch amongst other bits and pieces."

Jess took a deep breath and threw her arms up in the air. "So are you thinking one of her ancestors was a suffragette?"

"Suffra*gist*," corrected Emma automatically. "I haven't yet managed to put a tree together, so I can't be sure. Without more information I'm a bit stuck."

"Can't this girl tell you anything?"

Emma shook her head. "Her father won't talk about

the past at all. Which makes me wonder what he's hiding."

"Being too suspicious for your own sake again?" Jess picked up a stone and tried to skim it across the water, and shrugged when it sank.

"Maybe, but all the records that could link backwards are within the time periods closed for public research."

Jess nodded. "You had trouble sorting out some of my history because of that, didn't you? I distinctly remember you couldn't access birth records for 100 years, and wasn't it around 50 or something for the others?"

Sorting Jess's family tree had been one of the more difficult and fraught cases Emma had ever had to tackle. Most cases she took on ranged from interesting to humdrum. Jess's was full of the unexpected, with far too many dramas. Emma shuddered at the thought of the danger she'd found herself in and hoped nothing like that would happen to her again.

"Not bad. Yes. Fifty years for deaths and 80 for marriages," nodded Emma.

Despite the difficulties, Emma was glad she had been able to help her friend. Now free of her disagreeable ex-husband, Jess was thriving.

"I'm sure you'll find something eventually. You always do."

Emma kicked at a shell, picked it up to inspect it, and tossed it. "I've a gut feeling those pins tell me I should be searching for a line of activists."

"This girl sounds like someone after my own heart. What sort of campaign work has she done?"

"I didn't know you were a climate crusader," said Emma, turning to Jess in surprise.

Jess laughed. "I'm hardly that, but we can't keep doing what we're doing. Our infrastructure is shot and can't cope with the changing weather patterns, and we create far too much waste and pollution. We need to reset the environmental balance – and soon."

"You continue to surprise me. I didn't realise you were into politics."

Jess looked embarrassed. She stared at the horizon. "I'm not really. I don't do anywhere near enough, but I'll support those who do. Even those kids marching in the streets telling us it's time adults stopped talking and took action. There was a march last week."

Emma perked up. "Paige has been one of those kids. I bet she was part of it. She told me she joined the School Strike 4 Climate protests while still at school until her father found out and grounded her. She's a bit older now, so I think she's got a few other ideas up her sleeve. I know she's furious with him for investing in oil."

"Good on her! Fossil fuels have to go. They just need to hurry up and finish the research into cleaner fuels and develop more renewable energy."

Emma knew little about what was best. She left it to others to sort. "I doubt there are many people who don't think we should do something, me included, but there's many who don't know how, can't be bothered, or the enormous cost puts them off. There's no easy answer."

"Nothing worthwhile is ever easy, or cheap," said Jess. "But we have to do it."

On the return path, Emma suddenly felt as if all the energy had drained from her.

Jess frowned. "You've got that faraway look again. What's really bothering you? It's not Luke, is it?"

"No. No. Nothing like that," Emma reassured, hearing the anxiety in her friend's voice. "I promise, you'd be the first to know. I'm a bit tired, that's all."

"Okay. If you're sure." Jess glanced at her watch. "Better go. Break's over."

She dumped their coffee cups in the rubbish saying, "We shouldn't be doing that either."

"Paige would not approve," agreed Emma, as she waved farewell to Jess.

She sat in the car with her eyes closed, scared she was going to die.

10

Blind to distractions

As the month progressed, Lucy expressed her increasing dismay. "I fear the news isn't good," she began while she and Richard meandered arm in arm in the park. "The arguments are so divisive that I fail to see how an agreement can be reached. Have you heard the latest?" she asked, going on to explain the recent raft of amendments and the current tensions between the House of Representatives and the Legislative Council. "Did you know that approval for the franchise is now contingent upon women being bound to a postal vote?"

"Is it?" Richard sounded incurious even as he asked the question. "Why?"

They continued to stroll along the pathway in the Domain, a favourite haunt of theirs in the late afternoon when the weather permitted. It was an easy walk from the Young household in Parnell.

"Apparently, to relieve us of the inconvenience of attending a polling booth should the weather be inclement, and avoid the risk of being jostled, abused or

94

embarrassed by other voters. Isn't that just ridiculous? As if we are inferior beings in need of protection."

"Don't be too harsh, Miss Young. They mean well. It has been the traditional role for men to protect their womenfolk. I know you don't like to hear such things, but it's natural."

Lucy's eyes flared with derision. "Does that mean women can stop doing the chores when it rains then, or going to the shops to buy food for their hard-done-by masters?"

"That's not what I said at all. But I am looking forward to the day I can at least guard you from harm. Look at those. Aren't they lovely?" As they neared the band rotunda, Richard pointed to a row of trees that had developed some interesting branch shapes. "Shall we sit?"

Taking Richard's hand, Lucy lifted her skirt to step onto the rotunda.

"You look particularly charming today. Is your outfit new?" he asked.

She looked down at her dark wine cape draped over the large leg'o'mutton sleeves on her cobalt-blue dress, the latest creation from her dressmaker. "Thank you, yes. It is new. But what of it? There are far more important things to concern ourselves with."

She heard Richard sigh. If optimism was her strongest trait, patience was his virtue. "To you, maybe, and to me, obviously," he added hurriedly. "Since it matters to you so much, but can we not sometimes talk of other things? Like how fond I am of you."

She sat down on the bench inside the bannister, staring out across the lawn. She had become so subsumed by the political arguments of the franchise that little else interested her, and less distracted her.

"Be patient, Mr Harris. That time will come, meanwhile this postal vote provision threatens the whole process. If the clauses are accepted, the Bill will likely pass, but if not, and the Government appears opposed, then I fear we shall lose."

"Please believe me when I say I *am* being patient. Very patient, in fact, but what is so wrong with postal votes?" he asked. "I know that itinerants, the likes of shearers, sailors and commercial travellers, who are likely to be away from home at the time, can vote that way?"

"But we are none of those, and we are not away from home. Why should we be treated differently to the men living in the same household? That is the whole point of this argument. We want to be treated as equals." Lucy became more frustrated and more anxious as she outlined her concerns. "To top it off, I read somewhere that postal voters can be identified and a record will be kept of the way they vote. Is that true?"

"I don't know," he answered honestly.

"That's the trouble. No one knows for certain – or whether postal voting could be manipulated. Mrs Daldy says we can't take the risk. The whole idea we would be inconvenienced is absurd."

"So what happens next?"

"Mrs Daldy has sent a telegram to the Government stating that we expect to vote under the current system and consider the postal proposal an infraction of the secrecy of the ballot. In my opinion, and that of others, it is nothing more than thinly veiled subterfuge to kill the bill."

As usual, Richard became peripheral to Lucy's fixation on the details of the franchise. She'd become so besotted with the idea of equality that she hadn't noticed Richard becoming more besotted with her.

A week later, she and Richard sat in the parlour after a pleasant evening dining with her father, who was now in his study across the hallway.

"Look at this," she said. "Today's headline says, 'A Deadlock Imminent'. We are getting nowhere. I feel we shall lose again."

She took a deep breath, trying to calm herself, before she became even more agitated by the endless bad news. Richard tried his best to neutralise the issues and distract her but usually failed.

"Cheer up, my dear Miss Young. Progress has been made. People are far more aware of the need for enfranchisement than ever before. Now it's your turn to be patient. I can assure you all good things come to those of us who wait."

Ignoring his reference to her keeping him waiting, she surged on. "We have been patient! It is more than twenty years since Mary Ann Müller first raised the issue in her narrative, *An Appeal to the Men of New Zealand*. And Polly Plum wrote dozens of letters and articles to newspapers and politicians around the same time, drawing huge crowds to her meetings. Awareness is not enough. Not any longer. We must have action."

From then on Lucy read every article in the newspapers, taking note of who said what on either side. She went out every day, delivering pamphlets, posting more letters, speaking to women in the streets – anything to feel she was doing something useful.

"Listen to this," said Lucy a few days later. She and Richard were sharing a cup of tea one afternoon, under the watchful eye of Mrs Bush who was busy preparing the evening meal. "This report says Sir Robert Stout has received a reply to his telegram to Mr Seddon as Acting Premier." She paused to express her distaste. "Ooh, I don't like that man. I'm sure he is against us, unlike Premier Ballance. I hope he gets better soon. We need him back in Parliament." She picked up the paper again. "But Seddon is basically saying the proposed postal voting clause is creating what 'amounts to a disability for women and will destroy the secrecy of the ballot'. That's good news, isn't it?" Lucy queried before returning to the newspaper without waiting for a response.

"He also says the idea leaves the system open to abuse, and risks employers 'demanding to see a servant girl's voting papers'." Lucy crunched the paper in her hands. "That's terrible. The ladies of the League were right to be suspicious." She scanned more of the article. "He doesn't agree to the abolition of the amalgamated electorates either. He says that would 'strike a death blow to the democratic representation of the cities'."

"Most of the House is against the postal voting clause, from what I hear," said Richard. "But the Council won't give way. Neither will they like Sir Robert attempting to pull strings the way he's inclined."

Lucy frowned. "I know Stout isn't an elected member at the moment, but the ladies of Dunedin trust him."

Richard folded the newspaper he was reading and handed the page to Lucy. "Read that," he pointed.

"I think the biggest stumbling block will be these amalgamated electorates. The Council was happy to get rid of single electorates before the last election and now, here they are proposing they be reinstated. Ridiculous, I know, but by standing firm on that issue, the Council ensures women's franchise is effectively postponed for yet another year."

Lucy banged her fist on the table, making the tea things rattle. "This is all so frustrating. Men once again deciding our fate by playing silly politics."

"Let's hope, for your sake, that Ballance recovers from his illness soon and the franchise is approved. Maybe then we can take an interest in other things, such as our future together."

"Me too," said Lucy honestly, deaf to his overture and taking his solicitude for granted.

* * * * *

Throughout the first week of October the debate raged. Concessions were given on the postal voting within city boundaries, but the Legislature insisted on it staying in place for country areas. Seddon and his cohorts in the House were obdurate and refused to compromise on anything that would risk the secrecy of the vote. In turn, they suggested that post offices throughout the nation become polling booths, thus availing country women of a convenient opportunity to vote. The Council declined.

The newspapers reported daily on the slow strangulation of the Bill: 'There is an increasing lack of will on both sides to pass the law onto the Statute Books.

Despite last minute conferences with reappointed managers to re-argue the case, the managers on both sides report no compromise could be reached.'

"The reporters are scathing in their condemnation of the process," said Richard as he finished reading. "They write that every excuse is an utter and inexcusable falsehood."

Lucy suddenly stood and turned towards the fireplace. She clutched her hands tightly by her side, struggling to control the tears that threatened. "It doesn't matter what they write. It doesn't matter who accuses whom or points the finger of blame. None of it matters any longer. We've lost. Oh, Richard, we've lost."

"There, there, my dear. Do not despair." He crossed the room to where she stood and wrapped his arms around her, letting her head rest on his shoulder. He pulled a clean handkerchief from his pocket and held it before her. Her sobs finally broke free, and she relaxed into the warmth of his embrace.

At that moment, her father entered the room. "So, it is true!" he barked, a fierce scowl on his face as the young couple broke apart. "I didn't want to believe it, but it appears I was wrong."

Blushes of remorse and embarrassment suffused their faces as they turned towards Mr Young.

He pointed at Richard. "When I gave you permission to walk with my daughter," he thundered, "I did not give permission for you to be alone together in this house. How dare you molest her like that."

Lucy wiped the tears from her face. "No, Father. That is not what happened. Mr Harris was merely comforting me because I felt so disheartened."

"You should not have allowed him to comfort you, as you put it, in that manner. You are not yet engaged to be married."

"Mr Young, sir …" stammered Richard.

"Be quiet! I will deal with you later." He glared at the young man before redirecting his gaze towards his daughter. "Go to your room."

Lucy stood her ground. "I think not, Father. I have done nothing to be ashamed of. And you should not blame Mr Harris. I was simply in need of a moment of support. The women's franchise bill has been lost. Everything we've worked so hard for is lost …" Her eyes challenged him. "I was distressed."

Her father took two strides into the room. "I care not a jot for your reasons. I care about the impropriety. Now, go to your room."

Lucy lifted her chin. "No. I won't. You've always taught me to stand up for what is right. To be independent. To use my brain and question everything. I am questioning now. What is so wrong with what we've been doing?"

Her father bellowed, "There's far too much gossip around town about the two of you! I will not be talked about. Or have your reputation tarnished."

"You know Mr Harris and I discuss my work towards winning the vote. He supports me. You supported my involvement. You've never distrusted me before. Why now? Why, when I am already at the age of majority and free to …"

His voice rose as his anger notched up. "You are not free. Not while you are under my roof. You will not shame me."

"I have no intention of bringing shame on you,

Father. But a momentary embrace is not improper … not when … he and I …"

"When he and you are what, exactly?" he roared.

In the momentary silence that followed the battle of wills, Richard intervened. "I'd like to ask your permission to ask your daughter to marry me, sir."

Both father and daughter turned their heads towards Richard in astonishment. Flustered but not deterred, he got down on one knee and took Lucy's hand. "Lucy … Miss Young. Will you do me the honour of accepting my proposal?"

Lucy appeared flabbergasted.

"I promise I will look after you and protect you."

Lucy snatched her hand from Richard's. "So, I'm to be passed from one man to another who seeks to protect me. What if I don't want to be protected?"

"Don't be ridiculous, Lucy," said her father. "Of course you need a husband who will safeguard your reputation. Accept his proposal or give up your franchise work. Make your choice."

Lucy stared at her father in shock, her indignant thoughts clearly written on her face. Glancing between both men, she saw stubbornness in one set of eyes and pleading in the other. "Very well, Mr Harris. I accept your proposal. But I will not marry you until the day women are granted the franchise."

11

An emergency, of sorts

"Ems? Emma, honey. Are you okay?" Luke opened the car door and reached in to shake Emma by the shoulder. "I've been worried about you."

"Mummy. Whaddya doing?" asked Rosie, clambering into the passenger seat and leaning over to hug her mother.

Emma shook her head, clearing it of the shadowy thoughts that had been drifting through her mind. "What? Oh. Hi, sweetheart," she said, putting her arm around her daughter. Confused, she looked at Luke. "Goodness, what's the time?"

"Coming up four. I picked the girls up from school and dropped Livvy home. Jess said she'd seen you around two, so when I couldn't find you, I came looking. Have you been here all this time?"

"Um. I guess so. After our walk, I was feeling a bit whacked so I sat in the car mulling over things. I must have fallen asleep."

"That's some sleep. Are you all right to drive?"

"Of course I am. Don't fuss, please, Luke."

"I wish you'd see a doctor. Something's not right. You shouldn't be this tired."

Emma dismissed his concerns. Along with her own. Anything was better than the alternative. "It's nothing more than the after-effects of that bout of Covid. It'll pass. Anyway, the doctors are far too busy with really sick people to need me bothering them."

Rosie did her seat belt up. "I'll go home with Mum."

Luke handed Emma her seat belt and leaned in to kiss her. "Okay. I'll see you back home in a few minutes." He closed the door.

Emma smiled at him through the window as he raised his hand in farewell. She backed out of her parking spot wondering what on earth had happened to her. Despite her so called 'sleep', she felt shattered. She picked up the water bottle from the side pocket and took a long swallow while she waited to join the stream of traffic.

Rosie was talking but Emma couldn't quite grasp what she was saying.

"Yes, darling, that's fine," said Emma, hoping her answer would be sufficient.

"Can I really? Dad said no."

"What?" Emma almost jerked the wheel as she turned suddenly to look at her daughter. "I'd better talk to Dad first, in that case. You should know better, Rosie. That's not acceptable."

"Sorry, Mum. But I really, really want to join the march. Everyone else is. Even Livvy. Auntie Jess said she might walk with us."

Suddenly, Rosie's question made sense: the climate march. When did 10-year-olds get to be so know-all-ish? She thought that phase belonged to teenagers. She'd ask Paige what she knew. Maybe she could take the girls under her wing. That might satisfy Luke.

"Have you got everything?" she asked Rose as she pulled up in the driveway.

"I dropped it home before, when Dad couldn't find you. You okay, Mum?"

"I'm fine, sweetheart. Don't worry about me. Let's get a biscuit or something, and then I'll help you do your homework."

"Haven't time. Auntie Jess is picking me up soon for dance." She bounced along the path and into the house rushing to get ready. Emma realised Jess was doing a lot more with the girls than she was.

Sometime later, after Rose had gone and Luke had finished his phone call, he sought her out. She was wearily sprawled on the couch but promptly sat upright as he sat beside her.

"Ems?" Luke reached out to rub her neck. She moved into his hand as he pressed on the aching shoulder muscles. "This has got to stop. Look at you, you're pale and your eyes are red rimmed with tiredness and yet you napped in the car for hours. You had me so scared. I couldn't find you. We have to figure out what the problem is."

She pressed her hands to her eyes, trying to clear the lingering fog. "I've made an appointment with the optometrist. I think my eyesight might have something to do with it."

"That's a start, but would your eyesight make you this tired?"

She shrugged a shoulder, promptly realising she'd copied Paige's offhand shoulder hitch. "Could be. I've been getting a few headaches."

"Promise me then, depending on what the optometrist says, that you'll also see the doctor. You might have an iron deficiency or something."

She nodded but wasn't convincing enough.

Luke became stern. "Promise me. I don't like you neglecting yourself like this."

"Okay. Okay. Don't hassle me," she said, thinking how petulant and like Paige she now sounded. "Sorry. It's just so hard to think sometimes."

"Go lie down. I'll sort dinner and collect Rosie. I'll wake you when we get back."

Needing no second telling, Emma slouched off, leaving her phone on the coffee table as she left.

* * * * *

Luke shook her awake. "Hey, sleepyhead. I think you should check your messages. Someone's trying to get hold of you. I heard it ring and beep several times."

"What?" Emma tried to shake the dull feeling from her brain. Her eyes itched and she rubbed at them. She hoped the eye specialist could help her.

She looked at the sky through the window, trying to work out how long she'd been lying down. It didn't feel long. "What time is it?"

"A little after five."

Barely forty minutes. She quickly sat upright.

Luke handed her the phone. She punched in her passcode and four missed calls and six messages all from Paige popped up. Adrenaline pumped as she jumped from the bed, rushing into the en suite to wash her face and brush her hair. "It's Paige. I have to go. Something's wrong," she called out as she grabbed her phone and hopped about putting her shoes on. "Can you take care of Rosie?"

"Of course, but …"

Emma had gone. She was in the car and backing out the driveway by the time she saw Luke appear to watch her leave. Guilt at taking him for granted nudged her conscience, but her heart drew her towards Paige. She couldn't explain the feeling to herself, never mind anyone else, but her protective instincts kicked in. She knew the girl was desperately seeking an anchor. Something, or someone, to give her roots. Proof that her instincts were valid; that *she* was valid.

She found Paige huddled in a hoodie, under a tree in a nearby park. Sitting down beside her, Emma rubbed the girl's back, trying to sneak a peek at her face. "How long have you been here?"

Paige seemed transfixed. Her signature shrug came as a relief. She raised a tear-stained face. "Why didn't you come sooner?"

"I couldn't," she answered simply, unwilling to tell the girl the reason, and slightly miffed that she would think she could, or would, drop everything at Paige's beck and call.

"He's gone."

"Who's gone?"

"Ryan."

"You brought me here because of Ryan? This is your emergency?" Exasperated, she battled to keep her voice calm. She watched the children playing on the equipment across the grass, their squeals of laughter drifting in the breeze.

"You don't understand …" wailed Paige, sounding more like a two-year-old having a tantrum.

"I thought the two of you were getting on well?" Emma didn't have the energy or the patience to be caught up in some romantic squabble.

"We are. That's the problem." Paige mopped her eyes with her sleeve.

"So tell me what happened." Even to her ears, she sounded long-suffering but honestly, this wasn't her gig.

"He's going away …" Paige's words became a mumble through the sobs.

"I didn't catch all that – say again, why is he going?"

Paige raised her head and sniffed. Emma reached into her pocket and pulled out a hanky. The girl blew her nose and wiped her eyes. "He's gone to join the People Not Profit protest. He's even saying he might go to other countries and do some research too." She took a few shuddering breaths. "He's been frustrated at the lack of action, so he's gone to join Greta Thunberg's Fridays for Future groups."

Emma now understood. "And you think if he goes, he might not come back?"

The girl descended into sobs again while she talked. Gradually, Emma gathered Ryan wanted Paige to go with him, but she didn't have the courage. "Nor a passport for that matter."

"That's easily fixed, but it's bigger than that, isn't it?"

Emma stifled her irritation, aware that young love was often a painful passage. Paige was nowhere near ready to leave the security of her home, however bad she made it out to be, and go off with a boy – actually, a man of twenty-five – with no guarantees.

Paige nodded. "I want to go. I want to be part of the bigger picture. But I don't know how. I'm scared I don't have the answers … I'm so confused. They hold all these big conferences and stuff in fancy hotels that the guests fly to in expensive planes, gobbling up high-polluting fossil fuels – contrary to what we should do – to talk about how to fix climate change, and then do nothing. Or not much. I don't get it."

Emma understood the girl's point. It didn't make sense when we were supposed to be reducing emissions. "But isn't it about raising awareness and showing how much they support climate action so everyone will accept the need for change? What do they call them? Influencers?"

"Yeah. Pretty much, but it's not working. It's been decades since the Climate Change Panel came together in Paris and nowhere near enough has been done since. I don't know how to be an influencer, but I do know we need more than awareness – we need action." A loud hiccup escaped. "My father's right. I don't know anything. I'm useless." She folded her arms across her knees again and buried her head.

Vexed at such self-abasement, Emma tried another tack. "Isn't there a march here you could join?" Thinking of the one Rosie had talked about.

Muffled words came from the depth of the hoodie. "They all disappeared into the woodwork with the Covid restrictions. Nothing's happening, which is why Ryan is leaving."

"I bet something is. Have you even looked?" Emma fished her phone from her back pocket and googled. "I can see a Facebook post about wearing green on Fridays to show solidarity for the environment. And another one from International Women's Day earlier in the month, claiming climate justice." Even she recognised green-wash and trivia when she saw it, but kept searching. There didn't seem to much of anything worthwhile going on. "Oh look …"

She turned her phone to face Paige. "Is that the march Ryan is going to?"

Paige nodded. "It's a global protest."

"Why don't you join one here? My daughter was talking about one only yesterday."

Her one-shoulder hitch was the reply. "I used to enjoy the buzz of going on the marches with lots of people shouting slogans, but there's so many dissenting voices with different agendas, I got disillusioned." She raised her head and stared up at the fading blue sky through the leaves and branches serving as an umbrella overhead.

Her voice changed, she became calmer and sounded wistful. "I began to wonder what we should be shouting about, and what we should do. Slogans aren't going to change anything. We need to adapt. To change the drivers. But I don't see how. Not after all the failures. What good are marches?"

"But Ryan wants to march."

"Seems so."

"And you?"

"All I know is that during the lockdowns the natural world started to bounce back. Every country was reporting clearer air and cleaner oceans, demonstrating that all the arguments about reducing our emissions and waste streams will work. But as soon as we got back in our cars and trucks and planes, and started living life as usual, it reverted, and we're no better off than we were. There has to be a better way. There *has* to be."

12

Constant dismay

November – December 1892

If Richard's going to behave like that, maybe I won't marry him after all, thought Lucy after their recent tug of war. He could be so loving and understanding when he wanted to be, but at other times, he frustrated her.

The matter had come to a head after her father had tried to extract a promise that someone of repute was always in the house when they met.

"Like who, Father? Mrs Bush? She was there that day. She comes in every day late in the afternoon to prepare our evening meal, often at a time when Richard and I are doing our planning. Does she count? She didn't last time. Or you? You said Mr Harris could visit in the evenings when you were home. When can I rely on you to be here?"

The flash of anger that crossed her father's face almost reined in her attack, but insolent or not, she refused to be cowed. Winning the franchise was too important to her.

"That is enough, young lady. I won't be spoken to like that in my own home."

Lucy didn't like arguing with her father. She owed him so much, and she loved him but couldn't understand why his turnaround. They usually got on so well.

She softened her voice. "But isn't this also my home, Father? Isn't this somewhere I should feel safe and able to conduct my affairs with impunity? Especially now Richard and I are engaged." …

A month earlier, after her father had insisted on placing an engagement announcement in the paper forthwith to allay any further gossip, Mr and Mrs Harris were invited to the house along with an aunt and uncle, and Richard's maternal grandmother to celebrate the occasion.

Mrs Bush had created a delicious array of tiny sandwiches, cakes and pastries for the event. A glass or two of sherry was offered to the ladies, while the men partook of a quiet whisky. None of the Harris family ladies objected to the provision of alcohol, although Richard's grandmother had declined and chose an aerated water. As did his perpetually subdued mother.

Lucy handed her the glass. "Thank you, my dear. What a lovely girl you are." Grandmother Stone lowered her voice. "And don't let the men bully you. If I was younger, I'd join you in your campaign." She winked at Lucy who smiled back at the old woman, happy to believe the franchise had such broad support.

"To Richard and Lucy," Aloysius toasted, to which everyone raised their glasses.

Lucy suddenly realised she had a quandary to resolve. Who would stand with her if liquor was to be served? She certainly couldn't ask Hope to be her bridesmaid when, *if*, she reminded herself, the time came, and even Milly would feel compromised. While Mrs Daldy believed in the franchise more than prohibition, she was a staunch teetotaller and would not approve of Milly being so closely exposed to drinking.

"We shall hold an official engagement party, of course," said Mr Young. "To publicly announce the betrothal. You must give me a list of family and personal friends you want invited, and I will talk to Lucy about who she wishes to attend, but I'd like the commercial sector to see how our two businesses will complement each other."

"Must we, Father?" asked Lucy, her shoulders drooping despondently.

Shocked faces turned towards her.

"Lucy!" squawked Richard. "That's an ungenerous remark."

Speaking over Richard, her father said, "Of course we must. Why would you think otherwise?"

Lucy glared at both men, before addressing her father. "Because I don't want to be shown off like some sort of prize."

Gasps from Richard's father didn't deter her, but she modified her words. "I'm sorry, Father. I do not wish to appear ungrateful, it's just I'd like our engagement to remain a personal matter, and not some sort of add-on to a business arrangement."

"That's hardly fair, my dear," said Richard in an effort to quieten the storm before it erupted. "Our betrothal is much more than that, but to have our families and businesses united is a good thing. Isn't it? Could we talk about this further – in private – before we make a decision? I believe I would enjoy such an occasion."

Lucy turned on him, her eyes wide open as she glared at him. "May I remind you, my acceptance of your proposal was contingent upon women winning the franchise. As that is likely to be some way off, given the recent turn of events, our engagement could be a rather long one. It seems premature to me to be holding a gathering at this time. And, since the announcement has already been put in the newspapers, even people beyond this family group are well informed of the matter."

Grandmother Stone chuckled. "She's right, you know."

"Mother!" reprimanded Mr Harris. "You forget your place."

"I do not. The girl is right. Gone are the days when marriage was solely about making the right connections. If she doesn't want to be part of your business arrangements, then she doesn't have to be."

Lucy smiled at the older lady, mouthing 'thank you'. She'd made her point and she'd gain nothing by arguing further.

However, from that night on, her father seemed bent on keeping them apart. His latest attempt, requiring a chaperone at all times, was above and beyond reason.

What had infuriated her more was that Richard went along with it.

"Listen, Lucy, I can't always come to suit you. I have to make my way up the ladder in the business, and haring off whenever you want me to help you isn't right. My father needs me."

How convenient, thought Lucy, restraining any verbal response with difficulty.

"Best we restrict ourselves to the evenings, when your father is at home, and the weekends when we can walk out and attend the theatre. Isn't that better?"

She stared at Richard, appalled. He'd obviously been pressured by his father – and hers, she suspected. "That will not help with the composing of letters, or preparing banners, or attending meetings where a man's presence adds weight to the arguments with other men. When will we analyse progress and plan our next tactic?"

"You don't need me to write letters, Lucy. You are being ridiculous. And we can make banners at the weekends, if we must. Although, I have to say, I don't see the point in that any longer. And I do escort you to meetings and attend when I can, if my father doesn't need me. It's about priorities. And I'm sure Mrs Daldy and the others will have a better idea about tactics than either you or I."

She couldn't disagree with his arguments, but it infuriated her. He did need to make his way in the business and become respected in his own right to have an income to support them, but she railed against his offhandedness towards something that was so important to her. She considered it a moral duty to fight for the franchise. She wanted him by her side, fighting as strongly, prepared to make sacrifices, but it seemed he didn't want that any longer. Not since he'd won her hand.

Well, she'd see about that.

* * * * *

As the year drew to a close, Lucy learnt of the further difficulties they faced because of the obdurate Legislative Council.

"I am increasingly concerned about the health of our dear Premier, Mr Ballance," said Mrs Daldy as her regular group took tea. "The news has not been good and I fear our cause will meet many more difficulties should Mr Seddon be in charge."

Lucy fumed. "He is not at all supportive."

"He is not, dear," agreed Mrs Daldy with a sigh. "I do not wish to speak ill of the dead, may he rest in peace, but our former Premier, Mr Atkinson, did the country – and us – a major disservice when he and Governor Lord Onslow signed those papers."

"The way Atkinson pushed through the appointment of seven of his conservative cronies to the Legislative Council, himself included, just before his defeat was completely underhand," said Mrs Caradus.

Lucy was itching to speak her mind, saying they must protest in the streets, call out the shirkers and the naysayers, but she knew the WFL ladies would only take the persistently polite and peaceable approach with their meetings and their letter writing.

"I agree," said Mrs Rattray. "The Council has been a constant restraint ever since. Thank goodness Lord Onslow was replaced. Let us pray our new Governor, Lord Glasgow, will be more balanced in his views."

"It has certainly taken months of constant battle to get to this point. But it is hoped the recent appointment of more liberal-minded members to the Council will mean we will see some progress."

What else could she say? Progress was slow and with

Christmas fast approaching, there was less likelihood of anything happening until well into the New Year.

Lucy bit her tongue while she considered other options. She wasn't prepared to give up.

* * * * *

The lead-up to Christmas began in earnest at the start of December. Richard escorted her to several concerts and entertainments, either in the company of his parents, his grandmother, her father, or Milly and her sister, who all allowed them a degree of freedom while maintaining the proprieties of being chaperoned. In Richard's company, her love for him deepened, and her belief in their future together increased. They were so well suited. He was kind and generous, and she had utter faith in them being leaders of the community. Him with his work, and her with her causes, if only he would listen to her more than their fathers.

She had especially enjoyed the magnificent Scottish entertainment hosted by the Burns Club at the Opera House in the presence of His Excellency the Governor and Lady Glasgow. For once, feeling as if she had walked into a garden of spring flowers amongst the many stylish and bejewelled gowns befitting of the glamorous surroundings, she forgot about her worries. The subdued lighting flattered the ladies' complexions as fans fluttered gaily, keeping them cool, while the music from the orchestra roused their spirits. Chatter filled the auditorium as they waited for the show to start.

She'd taken extra care dressing tonight in an effort to please Richard. She'd swept her hair up and held it in place with a series of small flower clips; soft tendrils fell around her temples. Her silver-sequinned lilac gown shimmered with every movement, and she felt, if not beautiful, at least elegant, and charming. She'd been rewarded by the admiration in his eyes.

Although, later that night, once again, she had reason to be dismayed.

"How lovely to see you," said Richard, on their way out, to a couple Lucy didn't recognise. "May I introduce my fiancée, Miss Lucy Young. Lucy, this is Mr George Willis and Mrs Willis."

After polite greetings and congratulations had been exchanged, Mr Willis said, "I have the pleasure of knowing your father, Miss Young." He turned towards Richard. "I shall look forward to seeing an affiliation between Young and Harris. Sound business practice. Very sound."

Lucy's cheeks flamed. She glanced towards Mrs Willis for support, but the woman's attention had been taken by another and she was unaware of the exchange.

In reply, Richard said, "Indeed, sir. I'll look forward to doing business with you."

"Good lad." Mr Willis tapped him on the arm. "When is the big day?"

"A date is yet to be set, sir. But I'm sure my father will keep you informed."

"Is he here?"

"He is, sir. Over there, I believe."

"Congratulations, again, Miss Young," said Mr Willis as he rejoined his wife, and they disappeared from sight seeking Mr and Mrs Harris. Lucy found Richard's mother far too oppressed for her liking. The woman barely spoke, except in meek tones. She hoped Richard would never expect the same of her.

"Richard! How could you?"

"What have I done?" He looked genuinely confused.

"You put me in a most invidious situation. You didn't say anything about me at all. It was all about our fathers and their business dealings. Don't I count? Don't *we* count? Us, as a couple, about to embark on a lifetime together? Isn't what we do important?"

They followed the crowds down the staircase towards the exit, speaking quietly so as not to be overheard.

"It's not about us, Lucy. Of course we are going to make our lives together, but I will still have to work. Money doesn't grow on trees, my dear. I will not inherit sufficient wealth to live by my own means until my father dies. Hopefully, that is a long time hence."

"I know that, and I, too, do not wish either your father or mine to come to an early demise. But I believed we would make the decisions about the direction of our lives together. About our home, our children, and our work. My work."

Richard guided her towards the cab waiting at the kerb, curtailing any further conversation until they were settled. He sat stiffly beside her. "What 'work' do you refer to? I will not condone you working after we are wed."

"I'm not asking your permission, Richard. I will continue to work to gain the franchise, as we agreed. And when we do, then we can be married, but beyond that I wish to put my mind to causes that will bring about the betterment of women. I'm young. I'm articulate. I have a good brain, and there are women out there who need people to speak up for them."

Richard sighed. "I had hoped that you would be content to settle down after we married. I know I have to wait for you until after the franchise is achieved. And I'm hoping that will not be too far hence, despite continued setbacks. I support you in that. I believe women, like you, should be able to vote. But after that, can't you be happy with your church, your home and our children?"

Lucy sat quietly for a moment, considering her answer. *Women like me*, she fumed. *What does he mean? The franchise is for all women.* "No, Richard, I don't believe I can."

The rest of the journey continued in frosty silence as the pair considered what had been said and the effect it would have on their future.

"Goodnight, Lucy," he said politely as he assisted her from the cab. "I will think on what you have said and we will discuss it at a later date. I fear further discourse at this point would be upsetting to you."

Upsetting! Lucy resisted the impulse to snap back – she was slowly learning there were better ways to get what she wanted. "I agree, Richard. You do need time to think about my wishes and how you can accommodate them in the future. I will say goodnight, and thank you for a very pleasant evening."

He escorted her to the door before returning to the cab without comment.

She stood at the doorway watching him go, thinking she'd have to be more persuasive if she was to completely convince him.

Over the next couple of weeks, Lucy busied herself helping with decorations for the church, anything to take her mind off Richard. She loved this time of year when they put up the Christmas tree and the church was filled with flowers.

"Hand me another ornament," said Lucy, standing halfway up the stepladder. She didn't have the necessary skills to create the magnificent floral displays filling the huge urns at the front of the church, but she could decorate the tree with bows and shiny glass ornaments.

"Which one?" asked Milly.

"That one first." She pointed to the one in Milly's right hand.

From her vantage point she could see Hope working on the table stacked with flowers and lengths of greenery, alongside the more experienced women putting together the sprays that would adorn the end of each pew.

"How's it looking?" Lucy asked as she hung the last decoration.

Milly stood back and studied the tree from every angle. "Move that one there over a bit. Yes, that's right. Now straighten the angel on the top and we are finished."

Lucy climbed down and admired her handiwork. "Perfect."

She and Milly then began to make paper streamers and hung them along the walls, before turning their attention to making articles for the fête to raise funds for gifts for the poor. Some days, she was busy from morn until evening with barely time for a break, and happy she was contributing to something greater than herself.

Milly was a dab hand at stitching and quickly made a number of small gingerbread men and little stuffed rag dolls made from felt. Hope added the trimmings and drew the faces, while Lucy made cards and pictures with dried flowers and ribbons. Chatting non-stop, the three had a lot of fun together while they worked, often laughing at something, which earned disapproving looks from some of the older ladies, but no one could complain at what they achieved. She felt energised by all the busyness.

On Christmas morning, Richard arrived with a gift wrapped in pretty paper and tied with a ribbon.

"What's this?" she asked with a grin, happy to see him again, as Mrs Bush showed him in. She had forgiven Richard for their previous disagreement, deciding she had handled the matter badly.

"You will have to open it to find out." He smiled widely. His eyes looked adoringly at her, and her heart melted all over again, feeling secure in his love.

"Can I open it now?"

A mischievous grin gave her all the encouragement she needed. She had just rolled the ribbon up to save for another time when her father entered.

"I thought I heard your voice." His hand reached out for Richard's, and they shook. "Season's greetings to you."

"And to you, sir. Will you be joining us at church this morning?"

"If you'll allow an old man to walk beside you two young ones, I will accompany you."

Lucy continued to unwrap the present. "Of course you're allowed, Father. What a silly thing to say."

She smiled as she glanced at Richard's gift. "This is a wonderful keepsake," she said, holding up the Christmas edition of *The Auckland Weekly News*.

Richard put his hand in his pocket. "And with your permission, sir," he said to Mr Young, "I'd like to give Miss Young this." He opened a box to show a small bar brooch with a central ruby.

She took it from him and put her hand to her mouth to stifle the gasp of pleasure. "Oh, my. What a lovely surprise." She raced around the table, clutching the box tightly, and threw her arms around Richard's neck. "Thank you. I love it."

Blushing, she immediately withdrew and threw a quick glance at her father, wondering if he would be angry, thinking she was forgetting herself. But he looked content. She folded the wrapping paper to put away and wondered what might have been said recently to change his demeanour.

To cover her fluster, she flicked through the pages of the magazine, stopping now and then to look at the photos and read the odd caption. She would read the articles later at her leisure.

"Oh look, there's a photo of Mrs Daldy and the committee at the Opera House back in July. Remember that night, Richard?"

"I most certainly do."

The warmth in his voice forced her to meet his eyes, and she saw that all was well between them again. "In my excitement, I nearly forgot. I have something for you too."

She retrieved two parcels from the drawer of the dresser and handed one to Richard. "And one for you too, Father."

She watched Richard carefully as he untied his gift. She took the string from him and rolled it up and refolded the wrapping paper he dropped on the table. He lifted up the cravat, admiring the pin engraved with his initials. "Thank you, Lucy. It is truly elegant. It will become a favourite, I am sure."

"Thank you, my dear. A lovely gift indeed," said Mr Young, admiring his own cravat and engraved pin. "We'd better be off, or we'll miss the start of the service. Even if you aren't bothered, I am looking forward to Christmas dinner."

13

Much-needed reinforcements

Emma picked up her phone. She had an idea. "Hi, Jess, got a minute to talk?" Her pulse raced. Would Jess be willing? It was a lot to ask.

"Sure, what's up?"

Emma explained her 'emergency' with Paige the previous evening. Luke had not been at all happy and they'd argued, even though she was back well before Rosie had finished dance, and they ate dinner together. "I hate it when we row, but what was I supposed to do? The girl put out an SOS that ended up being an emotional crisis rather than a physical one, but I didn't know that until I got there." Emma doodled on her notepad while they chatted about the temperamental volatility of teenagers over just about everything.

"Our girls'll be that age in a few years," said Jess. "Think of it as training."

Emma couldn't laugh. The thought scared her. Motherhood was full of risk and worry. "Luke thinks I should cut her loose. He keeps reminding me I'm not her mother, but since she doesn't have one, or any other sympathetic female to turn to, I'm reluctant. She might be overly sensitive and get hurt easily, but she has some great goals, which got me wondering …"

"Uh-oh! What're you thinking this time?"

Emma's stomach churned. She shouldn't be putting Jess is such an awkward situation. She had more than enough to cope with. "The girl is bright. She's lapping up all the scientific evidence, the economic arguments, the zero emissions conversations and the technological innovations, but she's bogged down by too much theory and can't see the practical solutions going on around her. And …"

Emma paused. Maybe she was asking too much. She added to the doodles unsure if she was on the right track. Jess was a little bundle of energy. She'd more than bounced back from her marriage break-up. She was thriving in her new floral business, loving having her sister Lily back in her life once all the secrets had been untangled, and was a great mum to Olivia.

"And …" Jess prompted.

"Something you said the other day about backing anyone who wanted to protect the environment got me thinking, that's all."

Emma stared through the French doors seeing the shades of green of her garden, speckled with the bright spots of colour of flower heads framed in the window. The odd soft cloud scudded past in a forget-me-not blue sky that today was bright and clear. Skies should always look like that, she thought.

"And you think I can help?" Jess brought her back to the issue. "But how exactly?"

"I have no idea. I don't know enough about it to counter her doubts or push her in a direction. Her scientific boyfriend was the obvious answer, but he's missing in action."

"Any news on that front?"

Emma found herself copying Paige's one-shoulder hitch, even though Jess couldn't see her. "After I dropped her home, she texted me to say she'd heard from him and they were talking."

"Well, that's good. Isn't it?"

"Yes. Except he's overseas and she's staying here. For now. But she seems to have lost her focus. She's saying changing anything needs such a massive political and economic push, globally, that she no longer believes it's going to happen. Or at least, not fast enough."

"She may be right."

Emma's doodles got darker and longer. "And isn't that a worry?" She took a deep breath. "I don't know enough about any of this. I don't know what to advise her. Would you talk to her? Tell her what you see people doing to make a difference?" A momentary silence followed Emma's question. Her heart pounded.

"Sure, why not?" came the chirpy reply. "In for a penny and all that. If it'll help, I'll see what I can do to encourage her back on track."

Emma let out her breath. "I owe you one."

"Sure do." Jess's laugh had a genuine tinkle to it. Honest and caring.

They finished the call agreeing to meet up for coffee in a few days.

Emma turned off her phone, email and any other notifications. Freed from any distractions, within moments she was engrossed in writing up the last of Ruby's story. She wanted to finish it so she could begin the next client's family tree and concentrate on Paige a bit more, despite Luke's indifference. She understood his priority was her, and her health. She was grateful, but … and that was the problem, there was a but.

They'd drifted apart of late. Or rather she'd pushed him away, too tired to be bothered, if she was being honest. He didn't deserve that. Increasingly she thought there was more to her fatigue than mere tiredness through sitting at her desk too long, concentrating so hard her eyes were sore, or any hang-over symptoms from Covid. But she was too scared to find out.

Ruby's story had become more compelling as time went on. Her activity in the push for suffrage appeared minimal, although she may have helped collect signatures, but in the course of her day she would have come across many of the activists who were to become its leaders. Women who would become household names within and beyond their lifetime.

The more she researched, the more astounded she became at how organised and determined they were, and how long it had taken them to win the vote. The women of today needed to know, to understand, and not take anything for granted. Rights could be lost far more easily than they were won.

"Jean," said Emma when she answered her call. "I've discovered a lot more about the timeline of the suffrage movement. While it doesn't specifically relate to Ruby's activities, I would like to include it, if you don't mind. It seems very relevant to the time and the place she lived."

129

"That sounds interesting," said Jean. "As I said the other day, I know very little about what happened here. So yes, my dear. Go ahead and tell me about it."

Satisfied, Emma finished the conversation, turned her phone off again and started to write.

Ruby would have been a mere babe in swaddling in 1869, when Mary Müller, under the pseudonym Femmina, first published her article, *An Appeal to the Men of New Zealand* inspired by the great British philosopher and parliamentarian, John Stuart Mill.

From then on, women's suffrage was on everyone's lips.

After reading Mill's book, *The Subjection of Women*, Sir Robert Stout, the Dunedin teacher, lawyer, and parliamentarian, began to speak up about women's rights as early as the 1870s – often to much derision, but with a surprising level of support. Fellow parliamentarian, and Otago newspaper magnate, Sir Julius Vogel, did the same. Addressing the Otago Girls' High School in 1873 and citing Mill, he supported women having the vote.

Around the same time, Mary Colclough, under the pen name Polly Plum, wrote endless letters and articles supporting women's rights, and held widely popular and well-attended lectures.

In her infancy, Ruby could have gone with her mother to any of these meetings in support of the franchise, but without proof, we can only surmise. What we do know is Ruby was part of the successes of the 1890s.

Emma made a list of the names, recognising many – both political leaders and women's voices – and beginning to think that the coincidences of time and place with Paige's family were too great to ignore. Not only family, but also the parallels between the fight for what was just then and what was just today.

Stout introduced a suffrage bill to parliament in 1878, enfranchising women who owned property. It failed. Nine years later, in 1887, Vogel introduced another franchise bill which he believed would pass 'if the women would move' he told his wife Mary. It too failed.

Emma couldn't see why the women didn't act when they had the chance. Only a few years later, they were out in force. She'd like to think she'd have been brave enough to make a stand at the time. But it took guts – or desperation – to fight the status quo without the right backing. She thought about Paige, who believed the planet was at crisis point and was desperate to take a stand to protect it. Was enough being done? Emma pushed today's issues from her head and returned to the past.

At the time Vogel's bill was proposed, Kate Sheppard had held the position of National Superintendent for Franchise and Legislation in the WCTU for a few short months. The small numbers of WCTU women were campaigning for prohibition and, with little time to prepare, the mobilisation required to pass the bill didn't happen.

Four years would pass before the movement began to pick up pace.

Increasingly, Emma saw analogies between then and now. Paige and the youth of today were the modern counterparts to the activists of the past. The adaptive solutions to environmental issues required global assent, but the push needed to come from the populace if they were to succeed. Too many agreements and accords and meetings had failed because of a lack of political will, blocked by big business with moneyed interests.

She understood how important it was to Paige for people to speak up. Inspired, she carried on with Ruby's story.

Organised by Helen Nicol, the 1891 Dunedin meeting of the Women's Franchise League was the catalyst. It attracted an audience of over twelve hundred drawn from 'the elite of the grace and elegance and wealth of Dunedin'. Many women who had not joined the WCTU because of their rigid views on temperance happily signed up to the new league to focus on winning the vote.

What had Paige said? Too many conflicting opinions on the best way forward was holding everything back. Seems that wasn't a new phenomenon.

The similarities were becoming clearer with each paragraph Emma wrote. For democracy to function, and reform to occur, it needed voices – not only political voices, but those of the masses. Women won the vote because enough people spoke in favour. Climate action now needed its global citizens to speak up and add their weight to the debate. The time was right then; was the time was right now? Paige thought so.

She felt certain Paige sat with the majority, but, Emma sighed, they didn't need all the grandstanding. The environment was desperate for action. And money. Some days, the past made more sense.

Their most vociferous opponent, Dunedin politician Henry Smith Fish, did his utmost to undermine them using underhand tactics, but his argument that only a handful of spiteful women who wanted prohibition wanted the vote was proven false by the growing numbers of league members.

Fish! Emma stopped mid-paragraph. Why had she not noticed before? She scrambled amongst her notes trying to recall where she'd seen the name. She stared at the piece of paper before her, doubting the possibility. But there it was, in black and white: David Fish Frazer – Paige's father! What, she wondered, could she do with that titbit? Shoving it to the back of her mind to percolate, she carried on.

Incensed by Fish's devious antics, Ruby and the women of Dunedin campaigned against him when he stood for the mayoralty of Dunedin later that year. He was soundly defeated. Ruby would have been delighted.

He blamed the league – and rightly so. Imagine the marches, the banners, the camellias, the petitions, the quiet determination, and the celebrations.

Ruby's ally, Harriet Morison, found further success in Auckland working alongside the indomitable Amey Daldy to establish the Auckland League in June 1892.

With an inner smile at the demise of the disagreeable Mr Fish – and maybe a certain disagreeable descendant, if she could prove it – Emma made a note in the bibliography, citing her sources – *The Otago Daily Times*, Papers Past, and the New Zealand History website – and closed the file.

She hadn't known much about the suffrage movement beforehand, other than the great achievements of Kate Sheppard and her Christchurch cohorts. Now, she realised, many more women deserved recognition for what they had achieved – without taking any glory from Kate herself.

Emma switched on the phone and internet again, checked the emails and marked some to deal with later. She was surprised not to have heard from Paige.

After all the research into Ruby's place within the franchise movement, Emma began to speculate if Paige's ancestors could be similarly involved. The timing was right if she'd done her generations chart correctly – and variations of the naming pattern had been maintained. If not, she had even less to go on. She sighed. Only the badges in the trinket box gave her any indication these women might have been activists. That, and Paige's insistence that she came from a long line of troublemakers.

Emma was at a loss. She'd not found anything online to help, or in the newspaper archives. She needed their married names. One option was to purchase the relevant certificates. She didn't usually do that for clients. If they wanted to know, then they had to pay. But Paige was not a client. Paige was … what?

She wasn't a friend exactly; there was too big an age gap. Emma was more her mentor. She certainly felt if not responsible, then empathetic. Without asking her father and risk riling him further, Paige couldn't afford the costs. Emma knew they could run to hundreds of dollars for the number of certificates they might need as one led to another. Or worse, was the wrong person and led nowhere.

Emma harrumphed. If she wanted to know, she'd have to cough up herself, or forever wonder. She returned to the trinket box and set each item out on the desk. She'd already identified some of the badges and pins belonging to the various organisations, but it was hard to remember them all. She needed a system.

She reached into the stationery drawer for some light card, dug around for the scissors and began cutting the card into squares. Pinning a badge to one of the squares, she checked the image on the computer and wrote the name and span of dates it operated below. One by one, she put them into some sort of date order and laid them in the lid of a copy-paper box. She was left with the brooch Paige had recognised, pinned at the neckline of the 'still-to-be-identified' woman in the photo – older than the one in the locket – and various other bits of jewellery that surely had a story to tell, if only they could.

Emma picked up what she thought might be a tie or cravat pin. The long stick pin attached to the back was quite different from the usual bar pins with a swivel and catch mechanism on the reverse side of most badges. The gold had mellowed over time and was richer in colour than her modern gold ring. As she turned it to the light, she realised there were initials engraved on it. She found her magnifying glass and took it nearer to the natural light coming through the French doors. She couldn't quite make out if there was middle initial, but an R and H written in flowing script were clearly visible.

Who was RH? she wondered, and what was it in doing in amongst what was obviously women's jewellery?

14

Life is wonderful

January 1893

Lucy awoke on the first day of the new year eager and hopeful. She stretched against the pillows and yawned before snuggling under the bedclothes to reflect on what she considered the most romantic night of her life.

Richard had been at his most attentive and caring self as he escorted her, in the company of her father, aboard the paddle steamer *Britannia* for the moonlight cruise. She could recall every minute …

"Look Richard," she said leaning on the ship's rails and pointing as the *Britannia* steamed away from the wharf. "Look at the crowds. People as far as the eye can see."

Pennants gently flapped in the light breeze and light filtered across the decks from the public rooms, while music drifted in the air.

"All I can see is you," he whispered, staring at her as if she was the only one present, despite those milling around them and the throngs lining the harbour front all the way to St Heliers.

She returned his gaze and within moments was lost in his love. She felt as if they were alone in a world of their own. They danced around the ballroom, swaying to the music in a bubble, unaware of anyone else. She couldn't remember what they talked about, but his laughter rang in her head. Her heart and mind belonged to him and him alone as he whispered loving words in her ear. The hours disappeared in a breathless whirl.

They laughed when a sudden cacophony of sound burst the gauze-like cloud they'd wrapped themselves in.

"It's midnight," he said, pulling her towards the rails as the hooters blasted and the bells from every ship in the harbour began to ring, rockets were set off into the sky, amid gasps and squeals of delight, to announce the arrival of 1893.

"Happy New Year, my darling Lucy." His kiss was warm and soft and gentle; she sank into his arms and gave in to the intense feelings overwhelming her.

"It's raining," he laughed when they finally broke apart. He wiped the rain from her face with his thumb and continued to stare into her eyes. "You are the most beautiful creature and I consider myself extremely lucky."

Around them, people were dashing for cover and getting ready to disembark as the crowds on shore scuttled home. Her father appeared, "Hurry up, you two," he called.

Richard took his jacket off, wrapped it around her shoulders and with his arm around her, they hurried inside …

A knock on the door brought her out of her reverie.

"Get up, Lucy. It's breakfast time."

"Yes, Father."

Last evening's feeling of enchantment remained as she quickly scrambled into a pretty lemon blouse with a pleated front and the newer-look gigot sleeves. Humming to herself as she stepped into the plain bell-shaped navy skirt that fitted neatly over her hips, she realised she had not had reason to chivvy Richard about his propensity to talk business with everyone he met.

Maybe she had taught him a lesson in how to treat her after their early December falling out, and could at last allow herself to consider a few details about their nuptials. Surely, this year they would win the franchise. She couldn't wait to tell Milly about it all, and Hope, if she was at all interested since her own wedding was coming up.

She wrapped her hair up in a chignon and pulled a few curls loose around her face and hurried into the kitchen where they preferred to eat breakfast.

"Sorry I'm late," she said as she slipped an apron over her head and tied the strings behind her back. "Won't be a minute."

She unwrapped the muslin-swathed bread that Mrs Bush had baked the previous evening, giving it to her father to slice. Chatting all the while, she threw eggs and bacon into the large pan and made a fresh pot of tea. "We had such a wonderful time last night, I was still daydreaming about it this morning. I hope you did too. Richard is taking me on a picnic today, with his grandmother."

She quickly dished up the food, as Mrs Bush had taught her, and popped the plates on the table. Her father grunted, put the paper down and picked up his knife and fork. "Have you looked out the window? I doubt there's a picnic happening anytime soon. The forecast is for wind and rain for several days."

Lucy's heart sank.

Noticing her sorrow, he attempted to cheer her up. "You and Richard are welcome to come with me to the races. You would enjoy the ladies' fashions, I'm sure."

She shook her head. "No thank you, Father. I don't wish to be compared with the fashionable set. Some of the ladies are already complaining about Lady Glasgow giving tacit approval to such activities with her love of horse racing. But what is the point of watching the horses race if not to win?"

"You're a funny young thing. So strong-minded about the rights of women, yet you are not a prohibitionist like so many of them. You don't like gambling, yet you are amused by those ghastly theatrical comedies and enjoy card games."

"There's no harm in laughing, Father. I like to laugh. It's such a happy feeling, but I don't see why women should be treated as lesser beings when it comes to the vote." Lucy finished her mouthful and took a sip of tea. "I know as well as you the issues Parliament discusses, and how their decisions affect us all. It's something you taught me. After Mama died, remember? To make sure I knew what was in my best interests and not be pushed around. If it wasn't to prepare me for making my own decisions, I don't know why you bothered."

Aloysius Young cleared his throat and wiped his mouth on the napkin. "Your dear departed mother was the light of my life. And you have fulfilled that role since.

I failed to protect her and your baby brother, and I lost them," he said thickly. He cleared his throat again. "But I promised I would protect you. That's why I taught you all those things. So you can be objective. I've done my best."

"And you have, Father. You have, and I wholeheartedly thank you for it. And I thank you for the support you've given me with the franchise, but you do confuse me sometimes."

"In what way?"

"You teach me to be my own person. You allow me opinions. You make sure I am educated and informed, and yet you seek to use me as a pawn in your business merger, and marry me off. Why is that?"

He lifted his head and met her steady gaze head on. "Simply to protect you from the worst of society's narrow-mindedness and those who could destroy a single woman without protection when I am not here."

Dread settled in her core. Was her father warning her about an illness? That he was getting old and might die? She couldn't bear the thought.

"That is why you must marry, Lucy. I held off as long as possible, but it's time. Don't spoil it."

"But Father …"

"Enough. You will do as I say." He threw his napkin on the table and walked out, leaving Lucy speechless. She'd never considered that her father might be looking after her interests in that way. Maybe she had misjudged him – and Richard.

She cleared the table and began the clean-up to make sure the kitchen was as it should be. Mrs Bush had been with them since Lucy was a girl, teaching Lucy the basics of household management and how to cook the simple meals she'd prepared before she left for the day, but Lucy wondered now if she would know enough to run a household on her own.

She'd never thought herself special, but as she considered what marriage might mean, she realised that she still had a lot to learn about life. Would they afford someone to help, or would she be tied to the house doing all the chores herself? Heaven forbid. Did she know how, well enough? With no close female relatives to act as a companion for her, she had few options. She couldn't remain a spinster … her mind went into a spin … unless she acted as nurse to her father. Her stomach fluttered. Was he trying to tell her he needed her? Or that he wanted her settled?

She'd had so many questions without answers, and here she was again with doubts about her future. She bit her bottom lip, worried she didn't know the full story.

She would write her thoughts in her journal. She'd found herself thinking more clearly when she did. She couldn't say why, but she'd started writing down her inner most thoughts after the large and, to her, frivolous event her father had hosted to celebrate her coming of age.

At the time, she had wondered what being 'of age' meant. For men, a lot. The right to vote, amongst everything else. For women, a lot less. For her, it simply meant she was getting old and in need of a marriage partner sooner rather than later. She had bewailed the necessity. Why couldn't a woman vote, why couldn't they live and work as men did, if they wished, and have their own money? Why did they need the protection and approval of a man to exist? Why?

Richard arrived an hour later with tickets in his hand.

"Since we can't have the picnic we planned, I've booked us on the *Clansman* to take us up to the Waiwera Hot Springs. My parents will join us and we can enjoy the midday meal at the hotel."

"Oh, how exciting," she exclaimed, thinking how solicitous he was and maybe she need have little to worry about after all. She was less sure about being in the company of the usually verbose Mr Harris senior, who effectively silenced his downtrodden wife. Grandmother Stone was a much more interesting person. "How did you manage to get tickets at this late stage?"

He grinned. "I've know someone who knows someone. They helped me out."

"That's so thoughtful. Thank you. The hotel is magnificent and I hear the food is delicious. I shall also enjoy taking the waters." All thoughts of the difficulties ahead disappeared from her mind as she focused on the day ahead.

A week later, as she and Richard were on their way to attend an evening at the Opera House with Milly and one of her siblings in tow, Lucy was once again complaining about men and the unfairness of life.

"Parliament has been prorogued again! Until 13th April. We will never get the Bill before Parliament at this rate."

"Don't fret, Lucy, my love. It'll give you ladies more time to prepare. Won't it, Miss Ridley?"

"You may well be right, sir," answered Milly quietly, shrinking slightly under Lucy's fervent stare.

"I have every reason to fret. After our defeat last year, the Government needs to present the Bill to the next session at the first opportunity. But there's still no guarantee."

"I'm sure they will as soon as they can, but remember the deadlock between the Legislative Council and the House remains. Don't get your hopes up too soon. Didn't you say another petition was being considered?"

Lucy's eyes sparkled. "Oh, yes. That's right. They did say that. Milly, remind me to tell Mrs Daldy that I am willing to canvass again."

"Now that's settled, can we not talk about the Bill any more tonight, and enjoy the entertainment?"

"Of course, Richard. I'm looking forward to it."

They arrived at the theatre and took their seats. The curtain opened on the well-lit stage. The four spent the rest of the evening laughing at all the witty repartee, buoyed by the music.

On the way home, after dropping Milly and her sister along the way, Richard was still in high spirits. "After the excessively wet start to the year, I think we should plan some outings now the summer sunshine has returned."

"What a lovely suggestion. It has been wet, hasn't it? Father said the lawn at the New Year races was awash and the track almost dangerous. I'm glad we didn't go. He said all the ladies were sombrely attired and wrapped in their cloaks for the day, never once venturing from the grandstand."

"And we all know the ladies only go to see what the others are wearing," he teased.

"I don't," she said indignantly. "It sounded like

an utterly miserable day. Waiwera was a much more pleasurable option."

Richard rubbed his chin between thumb and forefinger as if contemplating something of great importance. "I was thinking maybe you'd like to go cycling. We could venture farther afield, enjoy the parks and have a picnic or two."

Lucy turned in her seat towards him. "That sounds wonderful," she enthused, repeating her catchphrase for the umpteenth time.

"Does anything ever sound less than wonderful to you?"

"Not much," she replied, giggling. "Life is wonderful most of the time, isn't it? And I do so enjoy cycling, except for some of those very big hills, and I love picnics."

Richard grinned. "And while we are at it, I thought we could take a petition or two with us and see if we can do better than last time."

Lucy briefly stared at him, her mouth open in disbelief. "Do you mean it? You'd come campaigning with me?"

He nodded and she immediately hugged him. "Oh, you wonderful man."

True to her word, Lucy wrote to Mrs Daldy offering her services, and those of Mr Harris, who would accompany her to areas she and Milly had been unable to manage alone.

Mrs Daldy replied she was grateful for such enthusiasm for the cause: *I will arrange to have petition forms made available. As part of a delegation of ladies from the League, I recently visited the Hon. Cadman, Minister of Justice, who assured us the Bill would be presented at the next session, which was good news, even with the reminder that the issues with the Legislative Council are still to be resolved.*

He seemed sympathetic and we left with a sense of accomplishment. Your letter is timely as our ladies in Dunedin and Christchurch are increasing their activities to gather signatures hoping to add more weight to the already compelling demand.

From then on, every Saturday half-day closing, and on some of the long summer evenings when he could get away, she and Richard went cycling together. Every time they gathered signatures to be added to a growing pile of petition forms, and at each outing she fell more in love.

"Why are you doing this?" she asked one evening as they sat in Albert Park admiring the gardens. Lucy trailed her hand in the water of the large fountain overshadowed by a statue of Aphrodite spouting water. The surrounding statues of dolphins, ridden by cherubs blowing horns, also gushed water into the pool.

"Because I'm selfish," he admitted honestly. "The sooner you win the franchise, the sooner we can be wed. Then I can turn my attention to the business and how I'd like to see it grow and develop. Right now, my father won't listen to me, so I have to bide my time."

"How will the planned merger between our fathers work?"

Richard shrugged. "Your father will continue to import goods, and my father will continue to sell them. I'm not sure anything much will change, except that they will both have guaranteed sources of supply and demand."

"And what do you want to see happen?"

He rose to his feet, pacing before her, speaking with his hands. "Like I outlined to you before, I'd like to see us open larger premises to display the goods in a far better light, one that would rival any other. In time, we could expand and have branches in other towns and cities." His voice rose as the ideas spilled forth. "But so far my father won't hear of it."

He looked so despondent, her heart went out to him. "I'm sure he will after we are married, when you are a man in your right with a wife and a home of your own." Lucy hesitated, unsure whether to ask the question about where they would live, which was uppermost in her mind, but she hesitated too long.

"Precisely," he said, pulling her to her feet, towering over her as he held her hands against his chest. "Which is why we have to gather the signatures that will win you the franchise."

She thought for a moment he would kiss her, but he broke away and held her bicycle ready for her to mount. "Come along. But on Monday, which, in case you have forgotten, is a public holiday to celebrate Auckland's 53rd anniversary, we are going to join in the fun of the Annual Regatta."

"That would be delightful."

Except the day had not turned out as she'd wished.

The sun blazed from a blue sky, and the winds, she was told, were perfect for a magnificent day on the harbour aboard the *Clansman*. She was tempted with delicate sandwiches and delightful cakes, and an array of teas and fizzy drinks while she watched the billowing white sails race each other around a set course, without any understanding of what was happening, either on the water, or why Richard behaved as he did. She came home flustered with her heart and head at odds. She turned to her journal.

I am so disappointed. When we are working side by side for the cause, gathering signatures, walking, or cycling, or sharing a meal, Richard is the perfect companion; kindly and considerate, interesting and, more importantly, interested in what I have to say, and oh-so-engaging. So why is it, when we are out and about in public, meeting people of note in business, and especially the wealthy, that he turns into the archetypal high-handed male?

I won't tolerate it. He is not to treat me like some sort of appendage. I am his equal in intelligence and ability. I know I am. But bound by rules that make no sense, I have limited options. That doesn't mean that he can lord it over me and control me. We will be a partnership, or we will be nothing.

There! I've said it. I will not marry a man who seeks to mould me to something I am not.

15

When patience runs thin

April 2022

Emma was lying on the couch in the family room, when Luke came in, freshly showered after his cycle ride.

"How's things?" he asked.

She felt his shadow standing over her before continuing to the kitchen.

She'd missed their five-o'clock catch-ups of late, before the rush of dinner. Between having little sense of taste and constant fatigue, Emma had no energy left to chat. The change in daylight saving time at the beginning of April back to winter hours wasn't helping either. It had upset her body clock even more. "Okay."

She knew she was taking advantage of Luke's good nature and, while not exactly neglecting Rosie, she was not fully engaged with her daughter's chit-chat and constant requests either.

"Didn't you have an appointment with the optometrist today?"

"Hmm," Emma nodded.

"And? What did they say? Is your eyesight part of the problem?"

Emma remembered the woman had tested everything, shining bright lights into her eyes, puffing air into them to create a reaction, and measuring behind the eye. She was exhausted. "No. My sight is excellent." Emma could hear Luke rustling around getting something ready for dinner, she supposed.

"Is that it?"

"I could wear off-the-shelf reading glasses if it helps, but that's it."

Something banged on the bench a little louder than the other sounds. She winced. Was that accidental or deliberate? Was Luke annoyed? She couldn't even drag her eyes open to find out.

"That's good news at least. But what next? You can't leave it at that."

She felt Luke approach her again; the sofa sagged under his weight as he sat down. His hand reached up to stroke the side of her face and hair. "I'm worried, Ems. Please go and see a doctor."

She opened her eyes to look at him and shook her head slightly. "Not that again. Will you stop. I read up again about long Covid. I'm sure that's what it is. It'll pass. There's nothing they can do anyway."

"You should try," insisted Luke, his voice tight. "It's been weeks. You should be feeling better by now."

She made an effort to pull herself up against the cushions. "Haven't you been keeping up to date with the numbers? They are still far too high and putting strain on the health service. They don't need me clogging the system."

Luke tensed and his tone changed. He wasn't as patient with her as he had been. "But what if it's not? What if it's anaemia or, or … I don't know …" he rubbed his hands through his hair "… something worse? I want to know what's wrong with you, even if you don't. It's not fair on Rosie, or me, for that matter."

She had little enough strength to argue as it was, and didn't need him on at her all the time. She flung her legs past him and pushed herself to stand up. "For heaven's sake, Luke. Leave me alone. I'm okay. I'm managing." Her voice sounded snappy even to her ears.

He was on his feet beside her in a second, gripping her arms, forcing her to look at him. "No, you're not. You're ignoring the situation. When was the last time you read a story to Rosie – or we sat and chatted about the news or watched a movie together? You force yourself to do whatever you think is important in that office of yours, and then you crash. I rarely see you."

Emma sighed. "I can't do this, Luke. I can't think straight. Please, just leave me be. I'm going to lie down."

He dropped his hands from her arms. "And it'll be the last I see of you until tomorrow – again. Have you forgotten Rosie's dance recital coming up? What about the trip we talked about for the school holidays? You can't go on like this."

Unexpected tears overflowed her aching eyes, as her body screamed with the tension in every muscle. She shook her head, flapped an insouciant hand and headed through the doorway. She heard a door slam as she fell on the bed.

To avoid alienating Luke further, Emma had started to take an afternoon nap so she could function through the crucial after-school to bedtime hours.

After a few days, she began to feel better except her night-time sleep increasingly became disturbed and mornings a trial. Light shone through a gap in the curtains as Emma tossed from side to side, her subconscious telling her something wasn't right.

Luke was missing from their bed.

Emma opened one eye to check the clock. 6.01 am. Where was he? She turned over and realised he'd not slept there at all. *Where was he?* A flutter in her stomach, and she was out of bed in an instant, racing towards Rosie's room.

She paused to quietly peek in to see her daughter still fast asleep. She closed the door again and hurried along to the spare room. A sigh of relief calmed her as she leant against the door jamb watching Luke. He wouldn't be far off waking. He was usually up around the half-hour, but she could tell by the tangle of sheets that he'd not slept well either.

He'd been right. She hardly saw him these days. He'd tucked her under the bedclothes at some stage, but she remembered nothing after that. Except for the dreams. Constant dreams. Vivid. Full colour. Confusing and enervating. Never mind how long she'd stayed in bed, she felt drained and every joint ached.

She left Luke sleeping and headed towards the shower, hoping to feel more refreshed. Before she'd finished, he'd slipped in beside her. Amid the hot water and the soap, they lovingly and laughingly made up for another uneasy row they'd had. The second in as many days. Thankfully, he didn't mention going to the doctor again.

"Are you ready, Rosie?" said Luke an hour later as he grabbed her lunch box, thrust it into her school bag and stood at the door.

With a piece of toast in her mouth, Rosie hobbled and shoved her way into her shoes. "Bye, Mum," she mumbled, giving Emma a hug.

"See you tonight, sweetheart." Emma promised herself she'd take it easy today and not let herself get so tired so she could spend time with her daughter after school. She had to admit she'd been lax.

Luke grinned at her. "Be back soon. I've got a busy day scheduled. Are you okay?"

Emma nodded. "Yep. I'm fine. Meeting Jess when she has her lunch break, but otherwise I'm going for a quiet day."

He winked, and hurried Rosie out the door.

Emma wandered into the library, her work place, her comfy place, surrounded by her books, her antiques and her photos. She resisted turning on the computer, as was her norm. The optometrist said her eyesight was unlikely to be causing her headaches or the excessive tiredness and brain fog she was experiencing. Instead, she suggested something medical and urged Emma to investigate the causes further.

She'd not told Luke that bit, and guilt at misleading him niggled at her. Stupid as it sounded, she didn't want to admit something might be wrong.

Ignoring the inner voice telling her to attack her fears head on and find out what the problem was, she went out through the French doors into the garden.

She collected her gloves and secateurs and began to deadhead the roses. No one had loved roses as much as Charli, who'd taught her how to care for them. Emma missed her grandmother so much, it hurt just thinking about her sometimes.

Luke returned from the school run and waved as he went into his container office, only to return a few minutes later to sweep her up in his arms. "Emma Grainger. You are the most important person in my life, next to Rose, and I am begging you to take care of yourself. For my sake, and hers." He kissed her deeply and left her stunned as he returned to work.

For long moments, Emma stood still staring into space, stifling the rising panic. She shook her thoughts away and continued with the deadheading, in total denial.

A couple of hours later, Emma carried her coffee into her office. She needed to check her emails, if nothing else, but, as usual, couldn't resist popping into Ancestry to see if there was anything new, and go from there.

It wasn't hard to find Henry Smith Fish and his thirteen children, some of whom died young. Beyond that, she found no clues to indicate his daughters might have handed the 'Fish' name down through the female line, as she'd believed likely. But it was still possible.

Another search revealed a Fish family of man, wife and fifteen-year-old daughter, arriving in New Zealand in 1876, who were unrelated, so without considerable and unwarranted research she couldn't prove her theory. Pity. By all accounts, Mr Henry Fish was considered conceited, unmannered and untrustworthy, with dubious morals. Dave Frazer more than likely wasn't.

She glanced at the clock remembering her date with Jess. Time to go. She closed all the searches down and headed out the door.

She'd enjoyed the brief flirtation that Paige's father was related to the underhanded Henry Fish. Amusing, if uncharitable, towards a man she didn't know. But she knew better than to speculate. Wishful thinking wouldn't get her anywhere. She'd keep her fanciful ideas to herself – for now.

"Hi, Jess," she called, seeing her friend sitting on the bench facing the beach, as she climbed out of the car.

"Aha! You remembered this time," quipped Jess, handing her a takeaway coffee and returning a hug.

"Thanks. And sorry – again – about last time. But don't be mean, girlfriend. I enjoy our chats."

"You're forgiven."

Emma sat beside Jess as they finished their coffees, then the pair made their way down the uneven steps through the soft, white sand onto the harder, honey-toned sand closer to the water. Before long they'd both shed their zip-fronted sweatshirts and tied them around their waists as they strode along the beach.

"So what happened with Paige?" asked Emma.

"What a lovely girl. But you're right. She's insecure, which makes her touchy, but her heart's in the right place."

Emma was soon panting. "I talked her out of going flatting … sort of … but I'm not sure … being at home, coping with her father's … put-downs … is not good for her either."

"She's strong enough to manage him. And I don't think he's as bad as she makes out. She just needs direction."

Jess pulled up a few paces ahead of Emma and walked back to her as she stood hands on knees, resting. "Are you okay? You seem very unfit these days. Is it still that Covid, do you think?"

"Think so … But it's taking its time."

Jess rested her hand on Emma's back, watching her breathing return to normal. "We can take it slower if you want to carry on."

Emma nodded, wiped her face on her T-shirt and began walking. "What ideas did you give Paige?"

"Basically, to focus on one aspect. Like that old adage of eating the elephant one bite at a time. You were right, she was looking at the whole picture and got lost in the noise storm."

"Such as …"

"Either water management or clean energy – we might have 80 per cent renewable energy in this country but the energy companies are still making huge profits using fossil fuels for the rest. And advocate. Write more letters to more people."

"I like that idea," said Emma, walking slower with each step. "It fits with what I've been discovering about the women of the past. Writing letters and articles to the newspapers, to businessmen, to the government – to any like-minded organisations – worked for them eventually. Her ancestors could have been one of those women. It took time, but the arguments about looking after our planet better have been going on for years, so the more voices, the better."

Jess agreed. "Better than protests, I told her, as they can be dismissed as rabble-rousing, but if we all emailed, used social media, signed petitions and raised our voices in print, the best arguments would eventually get heard."

"And did Paige like that?"

"She did. She remembered some of the advocacy groups she'd looked at earlier, and decided to take another look and see which ones were doing the most that she could add her voice to."

"Thanks, Jess. You're a blessing."

Jess blushed and shrugged off Emma's compliment. "It's nothing. I soon realised she was doing much more than all the basic stuff we've been told about for years, but she wanted a focus. Aimlessly protesting in the streets isn't her thing, but I think this could be. It's more direct."

"And simple – she'll soon be all over social media with her ideas." Emma had stopped again. "Can we sit over there?"

"Are you sure you're okay?" persisted Jess, sounding worried. "This has been going on for too long to ignore."

"My legs feel a bit wobbly, that's all. I'll sit here for a few minutes before heading back. But you go if you have to," said Emma, checking her watch.

Jess had other ideas. She glanced both ways along the beach searching for another road exit closer to where they stood. "You stay here and I'll go back and get the car. You look awful. I doubt you could walk that far."

"No, I'll be fine. Honest. You go. I'll make it after I've rested."

"*Stay put*. I'll be back."

Emma watched Jess head back along the beach at a brisk pace. Less than ten minutes had passed before she returned. Jess found Emma lying on the bench with her arm slung across her eyes to block out the light.

"Come along, you. I'm taking you home. Luke and I will sort out your car later. But you need a doctor."

Emma struggled to her feet and slowly made her way to Jess's car, fighting back tears of frustration, too weak to argue. What she couldn't control was her mounting fear that something was terribly wrong.

16

A day out

"Have patience, Lucy dear," said her father between mouthfuls of toast.

Lucy rose from her chair to pace. How many times had people told her that? She didn't want to hear it any more. "We have been patient. Extremely patient, and my patience has now run thin. It's as if we've come to a standstill. There's no movement in any direction. Both the regular and annual meetings of the League are cursory, at best, if not tedious."

She pumped her fists. "Whether it's the WCTU or the League, or wherever we go, we say the same things over and over again, make the same resolutions, are asked to stay calm, to remain civil while the machinations of Parliament go round and round seeking ways to stop it all."

"I cannot agree with your assumptions, my dear. Parliament is in favour. I can assure you. It is only the finer details still needing final agreement to ensure full equality. Remember, the Government has many other pressing concerns to deal with as well as the forthcoming election – notwithstanding Premier Ballance's health."

Lucy pulled up short at being reminded that Premier Ballance was not at all well, and her fears about who would take his place, should the worst occur, resurfaced. The battleground would be between Sir Robert Stout and Richard John Seddon. Mr Seddon was no fan of the franchise linked, as he believed, to prohibition, although she understood he might still support it, even if his connections within the liquor trade were lobbying against it.

"Let us pray he recovers soon," she said sincerely, "as even the number of signatures we're collecting has stalled. I'm so disheartened."

To top it all off, the ghastly case of Alexander James Scott, sentenced to death for poisoning his neighbour, the husband of his lover, had pushed many deserving activities from the news pages, including the franchise. The whole terrible situation was being drawn out in the papers with arguments for and against the sentence imposed. She was glad such a decision was not hers to make.

Mr Young folded his paper and rose from the breakfast table. "Chin up, my dear. The world will not end just yet." He kissed her forehead.

"Yes, Father." She watched him leave, wondering what she would do with herself as the empty day stretched before her.

After clearing the breakfast dishes and making a few desultory attempts to tidy up and write some letters, she pulled off her apron, deciding a frivolous day of shopping, and talking fashions and weddings, with

Hope and Milly would be better than the torture she was putting herself through.

Within the hour, the cab pulled up outside Milly's place in Hopetoun Street. Not expecting Milly to be ready, Lucy was about to pay the cabbie off and get another one into town later, when her friend appeared.

"Hold that cab. I'll just grab my hat and gloves. I've got some things I'd like to do."

Minutes later they were heading into Queen Street. "I'm glad you came by. It was such a lovely surprise to see you outside without sending a note first, but you saved me." Milly continued, complaining about the demands she was under, and how her younger siblings were unruly and wanting her attention all the time. "Unlike another person we know."

"Do you mean Hope?"

"I do. My … our so-called friend has decided we are not good enough any more."

Lucy wasn't surprised. She and Hope had never been that close, but Milly had been her best friend for many years. "That's sad. I had heard that Mrs Willoughby had fallen out with Mrs Daldy."

Milly looked out the window to check where they were. "She has – over the prohibition argument. Mrs W is insisting she will only support the franchise if prohibition is embodied. Grandma Amey wouldn't agree. It's ridiculous. Grandma Amey no more supports the liquor trade than Mrs Willoughby, but she knows women aren't going to win the battle with the liquor barons unless – or rather, until – we have the vote."

"And even then, the battle will be an uphill one. The men are attached to their liquor."

"Even your father and Mr Harris, I hear," said Milly.

"True. But only in moderation. I have never seen either behave badly with or without a taste of liquor. Oh, here we are."

She knocked on the cab roof and the horses were immediately pulled up at the kerb outside the Smith & Caughey department store. "I want a quick look at their summer sale," said Lucy, as they entered through the double doors into the haberdashery section.

"Good idea. I need some new gloves, but I might look at a new hat."

The girls spent a pleasant hour browsing, coming away with a few fripperies and Milly's new gloves.

Lucy shielded her eyes from the sun as they left the store. "I'd like to visit the new Direct Supply Company store next. Just to see what they've achieved after amalgamating the way they did. They've only just opened and there's a refreshment room and lavatories especially for ladies. It's just a short walk down to the corner with Victoria Street."

The girls were soon settled and admiring the spacious and elegant tearoom on the upper floor. "I rather like this," said Lucy. "We should come here more often."

Milly leaned forward and lowered her voice. "It is lovely, but I'm not sure I can afford to come often."

Lucy looked at the menu. "I think the prices are reasonable. But as I invited you to join me, I will buy lunch today for the both of us. Then you can save your pennies for next time." Lucy smiled gently to ease her friend's worries.

"Thank you," whispered Milly. "I don't want to be a bother."

"You're not. You're my friend. That's settled then. Now tell me the gossip about Hope. Is she still marrying that frightful man?"

"Lucy! You can't speak of Mr Fernley like that."

They were briefly interrupted by the waitress who took their order.

"Why ever not? He's a pinched-faced stuffed shirt in my opinion. She might think he's the catch of the century, but he's not going to be at all interested in her franchise work."

"I'm not sure *she* is any more."

Lucy raised an eyebrow. "Is that so?"

"Oh, she'll sign the petition and pretend, but in reality she just wants to set up home with the best of everything money can buy and become a society hostess. Mrs Willoughby is the one who wants prohibition. Hope pays lip service to her mother, but once she's married she won't be bothered any longer. You wait and see."

Milly sounded bitter and saddened.

"What does that mean for you?" asked Lucy, her voice softening in concern.

"She doesn't want me to be her bridesmaid either." Milly looked down into her lap where she was folding and unfolding her napkin, clearly distressed by the whole affair.

"What! That's scandalous. And very mean of her."

The waitress returned at that moment, setting out the tea things and a serving stand of delicately cut sandwiches, mini savoury pies and dainty cakes.

"Thank you," murmured Lucy, pouring the tea and handing a cup to Milly. "What did you say?"

"What could I say?" Milly accepted the cup and took a long sip. "She apologised for giving me the wrong impression but said she only ever intended to have her sisters and his to stand with her. But I'm certain she said she wanted me to be bridesmaid as well when she first announced her engagement."

Lucy pursed her lips. "I see. Well, in my opinion you are better off without being her attendant. She is already ignoring you. It would be worse if she publicly shunned you. She can be such a cow when she wants to be."

"Lucy!" gasped Milly. "I'm shocked. I've never heard you speak so harshly."

"Oh, Milly, my dear friend. It's because I see you are hurt and upset, and I only want to ease your unhappiness. But it's true."

Milly bit into a sandwich and refrained from answering.

"I have something to ask you myself," said Lucy, hesitating, knowing it would be a difficult choice. "Well, two things really. I wanted to come here today because this is exactly the sort of store Mr Richard Harris aspires to. A joining of forces so to speak, to be better together than individually, like this one. That is why my father is encouraging us to marry. He too wants to see the coming together of Young and Harris as importers and sellers – if they could agree on what to import and what to sell, and the manner of both."

Milly nodded, eyes wide, listening to Lucy's every word. Another dainty sandwich, and a small savoury disappeared from their plates while Lucy explained.

"My problem is, on one hand Mr Harris is fully supportive of my franchise role, as you know. He often comes bicycling with me, collecting signatures. But when he is with other men, and especially clients who mean money, he changes. He's … well. Let's just say he ignores me."

Lucy supped at her tea and ate another savoury.

"I'm sure that won't be the case when you are married, Lucy. Mr Harris is quite the gentleman, and I'm sure you will be very happy together. I think he wants to show you how clever a businessman he is and how well he will care for you."

Lucy tilted her head to one side. "I hadn't thought of it like that, but maybe. Showing off a bit. Hmm. As long as it doesn't become ingrained."

"What did you want to ask?" reminded Milly.

"Oh yes. I vacillate between wanting to marry Richard and thinking it's all a sham to tie the business up. Do you think I should?"

"What? Marry him?" Milly stopped to consider. "Yes. Yes, I do. I think you are well suited. As you said, he has aspirations, and that is good enough on its own. But more than that, I think you would have as much to say as he on the direction of a business partnership that you will one day inherit."

"I like you're thinking. So, if I do decide he's genuine about us being an equal partnership in marriage and in business, then will you stand with me?"

Milly's eyes filled, and she quickly pulled her hanky from her purse to dab at them. "I would be honoured, Lucy. Truly honoured."

"Not so fast, Milly, dear. You will need to think this through. If, and I still say if, because I made it plain I won't marry until women have the franchise, then my father and his father will want liquor available at the wedding supper."

Milly paled. "Oh, I see. Well, that is … I don't have to drink any, do I?"

Lucy laughed. "Of course not, but what would Mrs Daldy say?"

"Grandma Amey can be very daunting, I admit. But since I assume she won't be at the supper, and I am over the age of consent and can choose what I do, within reason, I'm not going to tell her."

Lucy grinned and tilted her head again. "That's one way to solve the problem. Thank you. You've just helped me make up my mind. In which case, we'd better get out into those streets again and keep gathering signatures until we get that Franchise Bill over the line."

17

Denial

When Jess had delivered her home, Luke had wavered between caring and frustrated, going from demanding to begging, from anxious to angry. Both Jess and Luke had insisted Emma see a doctor.

"No more arguments. I'm taking you and that's final."

Emma had been too distressed to argue.

The medical centre had not been able to give them an appointment until after the weekend.

Seated in the doctor's office, she did her best to answer the usual questions about how long she'd had the symptoms, about the aches and pains, what made her feel better/worse, what she was eating and how she was sleeping. Luke sat beside her correcting every second word while she tried to downplay her problems. "I'm sure it will pass. It's just a hangover from Covid."

"It could well be. It's been less than ninety days, so I'm hesitant to send you for further tests at this stage," said the doctor. "I recommend you record how you feel throughout the day, whether sleep or exercise or diet helps, and see if you can detect a pattern. The tiredness, muscle and joint pains could be Covid related. You can take paracetamol to ease them when necessary." The doctor handed her a prescription. "Come back in three months if there's no improvement."

Emma sat silently in the car. She didn't have the energy to say, 'I told you so', as Luke tried to persuade her to seek a specialist opinion.

"Not yet. You heard her. She said it's too soon to tell. Please, leave me to handle this my way," begged Emma.

Disgruntled, Luke extracted a promise: she would do less. "Rest, Ems. I'll pick up the slack. I want you better, so don't do anything to aggravate whatever this is."

However, she couldn't stop her thoughts whirling around. When she found it too hard to concentrate at her computer, she lay down and let her mind drift, as endless possibilities paraded past. To shut out the frightening worst-case scenarios she'd looked up online – she wasn't ready for those – she forced her thoughts back to Paige's story. She needed some sort of a breakthrough but couldn't quite grasp the threads. She just knew she was on the cusp of something.

The next day, Jean called to say how delighted she was with the additional historical storylines Emma had included but didn't know how to manage the others in the family wanting copies. "I'm worried about the cost. I can't afford to give so many away."

"You should ask people to buy their own," said Emma, knowing what Luke could do to help. "I'll email you an order form outlining three pricing options. There's the simple spiral-bound photocopy option, a softcover paperback, or the hardcover edition you want.

I've found people usually opt for the dearest one, but if they don't, the styles can be copied from the original without any trouble," assured Emma. "And if they don't want to pay, that's their problem, not yours."

Jean brightened immediately. "Oh, what a good idea."

"I'd like to finish the citations and acknowledgements and make sure I've covered everything, but I think Ruby's story is complete." Emma realised she felt relieved it was.

Once the final touches were in place, she would hand the file over to Luke to do the layout and printing. Her part was over.

"You've done a marvellous job. Thank you so much," gushed Jean. "It's so much more than I could have wished."

Emma's heart warmed at another satisfied customer. That was all she ever wanted: to hand people their family history to the best of her ability.

With that task completed, Emma made a decision. She emailed the next client and recommended another researcher to complete his tree or, if he was prepared to wait, she could look at it again in six months' time. She had to believe she'd feel better by then, but right now, she couldn't manage another client, not while she worked on Paige's history.

As if reading her mind, a text from Paige arrived on her phone.

Thnx 4 Jess. Ive news. Mtg?

Used now to Paige's text talk, Emma replied. *Tmrrw @10*

A thumbs up came back.

Emma returned to the trinket box pins. The story was in those badges somewhere, if only she could work out how, through the mire that clogged her brain. She took a photo of the tagged badges, then rearranged them to fit alongside her guesstimates of the likely women in Paige's past and took more photos. There was no doubt the dates fitted. She then compared the images of the woman in the locket with the woman wearing the brooch, and decided they were from different generations. She had a lot of research ahead of her to find out who these women were and what they did in life.

Decision made; her first task was to order a few certificates. She'd start with Paige's mother's birth certificate, as that was most likely to list the names of her parents. She'd order more as necessary. Why she felt so drawn to solving this mystery eluded her, but it was more than for Paige now.

That done, she opened up the trinket box to stack the pins back in place. As she carefully set aside the envelope containing the ancient newspaper cutting that had set her on this track, the velvet padded inset in the lid came loose and another pin fell out.

Eagerly she picked it up. It was a man's pin just like the other one with the initial RH. This one was engraved with AY, which told her nothing more. Taking a second look in the box, she spotted a newspaper cutting tucked behind the lid. She reached for her tweezers and gingerly lifted it up. Almost holding her breath in anticipation, hoping it would reveal something she could work with, she began to read the death notice.

> WILSON, Amelia Lucy (Amy) on 23 September
> 1977, aged 31. Treasured only daughter of Mrs
> Kathryn L. Wilson tragically taken as a result of
> a car accident. In death, you left behind new life
> and light to banish the darkness. Never forgotten.

A second notice appeared below.

> WILSON, Amy, respected friend and colleague.
> The National Organisation for Women (NOW).
> Sadly missed.

With mounting elation, Emma delicately placed the cutting in a clean envelope and quickly searched for her notes. She was certain NOW was an organisation she'd mentioned to Paige.

"There it is!" She grinned, circling the anagram using the Venus symbol as the O and opened up her computer to look at the photo of the badges from the trinket box. "And there it is, again." She'd found a link.

She immediately pulled out her large scribble block and began to mind map the generational diagram she'd drawn, but this time she started from the possible, probable oldest generations.

She read the death notice again. She hadn't been far out in her calculation for birth dates, or guessing at the naming pattern overall, but she'd been wrong about the name for Generation 3. The 'L' engraved on the trinket box could still stand for a variation of Lucy, she decided, as she amended her notes. At least she could now search for marriages and deaths with surnames to go by.

3 >   Kathryn L. (Lucy?) WILSON
       b. abt. 1921   m. abt. 1945   d. ??
       Approx. 25 when daughter born??
       Mother of …
4 >   Amelia Lucy WILSON (aka Amy)
       b. 1946 marriage unknown
       d. 23 September 1977 (aged 31)
       Result of accident.

She highlighted Generation 4 after she'd updated the information. This had to be the right person. Why else would Paige's mother have the cutting? Emma suddenly clicked that mother and daughter were both named Wilson. Kathryn was titled Mrs. It was possible Amy was still single at 31. The '70s were renowned for hippies, free love and feminism. She'd need to read up more about the history to be certain but thought it highly feasible. Especially as Amy had been a member of NOW.

Next, she tried to decipher the final phrase: In death, you left behind new life and light to banish the darkness.

Was it a religious phrase? Emma didn't think so, but googled it anyway. No results.

Adrenaline surged at another thought. Did it mean there was a child? A grandchild for Kathryn who provided 'light' and purpose in her life, after the emotional devastation of losing her only daughter? Emma understood how all-consuming that could be. She would never forget the death of her firstborn.

All supposition, of course, but worth investigating. If her guesstimate was even close, was there the slightest possibility that Paige's mother Lucy, was that child?

Emma's heart thumped harder, and her nerve ends tingled, but she deliberately forced back the thought.

Stop running away with ideas, she scolded herself. *Find the facts. The child could have been a boy, which wouldn't follow Paige's line at all.*

She drew more lines to what she knew and could roughly calculate. Because of the privacy laws, she couldn't look up birth records for that post-war time period, or marriages, which were blocked after 1942. But Emma might be able to find the registration number and birth year if Kathryn was over eighty when she died.

It was a start.

* * * * *

The next day, Emma arrived early at their favourite café. She wasn't feeling her best and knew her energy levels would fade soon, but she wanted to hear Paige's news first.

A few minutes later, the girl bounced into the café, her hair flying loose and flung herself into the chair looking at if she'd discovered the rainbow.

"What's got you so happy today?"

"Life. Isn't it wonderful?" Leaning back in the chair, she stretched her arms wide and wore a grin to match.

Emma internally shook her head at the capricious nature of youth. "It certainly can be, but why today especially?"

"Oh, it's not just today. It's from now on. I promise. No more down in the dumps for me."

Again, Emma didn't voice her thoughts, knowing promises like that didn't last.

"Because I've found my voice." The girl rattled off, more or less, what Jess had told her about their conversation. "Jess was bang on. Focus on one thing. So I did. Have." Paige explained all the groups she looked at online and what they were doing. "There's so many great things happening. R & D, future planning, much more than I realised – which is good, but it's scattered – and, like Jess said, I can't do it all. I liked best what I saw 350 Aotearoa doing – focusing on getting rid of fossil fuels to generate energy. Right here. Right now. I knew I was right. I told my dad so. Maybe now he'll listen to me."

At the root of all Paige's insecurities was her father. Emma had given up trying to be charitable about this man she didn't know. Paige felt overlooked and that was what mattered. Didn't he realise what he was doing?

Paige's excitement intensified as she prattled on. "It's so inspiring. I've talked to a few people and have started on a project already, and then Ryan said he'd heard about them, and … he's coming home, and maybe he wants to be with me and maybe we could do these things together and maybe …"

She paused for breath.

"Whoa. What's all this about Ryan?"

Fizzing with joy, Paige could hardly keep still. "He's coming home!"

"When?"

"End of the month after the mid-semester break."

"That's such good news. I didn't know you were still talking to him."

Paige blushed and reached for her phone as it beeped in her pocket. "All the time. We're always texting. That's him now."

"So what's brought about the change of mind?"

Paige finished her text and put the phone down. "He says it's not a change. He never meant to stay overseas forever, just that he wanted to go for the march. To be part of it. I got that bit wrong. But, like I said to you, I think there are too many people with different agendas tagging onto marches, so the message gets lost in the noise. He saw the same thing happen, and said he was always coming back to finish his PhD anyway."

"So … do you see a future?" asked Emma, thinking back to the 'emergency' call she'd received when Paige thought she'd lost him.

The girl hitched her shoulder. "Dunno. There's plenty of time, but at least we'll be together. Early days yet."

Emma breathed a silent sigh of relief. In amongst the exuberance of young love, and the yo-yoing of he loves me, he loves me not, sense also prevailed. "Sounds like you're back on track then." She stifled a yawn and stretched her neck. Her head was starting to throb again.

"Yeah. I am. We are, Ryan and me. Thanks, by the way. Jess helped."

Emma needed to wrap up the conversation. She'd have to explain about what she'd discovered and the NOW group connection another time. "I'm glad. Was that all the news you wanted to tell me?"

"Nope. There's more. I told Dad I'd taken the trinket box, like you asked." Paige pulled a face. "He was mad as hell that I'd gone looking. We argued, but then yesterday, he came into my room and threw this on the bed."

She pulled a photo in an old silver frame out of her backpack. "He said it's Mum holding Cam as a baby, with Grandma Kate. She died not long after, apparently."

Emma took the photo between her hands and stared at it. If Paige was right and the older woman standing at the back was Lucy's mother – by the name of Kate – then her suppositions were off track. Where did the deceased Amy Wilson fit if Kate was the mother? It was as well she hadn't said anything. She pulled out her phone and took a few photos of it, planning on a closer inspection later.

"And look," Paige pointed, "she's wearing that same brooch I saw in that teeny-weeny photo I sent through. Did you find it?"

Emma looked up at the girl in surprise, glad she had such excellent eyesight. "Yes, I found the brooch. It's lovely. Simple, rose gold, but stylish. And this means the brooch was handed down. What we still don't know is who was the woman in the first photo, and what's her connection to this one?"

Paige pulled her hair back and tied it in a ponytail, exposing another clue.

"And, for that matter, the one in that locket you're wearing," added Emma, suddenly feeling faint with weariness. She'd better start digging deeper if she was to uncover the answers before …

She stopped herself in time. Refusing to think about what lay ahead.

18
In mourning

Friday 28 April 1893

"Oh, Mrs Bush. Whatever shall we do?" wailed Lucy, biting back tears of rage and frustration. "The franchise is lost." And her wedding postponed. Indefinitely. She couldn't go back on her word. She couldn't, even though she loved Richard.

She had followed the newspapers throughout March and April, wishing fervently for an improvement in the Premier's health, but to no avail. John Ballance died on the 27th of April.

"I know you've yer 'eart set on the matter, Miss Lucy, but all good things come to those who wait." Mrs Bush continued to bustle around the kitchen.

Lucy held back the words ready to gush from her mouth. Mrs Bush had treated her well, taught her things a mother might have done, but never once made her feel as wrong-footed as she felt now. She didn't deserve the full force of Lucy's bitterness.

To make matters worse, she'd read in yesterday's paper that Sir John Hall had announced he would not be seeking re-election. What would they do if he was not there to advocate for them? Lucy had not been interested in the politics of much of his address, until the part where he had stated how much he deplored the disagreement between the two Houses that had wrecked – that was the word he used, wrecked – women's suffrage. And how vehemently he'd disagreed with the Council's amendment which clearly showed Mr Seddon's pretended alarm was a ruse to shelve women's suffrage.

And now, here they were, without the leadership of Premier Ballance to help it over the line, and facing the likelihood of Mr Seddon becoming Premier. It didn't bear thinking about.

Words that had been spoken over and over again for so long echoed in her head. Words she had used to amplify the urgency for the franchise, the reasons for it, and the ways in which women were treated as second-class citizens, had come to nothing.

All that work wasted.

"Not wasted, Miss Lucy. Nothin' is ever wasted."

Lucy realised she must have muttered the words out loud as Mrs Bush reminded her of her favourite saying.

"It's just sitting there ready to be used when the time is right. Does your Mrs Daldy think her time has been wasted? Nay, lass. She won't. Nor them other ladies you talk about. If anything, this'll get them going again. They's so close. I know. I hear about it all the time."

Lucy brightened. "Do you?" Her eyes glistened with expectation and unshed tears. Was there still hope?

Lucy hadn't considered Mrs Bush would be in the know. "Dare I ask if you support the franchise,

Mrs Bush?" conscious she had never asked Mrs Bush about it. She'd talked at her, constantly, telling her why everything was so wrong, but not *to* her. She was now mortified she had not sought her opinion or even asked for her signature.

"I do, lass. I do, and I've learnt the power of persistence. Don't give up just yet."

"What does Mr Bush say?" Lucy couldn't remember anything said about a Mr Bush either. She felt shame for taking the housekeeper for granted and treating her as unimportant, rather than as a fellow woman. She promised herself to do better in the future and remember The Golden Rule – treat others as you would want to be treated.

"He passed long ago. You wouldn't remember. You were just a little tiddler."

"And your children? What of them? I feel I should know more than I do. I'm sorry."

Mrs Bush stopped her busyness and stood before Lucy with her arms akimbo. "Don't be bothered, Miss Lucy. They're all grown now, and I wouldn't expect you to mix with my lot. No offence, but we're not your kind. We all work for the likes of your father."

Lucy blushed. "I'm ..." she stammered. "I didn't realise ..."

"Like I said, don't be bothered about it. But this 'ere franchise, I couldn't stop the girls if I tried, and the boys will know better than to cross me and their sisters."

Lucy had an idea. "Have you signed a petition?"

"I signed one a while back. Last year sometime. The girls said they did the same."

Buoyed, Lucy said, "We need more signatures this

179

year. We need as many as we can get, many more than we had in 1892 and thousands more than in 1891. Will you take a form, sign it and get your girls to sign again, and your neighbours and friends? Explain how important it is to keep up the momentum. Please?" She placed her hand on Mrs Bush's arm.

"There are Members of Parliament saying they wish to be certain every woman is in favour of the franchise before making their decision. How they think they are going to do that is anyone's guess, but the more forms we sign, the more we can send in, and the more we can prove it is something women do want. Would you do that, please?"

Mrs Bush grinned. "I thought you'd never ask."

* * * * *

In the days to follow, messages of condolence poured forth, expressing loss and sympathy for Premier Ballance's widow, and the country. The newspapers wrote in glowing terms about the achievements of the former Premier, while the drizzly weather reflected the mood of the nation. Lucy considered that, as a former journalist and founder of the *Wanganui Herald*, Mr Ballance would have been impressed with the many respectful and fulsome obituaries.

While flags flew at half mast everywhere she looked, people carried on life as normal. Business continued, transport plied back and forth, the theatre proceeded. On the night of his death, the opera house was packed. Although she'd read the orchestra played 'The Dead March of Saul' while the audience stood as a mark of respect before the show started in memory of the late Premier.

Everyone was moving on. Except her. She couldn't pull herself from her gloom.

Church on the Sunday morning of the funeral was a more solemn affair than usual. Lucy travelled with her father. Richard and his family met them at the entrance, and later, after the prayers and sermon, she managed to speak in whispers with Milly before the parishioners broke up early to attend their homes and mourn in private. Including Richard, as her father considered it unnecessary for him to visit that day.

The newspapers arrived early on Monday morning, and after breakfast with her father, Lucy spent the rest of the morning reading every version of how the sun broke through the clouds early on that Sunday morning as people gathered in the streets to watch the state funeral procession. Holding a handkerchief in her hand, she dabbed at any tear that escaped.

In her mind's eye, she saw the gun carriage carrying the coffin flanked by members of the Ministry acting as pall-bearers; the marchers, rank upon rank of soldiers and the navy; the sombre carriages conveying Mrs Ballance, the Governor, and the other prominent mourners, followed by the dignitaries of every council and province until the public could, at last, fall in behind.

In her head, she replayed 'The Dead March' as the procession made its way to the railway station to the beat of a steady drum. The coffin was then conveyed onto the train to be taken to Wanganui for the funeral service and burial. A second carriage was filled by relatives and dignitaries. The one name missing, Lucy noticed, was that of Sir John Hall, himself too sick to attend.

Please, don't let him die too.

Along the train route, citizens gathered to pay their respects. Its arrival was greeted by more dignitaries, and flags were dipped in solemn salute. Mourners flocked from all corners to be part of the sad, yet great occasion. The carrying of the coffin from the train to the cemetery was accompanied by the tolling of a Fire Bell and the keening sound of wāhine voices, as numerous pall-bearers changed places along the route. They were greeted at the site by the Masonic brothers who would lead the ceremony, which ended with a three-volley salute from the firing party.

By the time she'd finished reading, tears flowed down her ashen face, worn out with emotion.

Home for lunch, her father pulled the newspaper from her hand and gathered up the discarded ones off the sofa. "Enough, young lady. You have moped and mourned for three days. It's time to get to work."

"But Father …"

"No but Father excuses. You said you were committed to the cause. You said you would fight against all odds to win. You also said you would not give up. So what are you doing lying here? Get on with it."

Despite herself, she had to laugh at her father's performance. She rose from the chaise longue and gave him a hug. "Have I told you, you are the best father a girl could ever have?"

He disentangled himself from her embrace. "Enough of that, too. Now scat, and do something useful. Help Mrs Bush, if nothing else."

Lucy found Mrs Bush in the kitchen preparing luncheon. "Father sent me to help."

"Nay, lass, I don't need your help. But I tell you what, I have that form you gave me."

She dried her hands on her apron and retrieved her bag from the bottom of the pantry, pulled out the form and handed it to Lucy. "There's ten signatures on that. Is that enough?"

Lucy's tears were so close to the surface that she immediately choked up. "You are a marvel, Mrs Bush. In case I have not said it before, I couldn't do without you."

Mrs Bush blushed and harrumphed. "Go get yourself cleaned up, Miss Lucy. Luncheon won't be long, and I want to see those pretty looks restored."

* * * * *

Lucy rushed around to Milly's looking for gossip, hoping to see Mrs Daldy galvanised and ready to go, but despite being told about plans for a further push on signatures, motivation was difficult to muster. As the internal tussles in the House continued as to who would be the next Premier: Sir Robert Stout, as Ballance wished; or Richard Seddon, current Acting Leader. Lucy wavered between the two. Sir Robert was a great advocate for the cause but did not hold a seat, a situation that would need resolving first, which meant more delays. Mr Seddon was more conservative than either Ballance or Stout and only paid lip service to the franchise. He might not want it to pass through the House. Only time would tell.

A few days later, Richard finally put her back on track. "Your father tells me you have been morbid since the news of Ballance's death. Why?"

Lucy frowned. "Why shouldn't I be? The movement has lost a great ally."

"Was he, though? Never mind his other successes, what did he achieve for suffrage? He said he believed in the 'absolute equality of the sexes' back in 1890. He has been Premier since 1891. That year, the petition failed. The 1892 petitions failed. If the 1893 petitions are to fail, it will be through lack of public demand. You have to out-lobby the liquor barons, the stick-in-the-muds and the religious prohibitionists if you are to win. Stop feeling sorry for yourself and get out there and lobby! Besides, I have waited long enough. I don't want to wait any longer for us to marry."

Lucy stared at him with her mouth open as if he had said something completely outrageous. She wasn't feeling sorry for herself, just beaten, but she would forgive him for his borderline rudeness. He was right. No more half-heartedness from her. "Oh, Richard. I never thought of it that way." She flung her arms around his neck and felt the immediate jolt of attraction. She wondered if he would kiss her as she looked up into his eyes. His head moved slightly towards her. This was the moment. Her heart pulsed faster and louder. Sensations filled her body with expectation.

Until it was broken by the sound of Mrs Bush in the hallway.

They broke apart, blushing. Richard turned away and cleared his throat while Lucy wiped her hands down her skirt to straighten her dress. They looked at each other from across the room. The unfulfilled firestorm still brewing.

"I had better be going," said Richard.

"Yes, of course. If you must."

"I will see you later then." Reluctance heavy in his words.

"Yes …" Lucy paused, thinking of an excuse to retain him. "We … er … we said we would go to … the art gallery. Yes. We should visit the art gallery."

His warm smile lit her heart once more. "Your wish is my command. I will do my utmost to provide you with all your heart desires." He picked up his hat from the hall table and was ushered out by Mrs Bush.

"Better not lose that one, Miss Lucy."

19

Her worst nightmare

The thing Emma had dreaded the most happened moments after she'd allowed the thought to enter her head. After saying goodbye to Paige, she made her way through the crowded café. Now the final Covid restrictions had been lifted cafés, bars and restaurants were busier than they'd been for a long time. And noisier. She felt light-headed and hot, her heart thumped.

Grateful for the fresh air as she opened the exit door, she hesitated on the verandah. The few steps leading to the footpath swam before her eyes. She put her hand on the rail, closed her eyes briefly and took a deep breath.

"Emma!" demanded Paige, shaking her. "Emma."

Her panicked voice pierced Emma's consciousness. Why was she lying on the floor?

"Emma. Are you all right? Emma, wake up."

Emma's eyes flickered. Sounds billowed around her but she was too tired to care.

"Paige?" A man's voice. Not Luke's.

"Dad!"

The voices faded into a swirl of fog. Emma couldn't make out what they were saying.

A sound. Was that her voice?

"Emma?" Paige leant over her. "Help me get her up."

Arms lifted her onto a chair. Inside her head exploded, and she swayed with the pain. Someone held her upright as she dropped her head in her hands.

"The ambulance is here."

Surprised, she wondered what had happened to her. Had she fainted? And how long had she been out of it, if someone made the call. She didn't have the strength to look, even less to argue. But obviously longer than she realised.

Other voices asked questions, and she heard herself respond but didn't know whether they were the right answers or not. All she wanted was sleep.

The next thing she knew, she was jolting about on the gurney, then listening to the rattle of wheels as she was pushed along, screwing her eyes shut against the overhead lights in the endless corridors, surrounded by people in eerie protective gear, until finally quiet, apart from a myriad of bustling background noises of the hospital.

"Where …?" She licked her lips. Her throat was dry and her eyes ached.

"Emma. Oh, thank goodness." She recognised Paige's voice. "You're awake."

"What …?" She swallowed, but the words wouldn't come. Had the worst happened?

"You're in the hospital. Don't you remember? You fainted. At the café." Paige didn't wait for a response. "Dad's here with me. He wouldn't leave me on my own with you. I'm sorry, I opened your phone and I've called Luke. He had the same name so I assumed he was your husband. He's on his way."

Emma nodded. At least she thought she did. She tentatively opened her eyes and didn't feel too bad. She pushed herself upright, raising her knees to rest her head on her folded arms.

At that moment, Luke rushed in asking endless questions, which she let Paige answer.

"Ems, sweetheart? Are you okay?" He sounded muffled through the mask.

He sat on the side of the hospital bed, taking her in his arms, and hugged her. She clung on to him for dear life, aware of the plasticky feeling of the gown he wore as he whispered soothing words through his mask. Unbidden tears rolled down her face.

"Do you want to lie back?" He fiddled around raising the back of the bed and propped her up on pillows. "There, that's better, but you're so pale, Ems. I hope the doctors can tell us something."

Time passed. The monitor checked her blood pressure as lights flashed on the screen. Paige and her father left, Luke sat beside her, holding her hand, smoothing his thumb over her flesh. From time to time, she squeezed his hand. Needles pricked her arms. All she wanted was sleep, but she was plagued by vivid, senseless dreams. Tablets were given. At least she felt better than she had. The palpitations had gone.

"Luke?" Emma raised her head and looked around, trying to remember. "How long've I been here?"

"You're back. Thank goodness. Not all that long, given the chaos out there. Hours, but it's still today."

"Rose?"

"Jess has her. Don't worry. We need to find out what's wrong with you."

A doctor, covered head to toe in protective clothing, appeared at the foot of the bed. "Mrs Grainger, we're letting you go. Your vitals are now normal and we need the bed."

"But she's so sleepy," said Luke.

"Not surprising. But our tests show she probably fainted because of a drop in blood pressure, and she's a touch anaemic, but there doesn't seem to be anything to cause alarm. Have you been eating properly?"

She struggled to understand what he was asking.

Luke answered for her. "Not really, since she had Covid, she says everything tastes funny."

The doctor made some notes. "That's not unusual either. Nor is the ongoing fatigue. It takes a long time to get the coronavirus out of your system. Is your cycle normal?"

"Yes," she mumbled.

He made more notes. "I'd suggest a visit to your GP for a check-up and get some iron supplements. Drink lots of fluids. I'll sign the discharge forms and you can go."

After the doctor left, Luke and Emma looked at each other, feeling at a loss. If that was all that was wrong with her then she felt even more of a millstone. The diagnosis didn't seem enough to explain the exhaustion and all the aches and pains and the brain fog. Or why she was so tearful.

"Well, that's good news," said Emma, suddenly brightening at the thought that maybe her worst-case scenarios were not going to play out after all.

"Only if you do as he says. Go back to your doctor and do what *she* says. And eat. Promise?" He gathered her in his arms again and hugged her tightly. "You frightened me, Ems. Please. I can't lose you."

* * * * *

After a few days at home resting, Emma felt much brighter. Paige had texted or phoned every day to see how she was and even visited with some flowers and chocolates. Emma had been amused how easily Rosie had taken to her.

Luke had bought a bottle of iron tablets, and she managed to have a phone consultation with her doctor who had received the report from the hospital concluding she was suffering long-term after-effects of Covid. More severe than most, but not life-threatening. The GP advised her to keep up the supplements, increase her fluid intake and eat more often from a list of recommended foods she'd emailed through. She would see her again in a month.

"Not so bad after all," said Emma. "I did tell you it was a post-Covid thing. It'll pass."

Luke still needed convincing. "As long as it doesn't become permanent."

"Don't be such a worry wart. I declined my latest client, so I've only got Paige's history to worry about. I'll take it slowly, I promise."

"You do know she could do it all by herself, don't you? You don't have to be her researcher. Nice girl, though. I liked her. And her dad seems a nice chap, too."

"Her dad?" Surprised, Emma racked her brain.

"Yes. Dave was at the hospital. Apparently Paige didn't know who to call so she rang him and he came to the rescue. He picked you up off the floor, called the ambulance and followed it with Paige. He stayed until I arrived. They seemed to be chatting okay to me?"

Emma puzzled over Luke's assessment of the pair and wondered if she'd been led on. Was her father as bad as Paige made out?

"That's good to know. And yes, I know Paige is quite capable, but now I'm rather intrigued by all the women's groups I've discovered. I'd like to research them more, and if it fits with Paige's story, all the better."

"You never give up, do you, my little sleuth." Emma could hear the relief in his voice. "Just don't overdo it." He kissed her cheek and retreated to his office.

Setting the timer on her phone to one hour, she started on her notes. Mind-mapping what she knew and what she could surmise, Emma began to see some clear connections.

Her email pinged, interrupting her train of thought, but she was happy to see the information she'd ordered for Paige's mother Lucy arrive from the Records Office. Printouts of the original entry were often better that the official record. She downloaded the files and enlarged them on her screen. Anticipation tingled in her fingertips, and she bit her bottom lip as she read the details on the certificates.

Emma checked her chart and let out a little yip of glee. The names fitted.

One certificate proved Lucy's mother's name was Amelia; the father's name was blank. But since she was trying to follow the female line, that blank was actually helpful and explained that Amelia Wilson, known as Amy, had not married and chose not to name the father.

Emma would have to be careful how she presented that bit of information to Paige. She was used to coming across children whose parents weren't married. It wasn't unusual, but before announcing it, she needed to be sure how Paige would react to the news.

Fortunately, the statute books had changed the laws in 1969 to remove the stigma of children born to unmarried mothers. Before that, those children were listed as illegitimate, but while the law changed, people's attitudes to children born out of wedlock didn't always change with it. Not until much later.

Emma rewrote her list, highlighting the new facts. Now she was getting somewhere. Exhilarated, she tried another tack.

Paige said the woman at the back of the photo was her grandmother, called Kate, and she'd died around 1998, except that wasn't possible. According to everything she'd found, Paige's grandmother was Amelia, called Amy, and she died in a car crash in 1977. In which case … she remembered the obituary in the newspaper cutting for Amelia's death.

Could the woman in the photo be Paige's great-grandmother, Amelia's mother, known as Grandma Kate, and had she raised the infant child – the light in the darkness?

She was still guessing, but even now there was a chance if Papers Past came to the party.

She opened up a new search for weddings and WILSON. To cover her guess that the war had delayed a marriage, she set the dates for the beginning of 1944 to the end of 1946 and clicked Search.

Bingo!

Eager to follow the lead, she ignored the timer on her phone. She was so close, she couldn't stop now. She'd been right!

She changed her notes, certain now that Great-grandmother Kate had raised Paige's mother Lucy. And, more importantly, the naming pattern was her search anchor. She could now look further back.

Happy that that little mystery had been solved and she had some names to work with, she was convinced she'd find her way back to the suffragists of the 1890s.

Her next task was linking the photos, the names and the badges.

But not now. A wave of exhaustion washed over her. This time, she listened.

* * * * *

After an afternoon resting, Emma felt ready to meet Paige for coffee the following morning.

Emma laid her hand on her companion's for a moment. "Thank you for helping me the other day. I don't know what came over me. Passing out like that." She wasn't going to confide in the girl about her concerns.

Paige hitched her shoulder. "'Sokay. I didn't do much. Dad took charge."

"So I heard. Do thank him for me, won't you? But does this mean you and he are back on speaking terms?"

"S'pose. We weren't ever not speaking, but we argue a lot when he does his 'holier-than-thou, I-know-best' speeches."

Emma decided to try another approach. Something

that had been niggling for a while. "Are you sure you're not a bit hard on your dad sometimes? It's not easy being a parent. Have you asked him exactly what he does and shown interest in the business? Or included him in your research and studies to show him what you see, and what your concerns are?"

Paige fiddled with the cord of her hoodie. Her silence said enough as far as Emma was concerned.

"It takes two, you know, to build a relationship. If you won't share your interests with him, then how does he know what you're thinking, and vice versa."

Slouched in the chair, Paige didn't appear to have taken any notice.

Emma was about to change the subject when Paige said, "He's mellowing, I think."

Emma doubted her dad was changing much. More like, the girl was growing up. "In what way? About the climate situation?"

"Hell, no. He's still entrenched about that, but it's more about the past. He's been telling me bits about Mum that he's never talked about before."

Emma felt a small surge of optimism. Could Paige and her father begin to see eye to eye? And could she learn something about what her mum did in her short life? "That's good. Such as?"

"Nice things about her eyes and hair and stuff. And how she read stories to us kids. Cam says he has a few memories of her like that. He remembers her laugh, he thinks. Lucky him. I don't have any."

Just when she was thinking she should hand over what she'd discovered and leave Paige to do her own research on the rest, her empathy for the dispirited young woman resurfaced. She wondered why a man like David Frazer hadn't married again. But then what kind of man was David Frazer? She'd not even met him. All she had was Paige's version and Luke's comment.

But she'd said enough for now. It really wasn't her business. "Did your mum have any skills, go to uni or work somewhere?"

"He said she worked in the office where he worked in banking. That's how they met. But she didn't work after they married. Her job was looking after us kids."

Emma pulled a moue. "Sounds a bit traditional for the '90s for such a young woman. Nothing like the line of troublemakers you talked about?"

Paige fished into her pocket. "That's what I thought. Until he gave me this." She handed over a Nuclear Free New Zealand badge from the '80s. "He said she was very much against nuclear weapons and testing and such. He said the legislation came in in 1987, and she gave it all up to look after us."

"That doesn't sound right." Emma couldn't keep the disbelief from her voice. "She'd have been about 12! And it's more than a decade before your brother was born."

"Oh. I must've got it wrong somehow." Paige looked puzzled. "I'm sure he said she was anti-nuclear."

"That's still possible. I remember a lot of protests, here and overseas, about the French testing nuclear bombs at Mururoa Atoll in the '70s. Greenpeace was heavily involved and the whole nation supported them. In '95, flotillas sailed out to the island to block the test. You've heard about the bombing of the original *Rainbow Warrior* by the French in Auckland Harbour in 1985, haven't you? Your mum would've been a bit young to be protesting then, but she could've been in '95."

"Yeah, we learnt that stuff at school. But you've got me wondering. Could she have been with Greenpeace? Were there any other Greenpeace badges in the box?"

"No, but there's a feminist badge from the 1970s," Emma remembered.

The final clue dropped into place.

20

When innocence is lost

Monday, 1 May 1893

Lucy's dithering was put to rest once Mr Seddon was confirmed as the new Premier.

Rumours of underhand manipulation were raised in the newspapers but were quickly forgotten. Seddon had persuaded the House to elect him rather than risk splitting the party, and that was that. But the League now had a battle before them.

Taking Richard's comments to heart, Lucy began her lobbying in earnest. With the approval of Mrs Daldy, she wrote endless letters, even to the newspapers, hoping to put a different viewpoint forward – that of a young unmarried woman. Determined to be heard, she hand-delivered her missive, pushing her way past his assistant insisting she see the editor in person.

"I can't print this," he said, handing it back to her.

"Why ever not? It's a faithful account." She stared at the balding, middle-aged man seated at his overlarge, untidy desk, casually dressed in a shirt with a high collar and bow tie, and braces under his waistcoat.

His eyes peered at her over the rim of his small round glasses. "It is too brazen. Lower your tone and I might consider it. But as it is, the answer is no."

She snatched the letter from him, returning a short time later, having rewritten several drafts. She sat on the edge of the chair opposite, trying to control her nerves as she watched him reread her words.

He raised his eyes and looked at her over his glasses again, looked back at the note and sighed. "Very well, I'll print it."

"Oh, thank you, sir. Thank you."

She left the newspaper office in high spirits.

Every day she and someone from the League would catch the horse tram to another part of town, hand out pamphlets and camellias, and try to gather an extra signature or two. They rode their bicycles around the streets hoping to get women who had previously signed a petition to sign again. This year, the numbers mattered. Most days she was successful.

On occasions, Richard accompanied her, sometimes with Milly, sometimes the two girls went alone, or with one of the ladies on the roster, to traipse the streets.

"Everyone from the League is doing the same thing as us, Lucy," Milly told her on one of their excursions. "And I hear that Dunedin and Christchurch are garnering much support."

"That is such good news. Do we have any numbers yet?"

"Not that I am aware of, except they are greater than ever."

One inclement morning, Lucy found herself the only one willing to go out canvassing.

"You don't have to go out every day," said her father at breakfast. "And you must not go out alone."

"But I do, Father. If I stop, I will feel I have let everyone down. I lost heart once; I cannot lose heart again. I must try harder."

And try she did.

She decided to go on foot, staying closer to home, her father's words echoing in her head. *Not alone, do you hear me, Lucy? Not alone.*

The streets were slick with rain, although the cold wind had blown the worst of the clouds to another area for now. She fastened her coat up to her neck, wrapped her scarf tighter and held her umbrella low. The murky shadows darkened the streets between the houses in the unfamiliar narrow lanes, but while doors opened to her knock, she kept going. Sometimes she was invited into the warmth while a signature was collected; other times she was turned away.

"My 'usband's home. 'E better not see you," whispered one woman. "Maybe another day."

Lucy resolved to return.

With her trusty carpet bag safely carrying the signed forms, Lucy continued, head down, along the dark streets. She didn't see the man step out of an alleyway in front of her and walked straight into him. "Oh, I'm so sorry. Forgive me."

"What 'ave we 'ere then? What's a pretty maid like you doin' in these parts in this wevver?" slurred the man, clearly drunk.

His face and hands were dirt-streaked and stained, and his clothes filthy. She turned her head away from the stinking smell of stale beer.

"I don't think that is any of your business, sir." She pulled back, trying to wriggle out of his grasp.

"Ah, but I fink it is. You're on my patch now, ya see." He edged closer, wrapping his arm around her, and pushed her against a wall.

Lucy looked frantically up and down the street but saw no one. Panic filled her as she wrestled and wriggled, but the man held her tight. Suddenly a knee was pressed into her stomach. She gasped as he pulled her bag out of her grasp and began to search it.

Finding the papers, he screwed them in his hand. His angry faced moved closer, rain dripping off his cap, his foul breath filling her nostrils. "You're one of those wowser bitches, aren't you? Trying to take away a man's right."

"No," she exhaled.

"What are these then?" He thrust the petition forms under her nose.

"The vote. Not …"

Her breath was taken away by the punch to her stomach, followed by another to her ribs. Her knees caved and she slid to a crouch, her arms covering her head. Her hat fell off in the commotion.

He grabbed her wrists and pulled her upright, dragging her behind him into a squalid shed only yards away and shoved her inside. She landed awkwardly on a makeshift bed that tipped at one end.

Fear and anger sent adrenaline coursing through her veins as instinct kicked in. She couldn't flee until she got past him standing in the doorway, blocking her path. Anger won.

"Leave me alone!" she hissed through gritted teeth, pushing herself up with one arm. "My father …"

A backhander across her face was his answer. "Shut up. I don't want to hear nothin' from you. I'll show you who's boss."

He forced her back, pinning her down with one hand, cursing while he fumbled with his trousers. One knee sought to spread her legs, but he staggered and fell. The broken corner of the bed collapsed beneath his weight, landing him on both knees on the floor.

Fear gave her strength she didn't know she had. With her upper body now free, she braced one foot against the floor and pushed hard. Thanks to all the walking she did, her legs were strong and her boots sturdy. She fought back, punching, twisting and kicking, until another body blow cut off the air to her lungs. The second blow brought blackness …

She stirred. Something wasn't right. A weight. Wetness. Memory flooded her brain.

In a panic, she pummelled the sleeping head among her scrunched up petticoats on her stomach. She scraped at the blurry eyes suddenly inches from her face. He arched back in pain, sitting on his heels, his hands over his eyes. Seeing her chance, she jumped to her feet and ran through the door.

The heavy rain concealed her within a matter of yards. She slipped a few times, once crashing heavily to her knees, but kept running, fearful of pursuit. She ducked through an alley, then another, barely able to see where she was going and getting more and more lost with each turn. She thought she knew this area, but it looked different in the gloom. And he'd said it was his patch.

Panicked, she ran until she reached a T-intersection. She looked left and right. It was empty. Not a soul in sight. She had no idea which way to go. Her breath was coming in rasping, painful gasps but she couldn't stop yet.

Spying a garden to a large house on the rise across the way, she hurried through the picket gate and hid amongst the bushes, desperate to get her breath, and her wits, back. She took stock of her condition. Her hat had fallen off a long time ago, tendrils of hair stuck to her face and her chignon was hanging loose. She wrapped her scarf around her head although, torn and wet as it was, it did little to protect her. Her knees were throbbing where she had fallen, and she could feel bruises developing and a soreness she didn't understand. She suspected her cheek was bleeding where he had hit her. It was hard to tell in the rain.

She wriggled closer under the shelter of a tree in the corner, tearing her stockings to shreds, making sure she was still hidden from the road. At least her dark coat would not give her away. She began to shake with the cold and shock. Shuddering breaths sought to release the fear still twitching in her muscles. She had lost her bag with all the precious signatures, but that was the least of her worries.

She trembled at the thought of explaining all this to her father, and Richard. They would expect the worst. Could she persuade them she had not been violated? She closed her eyes and prayed to God for strength.

A plump, middle-aged woman appeared on the porch; a newspaper held over her head. "Where are you, you stupid animal?" she muttered to herself, then raised her voice to call, "Tippy, come here Tippy! Oh, dear. Tippy, where are you?" The woman tutted and turned to go inside but changed her mind and walked to the end of verandah near where Lucy was hiding. Except from that angle, she would be in plain sight. Lucy curled up in a ball, trying to make herself smaller.

The woman scanned the garden for her lost pet, and let out a squeal when she spied Lucy. "Oh heavens." She lowered the newspaper to peer more closely. "Come out, whoever you are."

Lucy scrambled to a crouch, keeping low behind the bush. "I'm sorry to intrude."

"Who are you, and what are you doing in my garden?" demanded the woman.

"I'm hiding … a man … he's chasing me," she said in a quiet voice.

The woman looked across the hedge left and right along the roadway. "There's no one there. You'd better come in. You'll catch your death of cold out there in this weather."

Lucy hesitated.

"Come on, girl. I'm not going to bite you. There's only me here."

Lucy scurried up the front steps and stood dripping on the porch, quivering, her arms folded around her.

"Go on, get inside," urged the woman. She closed the door behind them shutting off what little light the outside offered.

Lucy immediately felt the warmth of the house, and shivered.

"Give me that wet coat and let me have a good look at you."

Lucy undid the buttons, and her Good Samaritan peeled it off, removing her scarf at the same time. Her dress was soaked underneath.

"I'm Mrs Adams. Who are you?"

"Lucy Young," she stammered through chattering teeth.

Mrs Adams squinted at her. "Your father that importer fellow?"

"Yes. Do you know him?"

"Not personally. My husband, God bless his soul, did business with him a few times, I believe. Now, come along here where it's warm."

Lamps had been lit in the kitchen, adding to the homely feel. Lucy shivered again as the heat enveloped her. Mrs Adams draped the wet coat over the drying rack hanging above the range and pulled a towel from the shelf. Lucy noticed a tap that provided running water and, from a quick glance out the window, she could see what she presumed would be a water closet and bathroom added to the back verandah, suggesting her hostess was comfortably off.

She handed the towel to Lucy, who stood with her arms folded around it, shuddering. "Start with this, but by the looks of it, you are soaked to the skin. I will get you a dressing gown to wear while we dry those clothes."

She bustled out of the room, leaving Lucy to look around. A chair sat beside the coal range, providing a haven of safety and comfort. A pair of glasses and an embroidery hoop sat atop two books on the side table. Open shelves on either side were filled with various vases, crockery jars and bowls, while the dresser on the other side held the plates, teapot and cups. The round table was covered in a brown velvet fringed cloth. Two chairs sat neatly tucked underneath.

Mrs Adams returned carrying a dark-red quilted robe. "It was my husband's, but it'll keep you warm. Now, strip off that dress and put this on. Then I'll have your undergarments."

Lucy's teeth were chattering so much, she didn't argue. Mrs Adams helped Lucy undo the buttons at the back, and she slipped out of her bodice and dropped her skirt. Mrs Adams scooped them up, tutting at the state of the hem, which was covered in mud and had several tears, Lucy now noticed.

"You are so very kind," she mumbled as she wrapped herself up in the cosy dressing gown. It was too large but she felt warmer already. And it protected her modesty.

Keeping her back to Lucy as she cleaned the muddy hem and added the skirt and bodice to the drying rack, Mrs Adams said, "It's nothing. Now give me your wet petticoats and stockings or you'll freeze."

Inside the robe, Lucy stripped off the rest of her layers, leaving only her chemise and drawers, with their telltale stains. She wrapped her arms around her body again, attempting to stop the shakes.

Mrs Adams nodded. "It will be all right, lass. I'll have those things too."

Lucy did as she was told, too shocked to think otherwise.

Mrs Adams patted her shoulder. "Good girl. Now sit there next to the fire and get warm while I wash these things and make us a cuppa."

"I am so very grateful," said Lucy perching on the armchair, her heart thumping loudly and feeling sick to her stomach, "but I must not impose."

"You aren't. And I am glad for a bit of company. It has been lonely since my Sid died. That's why I like having Tippy with me. She was a stray who sauntered in one day and stayed. I would be all alone without her, but she's inclined to wander sometimes."

Mrs Adams poured the hot water from the kettle on the coal range into the teapot and popped a cosy over it. After turning it around a few times, she poured two cups of tea, handing one to Lucy, and reached for the biscuit tin. "Hungry?"

She nodded, surprised to find she was. Taking a biscuit, she ate it quickly and wrapped both hands around her teacup to hold it steady while she drank.

The woman pulled up a chair at the table and, after biting into a biscuit, turned to her bedraggled companion. "Now, missie. You'd better tell me what happened. We will need to let your father know where you are before he sends out a search party."

Haltingly, Lucy explained about her suffrage work and what she had been doing until she bumped into the stranger in the darkened alley. Tears fell as she tried to find the right words to describe what took place in that ramshackle shed. "He … he …" She felt so ashamed.

Mrs Adams patted her shoulder for a third time. "There, there, dear. Let's see what we can do, shall we?"

"My father will want retribution and my fiancé …" she sobbed, fearful and daunted. "What if he won't love me any more?"

"Don't fret about that, little one. Least said, soonest mended. You have nothing to be ashamed about. We will tell him you got lost in the rain and had a bad fall nearby and asked for my help."

Shocked, Lucy stared at her companion. "You think I should lie to my father?" Lying was a sin. Lying was deliberate.

"What part of that is a lie?"

Lucy couldn't answer.

"Do you want a fuss made?"

Lucy shook her head. She'd had no say in what happened, and it wasn't her sin. But she knew she was being silly. She would be condemned regardless.

"Do you want it to appear in the newspapers?"

Appalled at the thought, Lucy squeaked, "No!"

"Do you want to continue your suffrage work?"

Lucy nodded. "Yes. More than ever. If such brutality is what women have to put up with, then the sooner we have the vote and a chance to change things, the better."

"Good. In which case, it will stay our little secret."

"Even from my fiancé?" Lucy stared bug-eyed at Mrs Adams.

"Especially him."

But she thought keeping secrets brought such misery. To those keeping the secrets against all odds, and to those kept in the dark. For surely, sooner or later, all secrets were revealed. And she would be damned.

21

Revealing the truth

Emma decided the time had come to tell Paige what she knew so far, but she'd hedge around her mother's birth father for a while longer. "I'm glad you and your father are talking about things more. Honestly, the more you talk, the better. I promise you, it's much more productive than arguing. But listen, I've got news." She handed Paige a piece of paper that would help explain the first part of what she was about to say.

"This is you at the top …marked Generation 1:

1> Amelia Paige FRAZER, born 2003

Next comes your mother. I ordered her birth certificate which confirms her date of birth and who her parents were. I put your dad over to one side.

2> **Lucy Kathryn WILSON**
married David Fish FRAZER
born 1975   married about 1997   died 2006

Then her mother, your grandmother.

3> **Amelia Lucy,** better known as Amy."

"But that doesn't make sense," said Paige.

"Yes it does – when you know the rest of the story. Hidden away in the lid of the box was a newspaper cutting about her death on 23 September 1977. Amy was thirty-one, and sadly died in a car accident."

Paige lifted her head from the page, with a shocked look. "My mum was her baby? You're kidding?"

Emma shook her head and placed a comforting hand on the young woman's shoulder. "I can't prove it yet, but that feminist badge I mentioned, I think it was Amy's. There were a few other protest badges from around the '70s that would indicate she was part of the feminist movement. Which fits. It's a guess, but a fairly educated one, because from that death notice, I deduced *her* mother – your great-great-grandmother – was:

4> **Kathryn Lucy MILLS**, better known as Kate, born about 1921. "

Paige looked astounded. "Seriously?"

"She married Michael John WILSON in December 1945, who I suspect was a returning soldier. I'm absolutely certain she's the woman in the photograph with your mother and Cameron. You said she died not long after that was taken, in 1998?"

Emma pulled out her phone to show Paige the three photos they'd discovered lined up beside one another. "This one is of Kate, next to your mother, who I believe she raised after her own daughter's death, with Cameron as a baby. But look. What's that around her neck?"

Paige took the phone from Emma, enlarged the image and peered more intently. "It's the chain to this." She untangled the locket from underneath her hoodie.

209

Putting the phone down, she unclipped the chain and opened the locket.

"Which makes me think this photo …" – Emma pointed to the locket – "is of her mother Amy."

Paige's mouth formed a circle. "Wow! That's amazing, but how can you be certain?" Her eyes sparkled with anticipation.

"I can't, unless your father knows and can confirm it," Emma paused wishfully.

Eyes full of longing mixed with doubt looked back at her. A shoulder hitch. "Maybe."

Better than nothing, Emma thought, continuing her explanation. "But before I get to her, I want to go back to Grandma Kate. Remember I told you there was a Peace Movement badge and a Quaker badge in the box?"

Her companion nodded.

"I did a bit more research on the WILPF, the Women's International League for Peace and Freedom. In 1954, when Kate would have been about thirty-three, I think, Dr Kathleen Lonsdale visited. She was the British president of the league at the time, a Quaker, a brilliant chemist and long-time peace campaigner. She later became anti nuclear as well. From what I can discover, the group here had gone into recess during the war and was re-established after her visit. Their focus was the effects of war and nuclear weapons on the human body. In the '60s, they protested about our involvement in the Vietnam War."

"Are you saying *my* Grandma Kate was an anti-war campaigner?"

Emma could almost see Paige's brain putting everything into place, from her pacifist great-grandmother to her unknown feminist grandmother, to her anti nuclear protester mother.

"As I said, guesswork, but why else would all these badges be in a box engraved with 'L' on the top, and handed down generation to generation? Because I believe there's more."

"This is so exciting," said Paige. "I'm beginning to understand why all these things are so important. What more can there be?"

"Patience. I'm getting there, but it takes time."

Emma swallowed a glass of water. She didn't want to explain to Paige how much effort and time it took, especially now she was trying to limit her workload, rest more and spend more time with Rose and Luke. That part was working, but she was frustrated at not being able to work for as long, or as often, as she wanted to. Some days she just felt awful and couldn't do much of anything except rest, often crying herself into a fitful sleep. She'd have had this all done in half the time otherwise.

She'd also spent far too much time on 'Dr Google'. Scaring herself in the process. There were some seriously nasty and life-threatening diseases that could be causing her symptoms. She'd even found an article about research into long Covid, and whether it was linked to chronic fatigue syndrome, that sent her pulse racing. CFS was a long-term, incurable condition that drained sufferers of all energy. If she was going to feel like this for the rest of her days, it would curtail what she could do and life was going to be difficult. She dreaded the thought.

"What's this you've written here?" asked Paige interrupting her thoughts.

Emma looked. "Fish. Your dad's middle name is Fish. Didn't you know that?"

"No, I didn't." She laughed at the silliness of it. "I'd keep that to myself, too, if it was mine. But where'd it come from? What parent would be mean enough to call their child Fish?"

"That I can't answer. I haven't researched your father's side at all. But I thought it unusual, to say the least. For a brief moment and, I admit, as I was in a grump at the time about another man by the name of Fish I was writing about for a client, I wondered if there was any connection. But I doubt it."

"It's a real name?" She sounded horrified.

"Yes," chuckled Emma. "Originating from Anglo-Saxon Britain, defining someone working with fish."

Paige shuddered and pulled a face. "I'm glad it's not my name. Yuck. Who was this other man?"

"Someone with too much to say for himself, in my opinion. Amongst other things, Henry Fish was fiercely anti-suffrage and did his best to undermine the women campaigning for the right to vote. As a politician, I suspect he considered himself entitled to speak out on many matters he disagreed with, but the newspapers described him as sly. And that was one of the more complimentary versions. I read somewhere he was parodied as 'The Talking Fish'."

"And you thought my dad might be a descendant?" She sounded as if she was mulling over an idea.

This time it was Emma's turn to vacillate. "No, not really," she laughed awkwardly. "I don't know your father, so it's not fair to suggest he could be. But you were upset with him, and it was a moment in time when I thought disagreeably of both men."

"Would it be possible?"

"Anything's possible." Emma began to wish she'd never said anything. She hadn't expected to be interrogated to this degree. "He was survived by six daughters and two sons. It's the sort of thing a girl might do to keep her maiden name running through the male line, but there's no proof, and there're thousands of people with the Fish name around the world. The chances of any connections are slim."

"What did this man do?"

Emma decided not to tell the girl all she knew; it would be too exhausting. "Look him up and read about it yourself. He had a lot of fingers in lots of pies – mostly to feed his pride."

"Interesting …"

Again, Emma wondered what the girl was thinking.

* * * * *

"What gives?" said Jess, having dropped Rose home after school.

"What are you talking about?" Emma was evasive, not long having got up from a nap, as she prepared a snack for the girls.

Jess perched on the counter stool, watching. "You've been avoiding me."

Immediately defensive, Emma's heart rate notched up several degrees. "No, I haven't."

"Don't give me that bull. You can't fool an expert. You're dodging something. You called me out over my ex; I'm calling you out now."

Emma knew her friend meant well, but no one could help with this predicament. She was certain it would pass. "It's nothing like your situation. You were hiding abuse. I most certainly am not." She continued to put the snack together, opening cupboards and the fridge to look for something to add, anything to avoid looking at Jess.

"Okay, I'll go with that. I'd be doubting your mental faculties if you said Luke was being abusive. But there's something …"

"I'm fine," she rounded on Jess, and began to wipe the already clean worktop, keeping her head down.

"For Pete's sake!" fumed Jess, banging her palm on the kitchen bench. "One thing you are *not* is fine. You've just been in hospital."

Emma went to the door and called the girls to get their drinks and food. Seconds later, they ran in, grabbed their plates and headed back to Rose's room, leaving her without any more breathing room or excuses.

"I wasn't there long," she defended. "It's nothing. A bit anaemic. That's all. They were far too busy to bother with me. Coffee?"

"No thanks. Actually, a glass of water would be nice." Jess slid off the stool. "I'll get it." She chose a glass from the cupboard and filled it from the fridge dispenser, moving closer towards Emma. She leant against the U-shaped bench, sipping it. "But you still fainted. In public. And ended up with an ambulance taking you to hospital. That's not fine."

Emma folded her arms tightly across her chest, protecting herself, holding herself together, denying the possible.

Jess put her glass down and, crossing the narrow space between them, put her hands on Emma's upper arms. She ducked her head seeking those downcast eyes. "You are my best friend. I owe you for saving me from my ex. I don't like seeing you like this. Please, Ems, let me help you."

Emma raised her eyes, sparkling with unshed tears and defiance. "I don't need help."

Jess dropped her hands and turned to pick up her glass, putting it down again before taking a sip. She turned back to Emma who still stood, arms folded, mouth drawn and jaw clenched so tightly she was shaking. "You do, you know. Whatever this is, it's affecting everything. You're snappy, withdrawn, disengaged and ignoring what's around you."

"I don't need a character analysis from you," snapped Emma, proving Jess's point.

Jess sucked in her breath, keeping her temper under control. "Let me ask you something then. When was the last time you asked Rose about her dance recital? It's the weekend after next, by the way."

Emma started, but she refused to give way. "You said you had it all sorted and didn't need me."

Still calm, Jess replied. "I do. And I don't need your help, but Rosie does."

"Luke said he'd do the all the drop-offs and pick-ups," Emma continued, to justify herself.

"I'm not talking about that, I'm talking about you being interested in Rosie. Did you know she told Livvy that you didn't love her any more?"

Emma's heart flipped and her stomach churned. Had she pushed her aside to that degree?

"Of course I love her. She has no reason to think that."

"No?" challenged Jess. "I don't know why she feels you don't love her, but if she's told Livvy, then I suggest you show her she's wrong."

Emma's anger flared as the truth hit her. "Don't give me lectures on parenting. I know my girl better than you."

"Maybe you do. But you're not yourself right now. You're not behaving rationally. Why don't the three of you go away for the school holidays? Have a reset away from the pressures of work and whatever's bugging you."

Emma knew Jess was concerned and doing her best to be supportive but, feeling threatened by what was happening to her, she fought back. "Mind your own business! I don't need you interfering. Nothing's bugging me. Nothing's wrong. I keep telling you. I'm fine!" Anger and fear kept her tears at bay.

Jess put up her hands in supplication. "Okay … if that's how you feel, I'll go. But if that's you being fine, then get help."

"Leave me alone. Do you hear me? Leave me alone."

She heard Jess call Olivia, and as soon as the front door shut behind them, Emma allowed herself to burst into tears.

"Mummy?"

22

What will the future hold

May – June 1893

On Tuesday, the 2nd of May, and only a day since her terrifying ordeal, Lucy drew a deep gulp of air as she read the headline. She looked across the dining table, anticipation tingling every nerve, pushing away her darker thoughts. "Listen, Father. Mr Seddon has promised to make women's suffrage a Ministerial question and push the Electoral Bill through this session."

"There you have it. He'll keep his promise, I'm sure. Congratulations to you and all the ladies." He studied her for a few moments. "You've done something different with your hair."

Lucy patted the back of her head, knowing she had created softer curves and more tendrils around her temples to hide a nasty graze that only Mrs Adams had seen. "Have I? I don't think so. Maybe it's a bit looser this morning. I was in a hurry." She continued reading. "Oh no," she moaned.

"What now?" Her father sounded impatient.

"The article goes on to say 'while the Government will adopt female franchise as a plank, they will not permit any difference in the mode of exercising the franchise, irrespective of sex'. So if the Legislature continues to demand a separate voting regime for women, we are still lost."

She bustled from her chair, gathering plates and dishes to carry to the kitchen. "There's no time to waste. We must keep campaigning." Her voice faded into the walls as she disappeared along the hallway.

Mrs Bush was already in the kitchen. "How are you feeling, Miss Lucy?"

Lucy was conscious of the way Mrs Bush looked at her. As if she suspected something.

If she was being truthful, she would have said – should have said – 'traumatised'. Instead, she answered, "I am well, thank you. I slept well and feel fully restored, apart from a few bruises and grazes where I fell." She self-consciously fiddled with her hair, pulling a few extra strands loose to add to the effect.

Mrs Adams had insisted her way was the best way, otherwise Lucy would be wrapped in cotton wool and forbidden from doing anything without a male escort. She wanted to avoid that, at all costs. Only her journal would know her true feelings: of repulsion, of anger, of resolution. Overnight, she had made up her mind that she would work for the betterment of conditions for women for as long as she had breath in her body. Instead of weakening her, the attack had strengthened her. Richard would be in for a shock.

All she had to do now was quell the trembling affecting her insides and put on a brave face. "I'll be away from the house most of the day, Mrs Bush. I fear there is still work to be done."

"Your father won't be happy with you going out, and especially not alone, Miss Lucy."

"I'll be fine. I will take a carriage. There is still more rain to come."

"Be it on your own head. You've been warned," called Mrs Bush to Lucy's back.

Shortly after her father left, she quickly changed and before long the horse cab was pulling up outside Mrs Adams's Newmarket house. She knocked tenuously on the door, memories of the previous day still raw. She glanced up and down the street, seeing well-to-do homes and no sign of any brutish-looking men or workers' houses. She breathed a sigh of relief – it was unlikely that she would run into her assailant again. She must have run further than she thought.

"Hello, my dear," said Mrs Adams, opening the door and inviting her in. "I'm so pleased to see you. How are you today?"

"Rather stiff and sore, to be honest, but I couldn't let on to my father how much. I told him my knees were tender after taking the brunt of the fall. That part is at least the truth."

"Good girl. Sometimes, men just don't need to know these things."

She bustled around making the inevitable pot of tea while Lucy handed her a small block of lavender-scented soap. "A small thank you for what you did to help me."

"Tosh, girl. That's not necessary. I was more than happy to rescue you and brighten up my quiet life," Mrs

Adams flustered. "Oh dear, that came out wrong. That sounds awful. I didn't mean it that way. I am sorry."

Lucy took the older woman's hands in hers. "There's no need to apologise. If I hadn't appeared in your garden, life would have been different for both of us. As it is, we now have each other to brighten our days."

"You are such a generous-hearted wee thing." Mrs Adams patted the girl's cheek. "Now then. Tell me everything that happened after your father collected you."

With a cup of tea in hand and fruit cake set out on the plate, Lucy outlined the trip home, her father's solicitousness, Mrs Bush's nursing and Richard's protectiveness. "You were right. They were ready to confine me to my room to restore my health – Lord, grant me strength – and wanted me to stop going out, *and* working for the cause. I soon put them right on that front." Lucy dropped her head and lowered her eyes. "Thank you for helping me clean up my clothes, and um … well, you know. Nobody noticed anything untoward."

"Didn't I tell you?" Mrs Adams chuckled as she topped up their cups from the teapot. "So what are you planning? I am not at all sure I'm in favour of you being out alone, or in certain areas of town."

"I know. I had clearly wandered into unknown territory. I won't do that again. I promise." She shuddered. "But I lost so many signatures in the rain. I have to replace them."

"And I will help you."

Lucy stared at Mrs Adams. "You will? How?"

"I might look old and doddery, but I have my ways. You see, while I am not a member of the organisations you attend, I am a member of the Ladies' Benevolent Society. I cannot be overt, you understand, but I certainly can do my bit. I don't go visiting like some of the others, my poor legs won't let me any more. Thankfully, my Sid left me well off, so I provide financial support." She tapped the side of her nose. "Support which buys me a say in things. I'll introduce you to some of the ladies, and I am sure you will soon persuade them into not only signing, but helping collect signatures."

Lucy grinned. "That would be wonderful. That is another avenue I hadn't considered. Thank you. I am so happy I met you."

"So am I, my dear. So am I."

* * * * *

By the third week of the month, as news of petitions being carried throughout Wellington, Taranaki and Hawke's Bay filtered through, Lucy learnt that Mr Seddon was to visit Auckland before the next meeting of Parliament.

"Mrs Daldy has said she will attend his address, as there are rumours that the order to print the electoral rolls has been countermanded and she wants to know what that means for us. But she says we must not stop now. We have to keep petitioning," Lucy explained to Mrs Adams, who sat knitting in her chair next to the range. "Electioneering is about to start, and women's rights must not get lost in the commotion."

Lucy watched as Mrs Adams changed rows without looking.

"I agree. I read only the other day how the newspapers

are saying it will be the usual struggle between the classes and the masses, but this time the clash will be the most severe and bitter ever experienced. The masses are wanting change."

Lucy nodded. "And not before time, from what I have seen. Women deserve better. And the children. What a terrible life some of them have."

"It sounds to me that the arguments about equality and humanity, and the eloquent voices of Grey and Ballance, have finally been listened to."

"And aren't we glad of that," agreed Lucy. "The newspapers are encouraging every man to register so he may cast his vote equally now, since the 'one man, one vote' law came into being for the 1890 election. I pray that women may soon be able to register too."

Mrs Adams paused in her knitting. "Tell me, my dear. Why are you so passionate about this? You come from one of those wealthy backgrounds. Your father has very likely exercised plural voting, what with him owning more than one property. A privilege, I might add, that ensured business interests were met before social. Such practices have been highlighted many times as one of the ways in which the wealthy oppressed the masses, until now. So why are you for the masses?"

Lucy pondered the question. It was a good one, and one she hadn't considered in depth. "My father would argue we are not wealthy. We live comfortably, but not lavishly. He is a businessman rather than a political man. He has enjoyed the privileges of his position, but he's always valued his employees. Without them, he says he couldn't do his business. He says respect never hurt anyone." Lucy knew she hadn't answered the question.

"Admirable, I'm sure but, you have to agree, rather unusual. If you don't mind me asking, why did he never remarry?"

"I don't know exactly, except Mama was the great love of his life. He valued her opinion, so I think his views were swayed by hers. Mama was one of those who make society tick. One of the many women who run the church groups and the charities, the midwives and nurses, the fundraisers and the helpers like your Benevolent Society friends. Not all of them are wealthy, but they are not workers either. They want to be busy, and helping those worse off than themselves is rewarding."

She shrugged. That still didn't explain her reasons. As she fiddled with her fingernails, a word popped into her head and her eyes lit up. Now she understood. "Fairness," she said. "That's it. It is about the greater good, and being unselfish. I lose nothing if someone else has the same choices. Equality does not take from one to give to the other, it provides equal opportunities."

Mrs Adams smiled at her naivety. "Only if people take up those opportunities. They don't always. Too many, and women especially, believe they are not worthy of them, in my experience."

Lucy became more animated. "That's exactly why we need the vote. So we have rights. So we no longer consider ourselves undeserving. We might not want to be great philosophers or lawyers or, or … something, but we should have the right to do so."

"Well said, young lady. Now you know why you support the masses, and you are already in the middle of how, by trying to change the situation. My question now is, what next?"

Lucy looked blankly at her. Was she a mind reader? Only recently had Lucy given the future any thought, beyond getting the vote. "I promised Richard I would marry him when we won the franchise." Lucy saw an opening to ask about what was worrying her the most. "What if … there are … um …" she stammered.

Mortified, she could only nod at Mrs Adams's question about the arrival of her regular menses. "In which case, there will be no consequences to be concerned about, and life will continue as normal."

Relief, liberation and remorse jumbled inside her head as moments of that day flashed. She had buried it as best she could, not wanting to allow a single second to obtrude, but would she ever rid herself of her self-reproach?

"So, I repeat, what next?" continued Mrs Adams as if nothing at all had happened. "If you intend to marry this young man of yours, is he the sort to control you or will he allow you your freedoms?"

"He's supported me so far. I assume he will do so in the future. I certainly will not let him dictate what I can and can't do, even though he would like me to give up campaigning. I want to do something more to help women who are worse off, but I don't know what exactly. What can I do of any worth?"

"That's for you to decide, my dear. But you must do something."

"Look, Father, look. They are calling it the Monster Petition." A week later, Lucy stood behind his chair as she put the newspaper down in front of him. She

224

pointed. "The Napier petition alone measures fourteen and a half yards and contains 1,442 signatures. Isn't that wonderful?"

"It is indeed, Lucy, my dear child. I would be very surprised if you do not succeed this year. The time is right. And so, too, is the time right for you to consider arrangements for your nuptials."

"Oh, Father," sighed Lucy, a sense of panic creeping in. How would she pretend during such intimacies as marriage required? "Must I? Can it not wait until after we have voted?"

"You agreed to wed after you'd won the vote, not after you'd voted. There's a big difference between the two. You must at least start the preparations. You can't leave it all to the last minute. That's not fair on the guests."

Lucy muttered under her breath about having better things to do than worry about what the guests might want. "Very well. I'll think on it."

The news that Sir Robert Stout had won the Inangahua seat and would be returning to Parliament lifted Lucy's spirits. His was another voice in favour. Maybe she could plan for life with the vote after all.

But it wasn't her wedding she was thinking about, it was what Mrs Adams had said.

What would she do in the future?

23

Losing control

Remorse at the way she and Jess had parted company, and the accusations laid at her door, Emma decided to prove her wrong.

"I'm so sorry, Rosie," she apologised profusely for upsetting the girl who stood trembling by the kitchen door, and gathered her into her arms. "Don't be upset, baby, it's not your fault. Mummy's sorry. I love you, so much. I will always love you." She remembered through the sobs promising the child everything would be all right. Although, how that would be possible, Emma didn't know.

After she'd read Rosie a bedtime story, again promising that all was well and she was the most precious of things in her life, Emma sat next to Luke on the couch. "You know how we talked about going away in the holidays. Did you have somewhere in mind?"

Luke muted the TV and turned towards her. "No, I wasn't sure you were interested, or fit enough."

Her hackles rose and she shook herself to settle her irritation before she answered. "I was thinking, we could take a road trip – after Rosie's recital on Saturday."

Luke turned the TV off, and settled himself better to look at Emma. "Are you sure you're up to it?"

She bit back a retort, resorting to one word. "Yes." Sharp and to the point.

"How about Rotorua, then? If you're sure." He clearly wasn't. "That's not too far. Rosie would enjoy the hot pools and the redwoods are nice."

Emma shook her head. "I'd prefer to go to Wellington."

Luke looked surprised. "Wellington? That's a long road trip. Unless we fly. Why?"

"I'd like to show Rosie some of the historic sights like Parliament, and the National Library."

"That sounds a bit boring. I'd go with Te Papa Museum, and all the *Lord of the Rings* stuff, and even the cable car, as things that might be a bit of fun, but not those other places. She's a bit young."

Emma bristled. "You are never too young to learn history."

Luke frowned. "What's there you want to see?"

"Nothing in particular," she hedged.

He raised an eyebrow. "Yes there is. I know you too well. Out with it."

"I was talking with Paige ..."

"Not her again," he sighed. "When are you going to make the break with her? You can't keep doing all this work, not when you're clearly still unwell."

"I thought you liked her?"

"I do – so does Rosie – but she's no help to you."

"Can you not let me decide what I do or not do? It's my work. It's nothing to do with you."

"I disagree. It has everything to do with me when

227

how you are and what you do affects us as a family."

Emma tried to block out the same charge Jess had levelled at her. "I'm doing my best."

"Well it's not good enough, Ems. Not by a long shot."

Unable to withhold the surge of fury, or her sense of failure, she flounced off the couch, retreating to the bedroom, slamming the door behind her.

* * * * *

Emma was aware of Rosie watching the frosty interchange between her parents over breakfast and tried to make light of it. "Aunty Jess says I'm not allowed to touch your dance costume in case I break it. Is that fair? Could I really break it?"

Rose giggled and shook her head. Her eyes still darting between the two.

Emma said, "And Dad says they are keeping it all a secret from me. No peeking. Not at rehearsals, or at your costume. It's to be a surprise."

Rose brightened. "It'll be a great surprise when you see it." Until doubt set in. "You are coming to see it, aren't you, Mum?"

Emma's heart filled with pain. "Of course I am, sweetheart. We've got our tickets all ready. Now, off to school with you. Love you heaps."

She handed Luke the school bag, filled with Rosie's lunch box, sports gear and books, and waved them out the door just as her phone pinged.

"Hi, Paige. How's things?"

"Dunno. A bit out of sorts. Can we talk? Please?"

She had no desire to go out and be around people, but

Paige sounded forlorn. Against her better judgement, knowing Luke wouldn't like it, she weakened. "Sure. But can you come here? We can talk in my office."

An hour later, Emma let Paige in through the French doors. "So, what's this all about?"

"Wow. Beautiful room." Paige looked around and out to the garden. "With a lovely view. No wonder you like working from here."

"You didn't come for the view." Emma heard the irritable tone and tried again. "Sorry, but what was it you wanted to talk about?"

Paige settled herself into one of the wing chairs, putting her helmet on the floor, throwing her windbreaker on top. She somehow pulled her legs up into a cross-legged position Emma envied. "Dad, actually."

Why did that not surprise her? "What about him? I'm not sure I can help. I've never actually met your father, remember. And I never had one of my own so I can't make comparisons."

"You didn't have a dad? That's sad. They can be fun when they want to be."

Emma let the pause lengthen. If Paige had something to say, then she'd have to say it all by herself.

"Thinking back, Dave was a fun dad when we were little. It's only since I've grown up he seems, I dunno, awkward sometimes, and bossy. It's always got to be his way." She sighed dramatically. "That's why he and Cam get on. My big brother likes the things money can buy, and since he's the son and heir, and will continue the Frazer brand, he gets away with murder."

"He's also older," Emma reminded her. "He's done

his growing up, finished his degree and is learning the business, correct? Whereas you, I suspect, will always be Daddy's little girl in need of protection."

"It's not fair." Paige indignantly acknowledged the truth. "But that's exactly how he treats me."

"Have you talked to Cameron about it?"

Paige shrugged one shoulder. "Sometimes, but he didn't seem to see my point. Business was business, and nothing they did would make any difference to climate change, so what was my problem?" She hesitated, looking around the room as if seeking assurance. "Then the other day, he came and sat on the deck beside me, handed me an RTD and started to talk."

Emma remained silent. She recognised the girl was about to offload something that had shifted her thinking, and didn't want to distract her.

"He said he genuinely didn't know that Dad had shares in oil. Everything else they'd invested in through the business was in buyouts or managed funds of mostly private firms. But those shares had been bought in the name of one of the subsidiaries that only Dad had control of. I gave up trying to understand everything he told me, it made no sense, except I discovered that Cam's more pro the environment than I realised. That's when he started to tell me about his ideas for the future."

Emma listened to an astonished young woman outline her brother's plans for investing in clean energy and transport, infrastructure design and many other environmentally friendly activities. "It's still about making money but with a focus on sustainability, he said. I nearly fell off the lounger."

"That's good, isn't it?"

"Yes. At least, I think so. I hope so. He hasn't talked to Dad about it yet."

Paige unravelled herself from the chair and wandered over to the bookcase. She ran her fingers along the spines, checking the titles.

"So, what plan did you two hatch on how to approach your father?"

"We haven't yet. But something else happened."

She continued to look at the books. "I remember this one." She pulled Jane Austen's novel *Emma* from the shelf. "We studied it at school. Most of the class hated it, but I rather liked it. Silly, feisty, romantic."

Emma's patience was being sorely tested. She didn't have the energy for this level of procrastination. "I don't mean to sound rude, but either tell me what you came here to say, or leave. I don't have time for this."

The expression in Paige's eyes changed from bewilderment, to dismay, to distress. "But … I thought. You said …" Paige began to collect her belongings, her vulnerability showing. "Sorry, I thought you wanted to know. I didn't mean to be a nuisance."

"Paige. Stop." Riddled with guilt for upsetting the girl after she'd clearly offered to help her, and someone who was becoming a familiar part of her life, Emma retracted. "You're not a nuisance. It's just …" The words were in her head but she stumbled over them as she spoke. "Not feeling … the best. Can you … say what you want … or … maybe another day?"

In a flash, with the hastiness of youth, Paige was all apologetic and solicitous. "Sorry, I didn't realise. I should go and leave you until you feel better."

"Stop," repeated Emma sharply. "Stop apologising

… get on with it. I won't rest until I know."

What on earth was wrong with her? Behaving like this. Grumpy and impatient about everything. Now she couldn't even complete a sentence properly. After a couple of deep breaths she felt more in control. "Okay. Tell me what happened." She closed her eyes and listened to Paige recall the meeting with her father …

"Dad," Paige queried in a light tone. "Will you tell me more about Mum?"

He never even raised his head from the report he was reading. "What good will it do? She's gone. You have to make your own way in the world."

That wasn't good enough. She wanted to know. "But that's the problem. I don't quite know which way is my way. I thought if I knew more about what my mother and grandmothers did in their lives, it might help me decide."

"Times have changed. There are jobs available now that were not even heard of in their day. Think ahead, girl."

"I'd like to, if you'd help me."

She sat down on the perfect white couch across the coffee table from him and placed the photo of Grandma Kate, her mum and Cameron on it. He briefly raised his eyes, then lowered them again.

"You must have known Grandma Kate. If you didn't want me to know anything, why give me this?"

"You're wasting your time. Stop dwelling in the past."

"Why is your middle name Fish?"

This time his eyes opened wide and he stared at her. "It's not important."

"'Tis to me," she paused, eyeballing him. "You're not getting off the hook that easily. Pun intended."

"My business. Not yours." He scribbled something on the report and turned another page.

"Ah, since we're talking business. Those oil shares sound a bit fishy to me, Mr Fish. Doesn't sound like they were a legal catch at all."

"What are you talking about?"

"Just something I heard about shares being bought under a subsidiary, effectively hiding the true owner. Does that sound fair to you?"

His knee started to bounce as he underlined words and blindly turned back a page then forward another. He threw the pencil on the coffee table and sat back, one leg folded across the other.

"What are you on about, Paige? I've work to do," he demanded, getting quite irritable.

Having clearly flustered him, she pushed her point. "I want answers."

"Well, you're not getting them from me." He clenched and unclenched his jaw and a pulse throbbed at his temple.

With a one-shoulder hitch and pulling a face, she said, "Suit yourself. I could always mention it to a few influencers. They'd love a bit of gossip. And even if they dig deep and find – as I'm sure you will tell me – nothing, and that all is above board, gossip is hard to stop."

"Are you threatening me?"

"Dad! Would I do that?" She smiled. "But right or wrong, gossip spreads, oozing its way into social media threads you'd least expect, like Greenpeace or the clean energy groups. I wonder what they'd do with a titbit like that? Even unfounded."

"That sounds like a threat to me."

"No, Dad. It's a fair exchange. You tell me what I want to know, and I won't tell anyone what you don't want them to know. Easy really."

He stood and looked out the sliding doors to the harbour view. One hand propped on his hip as thoughts flickered through his mind. He rubbed his fingers through his hair as she spoke again.

"I read up about a certain devious Mr Fish the other day." Her voice was casual but her words, aimed at his back, were precise. "He appears to have been quite unscrupulous, and decidedly pompous and verbose when cornered, I believe. The suffrage women certainly didn't like him. Have you ever heard about him?"

"Why would I know anything about that?" His shoulders sagged as his hands dropped to his side.

"Something you once said about me being from a long line of troublemakers. It sounded to me like Mr Fish didn't like women, and especially women who caused him a great deal of trouble. I just wondered whether the current Mr Fish had inherited any characteristics."

"For Pete's sake, will you stop!"

While he'd been riled to anger, she remained calm. She was determined not to fight with him. She'd get more information if she was reasonable and rational.

"Yes. I will." She removed the locket and chain from her neck and laid it open on the coffee table. "When you answer my questions. Like, is this locket an heirloom handed down from mother to daughter? And is this woman in this photo the mother of Grandma Kate? And what happened to my mother?"

He turned and walked back to the coffee table, looking down at the locket but not touching it. He remained silent, then his eyes drifted to the photo of the three generations. She watched his face closely for a hint of recognition, for a moment of giving in.

Their eyes locked. He sighed as he closed his eyes tightly trying to stop a tear escaping. He wiped his face self-consciously as she went to him.

"Tell me," she whispered. She wrapped her arms about his torso and he fiercely hugged her to him, his head resting on the top of hers.

"I failed to protect your mother, and lost her," he breathed into her hair. "I can't lose you too."

24

In need of reassurance

Her task was done. At least, for now. Petitions from around the country were being collated, mostly in Christchurch by Kate Sheppard and her team. Others from Dunedin and all over the North Island would be bound and sent direct to the House and into the hands of Sir John Hall.

Mrs Daldy called a meeting for the 18th of July at City Hall as a final push to persuade doubters to support the movement. When Lucy arrived, throngs of people had already filled the hall. Notably absent was Hope who, as Milly had suspected, wanted nothing more to do with campaigning. With growing resentment, Lucy sat between Milly and Richard listening to the same replicated entreaties about equality and fairness amid quiet murmurs of assent and suppressed applause she'd heard so many times before.

Then Mrs Daldy proudly announced, "Auckland has collected over 3,300 signatures."

Lucy's sense of failure mounted. Surely they had

collected more than that? After all she had done, all she had suffered, and the burden she was now forced to carry.

Gasps of wonderment met the news that the petition being sent from Christchurch would surpass every other one in length and numbers, having gathered close to 26,000 signatures.

"Isn't that wonderful!" Lucy could hardly believe what she'd heard. So many. A truly monster petition of massive proportions. So why was she feeling let down?

Thanks were offered to Kate Sheppard, Helen Nicol and so many others, including Mrs Daldy herself. The total number of signatures collected was in excess of 35,000 and would surely carry significant weight in discussions in Parliament.

"I'm so relieved I could cry," she whispered as her eyes filled with tears.

While her personal disappointment did not lessen, ambition surged amid the prolonged applause. She glanced at her companions listening avidly to the discussion, and who appeared buoyed with the numbers. She studied Richard's profile and was instantly beset by uncertainty. She had changed since her ordeal. And had hardly slept while she battled the endless questions without answers.

Should she still marry him? Or should she shun him completely? Would it be better to let him think her callous but still respectable, and live the life of a spinster? Should she confess her shame and risk losing everything? How would she face his utter rejection and scorn, and that of her father? Would he allow her to live in his house after that, or would she be forever cast aside? Could she keep her secret and marry Richard as expected anyway?

It didn't matter which way she looked at it, she was defeated.

Mrs Daldy's voice filtered back into her consciousness. "And I'm delighted to say, there is a separate petition signed by a more than 1,200 men, requesting that the just demands of women are granted."

The three of them added their applause to the acclaim her words created, but those words also ignited the ire of the political agents, stirrers and well-known anti-suffrage bigots.

From then on, every speaker was interrupted by shouts and slogans, counterarguments and interjections, none of which made the slightest difference except to agitate the crowd. Lucy's natural optimism turned to disappointment and a growing sense of defeat. Her spirits drooped further.

The commotion in the hall necessitated a raise of voice as a motion was put from the stage by Mrs Kerr-Taylor. "We hereby call on the Legislature to immediately enfranchise all members of society."

Rising in support of the motion, Milly's grandfather Captain Daldy, attempting to ignore the noise, said, "The franchise is but a small link in the chain of women undertaking the necessary social and moral reform throughout the world. As husbands and fathers, we must support them."

A man called out, "Women are a menace!"

Instantly, Lucy became enraged. "That is a lie!"

Women were not the menace. Men wore that badge. Some more than others.

In response, Captain Daldy chuckled. "Then we must conclude that men are cowards if we are frightened by them."

A roar of agreement echoed around the hall.

Lucy completely concurred. "Cowards!" she yelled. Men were indeed cowards – some men, she corrected.

Above the commotion, she barely heard Mrs Daldy state she was unsurprised the franchise had failed in the past if that person was a specimen of mankind in Auckland.

To Lucy's ongoing dismay, one of the more voluble objectors began remonstrating at length.

"Not again," she sighed. "Not again."

Only the intervention of Constable Jones, who removed the man, prevented a physical scuffle. No sooner had he been dealt with when another man forced his way onto the stage waving a piece of paper, demanding the right to be heard.

"We will not be accepting amendments from the floor," said Mrs Daldy, her voice drowned out by the ensuing uproar. Amidst the stamping of feet, the hissing and hooting, shouts from rival factions on one side clamouring for the amendment to be read, vied with calls for the intruder to be ejected.

Sudden shrieks of laughter attracted her attention. "What's happening?"

Richard pointed to the cause. She stifled her unexpected giggles while he laughed out loud as a woman from the audience went sailing forth towards the offending gentleman who, by this point, was firmly seated on a chair at the front of the stage. Grabbing hold of his coat-tails, the woman attempted to bodily pull him off the platform but he hung on to the chair with one hand while gesticulating wildly at Mrs Daldy, much to the amusement of the audience . However, he was not to be unseated and refused to budge.

"I hope he gets his full comeuppance," said Lucy, her spirits drooping again.

During a small lull Richard again pointed. The man had thought better of his position and had retreated to a safer place nearby, from where he continued his onslaught.

"Very well," Mrs Daldy concurred. "For the sake of a more peaceful resolution we will put the amendment – which, in my opinion, can hardly be considered an amendment as it is so contradictory. The motion reads that: 'In the opinion of this meeting, the question of allowing the franchise to females should be remitted'. Those in favour say aye. Those against, no."

"No!" Lucy called at the top of her voice amid the uproar. She'd never known such anger before. It was a feeling she didn't like. Rage burnt inside her, distorting what had been good into something ugly.

The motion was overwhelmingly lost and after a time, comparative calm was restored. The meeting continued with the restless audience now more well behaved. It concluded its business with further resolutions in support of the female franchise.

On the way home, Richard laughed at remembered interjections and encouraged her to perk up. "You should be heartened by the positivity of tonight's event, despite the malicious attempts to defeat them. I am glad that it had ended well. Aren't you?"

She smiled wanly. "I am."

"Then we should celebrate. What say we dance around the square in the moonlight?"

Despite her mood, she laughed. "You are silly sometimes," but her heart lifted.

"I love it when you laugh," said Richard, running a finger along her jawline. Her spirits ignited to fervour at his touch. He leant closer as the cab swayed. She closed her eyes in anticipation and lifted her chin ever so slightly in the hope he would kiss her.

But the moment was lost. The carriage suddenly lurched. Lucy fell back against the seat and Richard was thrown on top of her. Instinct kicked in as memories of her attack returned.

"Get away from me. Get away!" she screamed. Pushing him off, she struggled to regain her balance. Her breathing came hard and fast, and her heart pounded. She placed her hand on her chest, trying to recover her equilibrium.

"Lucy? Whatever is the matter?" Richard sounded so hurt and worried she was tempted to explain until she remembered she needed to keep what happened a secret. She couldn't risk him turning away from her, not loving her any more. She couldn't bear his disdain. Or her father's disappointment.

Breathing deeply through her nose, she tried to control the tremor in her voice. "I'm sorry, Richard dearest. I don't know what came over me. I couldn't breathe and I panicked. It's nothing. Please forgive me." She attempted a smile. Hopefully, in the dim light he wouldn't see how false it looked.

"There's nothing to forgive, my darling. You are perfect as you are."

Shame flooded her entire being. She was not perfect. Not any more. She wasn't who he thought she was. She was not worthy of his love.

* * * * *

At the end of July, Aloysius Young came home to find his daughter, her friend Milly and Mrs Bush holding hands and dancing in a circle, laughing. "Am I allowed to join the party?"

The trio broke apart and Mrs Bush hurried back to the kitchen to get his dinner ready.

Lucy rushed up to her father. "Did you read what happened? Isn't it wonderful?"

An indulgent father, Aloysius smiled. "I am sure I have, but why don't you tell me all about it."

She pulled his arm and led him to the sofa where she sat beside him. Lucy didn't know anyone who had been to Parliament, not even her father, and only had a vague idea what it looked like from newspaper reports. "Sir John is, without doubt, our champion but it seems he went to extraordinary lengths to present our case. The reporters are far more eloquent than I could ever be but I've read every one describing the occasion. Oh, I wish I could have been there to see it. Such a momentous moment in history. But I shall have to imagine it all."

She understood the debating chamber was long, with a large hand-carved chair at one end and rows of seats on either side, divided by a sizeable table in the centre, leading to elegant, glass-paned double doors at the opposite end. She had no knowledge of the pomp and ceremony or traditions.

"Get to the point, my dear."

Lucy clasped her hands before her while Milly sat quietly opposite, but the excitement in her eyes spoke volumes. "Sir John rose to speak in favour of the Electoral Bill." She paused as a query interrupted her line of thought. "Why do they call him the Knight of Ellesmere?"

"Because Ellesmere is the name of the seat he won at the last election."

"I see." Satisfied, she returned to her account. "Sir John held two smaller scrolls representing 600 ladies appealing for the franchise. Before him lay a far larger scroll – I didn't know they'd done that," she added as an aside. "Anyway, he set the small scrolls on the table and returned to his seat. Placing a hand on top of the large scroll, he announced it held a further 25,570 signatures. The House cheered. Did you know that Father? The House cheered. Imagine that."

Lucy stood up and retrieved the newspaper from the table to be certain she could retell the tale perfectly and sat down again. "Look. It's all here."

Her father took the paper and patted her hand. "Go on."

"He said it was the most numerously signed petition of its kind ever presented in Australasia and he was honoured and privileged to present it." Lucy could scarcely contain her excitement. The thought of finally winning the franchise overriding the melancholy that had settled over her since 'that' day. "However, he apologised to the Speaker for asking, but its size necessitated assistance," she chuckled. "Two liveried messengers arrived. Taking one side of the cylinder each, they began to unroll the ribbon of paper, but it went on and on. Let me see. What did they say exactly?"

Lucy picked up the paper again, scanning the column until she found what she wanted. "Oh yes. 'They unrolled and unrolled until the great ribbon of paper lay stretched like a little pathway of white-and-black-veined marble from the Speaker's chair to the door at the end of the aisle.' Can you imagine it? I wonder how long that is. They had to stop at the door, but the scroll was barely smaller than when they began."

"I believe the petition was some 776 feet in length, comprising 546 separate sheets glued together in a continuous roll," said Mr Young.

"You read about it, too? Oh thank you, Father. Thank you." She hugged him, full of enthusiasm and joy.

"You missed the best bits," said Milly quietly. "The part where the House silenced Mr Fish and when Mr Taiaroa, the Māori who opposed us last time, said he would now support the vote."

"I also read," said Mr Young, "that the Hon. Richard Oliver of Dunedin and a member of the Legislature is in favour of extending the franchise to women. I believe you will be successful, my dears."

Lucy clapped and laughed ebulliently. "The papers have nicknamed Sir John the Knight of the Paper Cylinder. Isn't that wonderful?"

Except, Lucy realised, it brought her wedding day closer and she was nowhere near ready for that.

25

Tired of being tired

April – May 2022

Looking back, pretending had been the hardest part.

Rosie's dance recital had been a trial. Emma had promised to be there, time and again. She'd even made a point of showing Rosie where she, Luke and Jess would be sitting, but while their teachers had done a fantastic job of the choreography and the girls had excelled, the volume of the music and the flashing lights had set Emma's teeth on edge.

She'd surreptitiously pushed ear plugs in and resorted to shielding her eyes from the brightest lights, but she still came away with a thumping headache.

"That was brilliant, my darling," she'd enthused genuinely, wrapping her arms around Rosie as she'd bounced out of the dressing room, still with her stage make-up on and her hair tied back in a bun, glued in place by half a can of hairspray. "Congratulations, you looked wonderful."

"Are we going on holiday tomorrow?" asked Rose.

"Can Livvy come?"

"Yes, we leave in the morning, but no, darling, Livvy can't come, not this time," Luke had answered in her stead. "It's just for the three of us, to give Mummy a break away."

Rosie looked disappointed but, in the way of children, soon found something else to look forward to. "Can we go to the movies?"

"We'll see," grinned Luke, which saved Emma thinking about the trip ahead. 'I've mapped everything out,' he'd said a few nights after their argument. 'We get to spend two nights everywhere we go, so we have time to see the sights and take time to 'smell the roses', as Charli used to say.' He'd also booked all the accommodation and activities. Emma hadn't the brainpower to think about how it would go.

When they finally set off, the trip had been harder than she'd expected. Luke had been so understanding – more than she deserved, if she was being honest – and Rosie so exuberant and having so much fun, she couldn't begrudge them a moment. Even though she'd managed the fatigue better than she anticipated, thanks to Luke's thoughtfulness, it was pretending to be happy that almost destroyed her.

The more kind and considerate he was, the more unworthy she felt, the more she withdrew. She slid into a world of sorrow and self-blame. Why was this 'thing' taking so long to pass? She was *so* tired. Tired of being irritable. Tired of the days when pain in her aching muscles and joints slowed her down. Tired of *being* tired.

The trip to Wellington, through Rotorua, Napier and Wairarapa, was designed to cater to everyone's needs. They fell into a pattern of travel, rest, enjoy. If she had a rough start, they could do the short hops in the afternoons. Some days she felt almost normal again.

Despite her protestations, Luke took Rosie to all the adrenaline-pumping activities. "So you can have some quiet time to read or do whatever takes your fancy." He'd smile and kiss her on the forehead before taking off.

Sometimes, she slept. More often she was beset with doubts about the future. What did it hold for her? Frightened that the lethargy, disinterest and moroseness would become the norm in her life, she began to think up ways to insulate them, afraid she was becoming a burden. It wasn't fair to inflict that on Luke and Rose.

Her frustration was growing as the days went by. Unbeknown to Luke, after her falling out with Jess, she'd asked medical experts questions, only to be told she would have wait for at least six months of recording symptoms before they could begin a diagnosis. She was only halfway through the process. After being pushed, they'd conceded it could simply be the anaemia or low blood pressure she was being treated for, or a long Covid that would more than likely improve. Or, as she'd already discovered from Dr Google, something far more frightening and life-changing in the form of an incurable chronic condition. She'd blocked out all references to cancer. No one had any idea. None of it gave her a lot of confidence, and even less hope.

She began to write her worries in a journal, picking out the pros and cons of what she offered to the two people she loved, and how she could manage this … illness, whatever it was … in the days and months ahead.

The first week had gone in a flash.

"Thank you," she whispered as she and Luke curled up in bed one evening after an enjoyable day. "This is just what the doctor ordered."

"Anything to please," he chuckled, moving closer and kissing her gently. She knew he was testing the water. That was another part of their life affected by her irrational moods, but tonight she felt better than she had in a long time. Maybe the complete break away from her routine was paying off. She murmured in his ear and stretched out against him, kissing him more ardently, responding to his attentions.

They'd decided on three days in Wellington, as there were so many places they wanted to see and things to do.

"Can we go to the movies? Please?" begged Rosie, excited to see the latest Pixar offering, a Harry Potter spin-off, or so Emma was told.

Luke's ideas were far more varied, as he ticked off his fingers. "Zealandia, Weta Workshop, Te Papa, Mt Victoria, the cable car …"

"I want to go to the He Tohu exhibition at the National Library," interrupted Emma.

Rosie groaned.

Luke raised an eyebrow. "Didn't I tell you? I knew there was a reason. Why?"

"I want to see the Suffrage Petition." Wanting to see it for herself had become important in her mind. A 'must-do' at all costs.

If he wasn't a grown man, she'd have sworn he rolled his eyes, but that was the sort of thing Rosie did.

"I've had two clients in the last few months who both have connections to those days, and I knew little about any of it. The more I read, the more fascinating it became. It was dubbed the Monster Petition. I want Rosie to see it, to understand that women have always stood up for their rights. It's important for her to realise that today's issues are not new, but that together women can make changes for the good."

Emma could have said a lot more, but she thought her explanation enough for the time being. She might be able to explain, when they were looking at it, about the loss of all the earlier petitions; how only some of the signatures are searchable, as several pages were missing; who Sir John Hall was and his involvement; and so much more.

How Luke kept up with Rosie's 'energiser battery' was a mystery to Emma. She put it down to his cycling, something he did as often as he could. She happily let them go to the movies without her, on both occasions, and only managed some of Luke's list, as her spirits drooped further. She was more than tired. She felt heavy, as if each movement was a mammoth task.

The morning they planned to go to Zealandia, she'd barely been able to get out of bed.

Luke was so kind and understanding, she wanted to burst into tears, but she just nodded and accepted his offer. "You stay here and get some extra beauty sleep. Rosie and I have plans. Don't we?" He smoothed Rosie's hair back as she looked up at him so eagerly, Emma almost felt left out and not needed any more, which was ridiculous. "We'll go to the library this afternoon. Promise," he added as they raced out the door.

Emma had no idea what she expected, but she was blown away by the complexity and detail. The exhibition not only held the 1893 suffrage petition, but also the 1835 Declaration of Independence of the United Tribes and the 1840 Treaty of Waitangi.

Suddenly ashamed that she'd never taken the time to visit these defining documents of New Zealand's history before, she took in every aspect of the magnificent portraits of signatories to the documents, their biographies, the video clips and the wall plaques. She didn't need to explain anything. The exhibition did that for her.

Too soon, it was time to go. Rosie had skipped around the displays, taking in enough to give her an understanding but not enough to give her the deeper knowledge that Emma took from the visit. She'd loved it and it had given her vague ideas about a project she could possibly tackle in the future.

The following morning, they began their journey home. She was dreading the thought of long days in the car and having to force herself to make conversation. Her thoughts were so foreign, so frightening, how much longer could she pretend everything was okay?

As they were leaving, Luke added in another adventure. "Our next stopover is a secret. But on our way, I'm going to show you a windmill."

"Don't be silly, Dad," said Rosie. We don't have proper windmills. They're in Holland."

"Ah, but that's where you're wrong. We have loads of windmills. You see them all the time at the top of metal towers, going round and round, giving us power and water."

Rose still knew better. "They're called wind turbines, Dad. And they give us clean energy. Not like the ugly coal-burning power station in Huntly. We need to ban all fossil fuels and only use renewable energy."

Emma smiled at Rose's determined, if unformed, declaration. She'd obviously been talking with Jess, and the subject was clearly something they discussed at school.

"The small ones with vanes are still called windmills, honey, but I'm talking about a real windmill," smiled her dad.

Emma had to ask them to turn the radio down a couple of times as Rosie and Luke sang along to some song or other they both knew, but the pretence of wanting to do all these things, when all she wanted was to go home and be left alone, was taking its toll.

A short hour and a half later, Luke pulled off the main road in the township of Foxton and pointed. "There! What did I tell you?"

Rosie's mouth fell open. "It is a real windmill!" She was suddenly excited. "Can we go inside?"

"I believe so. Let's find out."

Luke parked outside the café and before long they were on the upper floors of the 17th-century replica flour mill. Emma was interested in how their speciality stoneground flour was made, while Rose tried out samples of the liquorice. The coffee was excellent and the baking delicious.

"Thanks, Dad, this was cool."

"Are you okay to go further?" asked Luke, checking on Emma's welfare. "It's about another two and a half hours to our next stop via the Paraparas, or we can stay out at the beach tonight if you'd prefer."

What could she say? In reality, the idea was depressing, but she had no option. "I'm fine. Let's keep going."

Maybe because she wasn't driving. Maybe because she had rested more since they'd been away. Maybe because time was passing and she was getting better. Emma didn't know the answer, but she enjoyed the journey. The scenery was beautiful and with less traffic on the road, she felt more relaxed. She had no idea what Luke had planned or really where they were heading. He wouldn't answer her questions.

They stopped a couple of times to take photos, before joining the main highway. Luke filled up with fuel at National Park Village, bought a drink and some chocolate for them all. Emma tilted her seat back and closed her eyes dozing off into uncomfortable dreams.

"Ems. Sweetheart. Look."

She opened her eyes. Her mouth fell open at the sight of the beautiful Chateau Tongariro before her. "Are we staying here?"

Luke nodded, grinning all the time.

"What a lovely surprise. Thank you. I've always wanted to come here. It's so gracious and old-worldly."

As they drew closer, she studied the four-storey colonial-style building with its distinctive blue roof, dark-red upper storeys, and mustard-yellow lower floors, which opened in 1929.

After parking the car and collecting their luggage, they passed between the Georgian-style columns supporting the upper balcony and into the grand foyer.

Emma felt she'd stepped back in time. "Oh, wow. Look at that," she sighed. Through the massive window, the view of the mountain was magnificent. Everywhere she turned, she glimpsed images of the stunning landscape or small corners of flora and fauna. A man played the grand piano in the graceful sitting area as they were shown their room, and Emma was overcome with a sense of timeless elegance in the red-velvet drapes and comfortable-looking furniture. "This is just lovely."

"Tomorrow, we can take the gondola up to the ridge …" Luke's voice faded into the background as he ran through his ideas, but Emma hardly heard him. Suddenly she felt she couldn't go on pretending any longer. Something had to change.

While Luke and Rosie fulfilled their plans, Emma sat by the huge picture window, staring at the mountain, contemplating her future. Complex emotions filled her mind as she staged an inner war. If this was her life, it wasn't fair on Rose and Luke. She couldn't encumber them like that. She hated the thought of being the nuisance who held them back. She railed against not being her normal self. To party if she felt like it, not that she did that much, but that wasn't the point. She rebelled against the thought of having to change her lifestyle and not be able to enjoy a glass of wine or indulge in great food any more. The small, silly things were building up to be big things in her mind. Insurmountable objects destroying the prospect of living what she'd considered her perfect life to the full.

The last few days had cemented her views.

The Chateau had been her treat, Luke's way of spoiling her, saying he loved her. Hobbiton was Rosie's. She'd adored every minute of the tour, giggling at the round doorways in the miniature houses set into hillsides, the quaint village settings, and The Green Dragon Inn. Although Luke was just as thrilled. He'd loved all *The Lord of the Rings* movies and the follow-ups, spin-offs and sequels. The pair were in their element.

By the time they had returned home on the first day of May, no one could argue the holiday hadn't been a huge success. Rosie was keen to tell Olivia all about it. Luke had a satisfied look about him.

"It's great to be home but wasn't that fun. We should do something like that every holidays. There so much to see in this country. The ocean, mountains, rivers, beaches, and all the history is sure to keep you writing for years to come."

His words tore at her. If the last few weeks had shown her anything it was that her work was over. She couldn't concentrate enough to do the research, and she struggled to bring the right words to her mind to create the story. Her life was irrevocably changed. All was lost.

And because of that, she decided she would leave. Leave her marriage. Leave her home. Leave the life she'd known.

Anything was better than seeing pity in Luke's eyes.

26

A moment of truth

August – September 1893

Why, oh why, is everything so hard? Just when I think we have won, we are once more at risk of being denied what we deserve. I will never understand the minds of men. What possessed Sir Robert to take up with the prohibitionists so volubly at a time when the franchise hangs in the balance? He cannot appease both sides. We are so close. So very close. I pray we shall not be defeated again.

Lucy paused in her writing. Winning the franchise had become even more personal and important to her since 'then'. She hated writing about it, thinking about it, but found it lingered in her mind, returned in her nightmares, and interfered with her relationship with Richard.

She loved him – she knew she did – but one moment she would yearn for his kiss and the next, shrink from his touch. Since the occasion in the carriage on the way back from the theatre, she'd avoided spending time with him, even with her father reading in the study across the hall.

Until yesterday …

"What is the matter, dearest Lucy?" Richard's voice was soft and gentle. "You seem so out of sorts these days."

"Do I?" she prevaricated. "I don't know why? But I am concentrating on the proceedings in Parliament. That has taken much of my attention."

"I can see that," he chuckled. "But I feel it is more than that. Have I done something to offend you?"

Lucy thought about it for a moment, wondering if she could invent a perceived offence to keep him at bay. He was such a wonderfully patient man, kind and considerate, wanting only to please her. But she had let him, and herself, down. Maybe she should call off their engagement altogether, until she could control her thoughts. "Not exactly. But I would like to consider delaying our nuptials – for a time, at least. Until I can settle to the idea and find time to make the necessary plans."

The distress that crossed his face almost made Lucy retract. She didn't want to cause him pain, but how could she face … She shuddered. Time was not dispelling her self-loathing. She didn't deserve his love.

"Are you cold?" Richard took her hand and led her closer to the fire. "You will be warmer here."

Holding her hands out to the heat, watching the flames leaping, Lucy valued his caring nature. She prayed she could train herself to accept his advances. She turned and suddenly he was there, up close beside her. His eyes burned like the flames in the hearth. Lucy gasped. He moved closer, a gentle finger on her chin. Involuntarily, she leant back a fraction, fighting the urge to run. The movement served to inflame him further, he gathered her in his arms and began to kiss her neck, her hair, her temple. Her arms, trapped between them, rested against his chest, but she had no voice. No words would come. Only a trembling in every pore. In her stomach and down her legs. What was happening to her?

"Lucy, my darling. Please, I beg you, don't delay our wedding. I could not bear it."

He kissed her lips, gently at first, then more probing, seeking her permission. One part of her said this was what she had always wanted, had yearned for. His kiss ignited feelings she didn't know existed. Another part, the rational, honest part of her, told her to deny her feelings, reject his avowal. He should not be dishonoured by her shame.

She attempted to push him away, but he held her tightly, kissed her more deeply, and sensations she didn't understand and had never experienced before stayed her flight. She staggered as he suddenly let go of her.

"Forgive me," he stammered, blushing to the roots of his hair. "I was forgetting myself. I should not have taken advantage of you like that until you are ready. It was most reprehensible of me." He picked up his hat from the table. "I will take my leave." With a curt bow, he disappeared through the door before she had gathered her wits …

As she sat at her writing desk, she wondered if she had any wits at all. Her dreams last night had been confused. Swirling from darkness to light, from dispirited to hopeful. No, hopeful was too definite, what was *possible* maybe. She'd woken in the middle of the night and lay there going over and over her plight. For months, disgust and loathing had been her companions, and rightly so. Shame was her burden. So why did she now feel a lightness she couldn't explain?

* * * * *

Her dilemma clung to her like a cloak. The same questions circled her brain day and night: should she speak up, or stay quiet? By the middle of the month, Lucy had reason to allow optimism to rise once more.

"What's this you're telling me?" she demanded of Milly as they walked back from church.

"I am surprised you haven't read it for yourself. Mr Shera –"

"Who is he? I don't know him."

"Me neither, but Grandma says he's an Auckland MP whose wife is part Māori."

Lucy nodded. "What about him?"

"It seems he put an amendment to the House that might just secure the franchise."

Lucy's hopes shot up. "How? I don't usually like amendments. They are often unfavourable. Why is this any different?"

Their steps had slowed to a dawdle as they talked. Milly put her hand on Lucy's arm and they stopped walking altogether.

Looking at her friend earnestly, Milly said, "I don't know the exact wording, but he has suggested the franchise should be extended to included Māori women."

Lucy frowned, considering the advantages. "I have no objections, but how does that advance our cause? After all, Māori are not always well regarded. Others might not be so agreeable towards the idea."

Milly nodded. "What matters is the House accepted it. I am told even Members who oppose the franchise voted for it, in the belief – mistaken, as it turns out – that extending the franchise would effectively kill the Bill. Except … remember those two councillors who voted against us previously …"

"Oh yes, the Honourable Mr Taiaroa and Major Rōpata," interrupted Lucy, who knew the names of all who voted against them. "What about them?"

"Will you stop chattering and let me tell you," scolded Milly. "Both men said they would support the franchise if it is extended to Māori women. So there you have it. Two more votes. Enough to sway it."

Lucy hugged her friend as they grinned and bounced on the spot, each as ecstatic as the other.

"We are going to win, Lucy. This time we will win."

A few days later, Lucy's optimism took another dip. The debate on the women's franchise had been adjourned because the order of papers to be debated clashed between the Houses. Sir Robert Stout's Licensing Control Bill had gained in importance, and she feared it would be muddled with the franchise and further antagonise the anti-prohibitionists against them.

And it is we women who will be held responsible, she silently fumed, as the arguments over the rights of itinerant workers, who may be away from home for long periods of time, continued. *What that has to do with women's franchise is beyond me.*

Would the shilly-shallying never end?

Thinking of which, she too needed to stop vacillating, sooner rather than later. She had not repeated her suggestion to Richard that they delay the wedding. Partly because he had aroused thoughts contrary to her feelings of alienation, and partly because her father would never allow it. He was firmly of the opinion that the Electoral Bill would pass and the vote for women would be won, and there was nothing to stop the wedding. How could she tell him otherwise?

Except she had yet to resolve her moral predicament.

By concealing the truth, she was destined to carry the sinfulness of perfidy on top of the burden of shame forever more. If she were to rid herself of one crime and confess her transgression, the burden of shame would remain but would be magnified tenfold by the contempt in which she would be held by those she loved, and the risk of damaging her father's business reputation would be too much to bear.

Either way, she was doomed.

* * * * *

Early September brought outrage, tempered only by relief, when news of Premier Seddon's perceived chicanery came to light.

"We shall be forever thankful," said Mrs Daldy at a hurriedly held meeting of the Franchise League ladies, "to Messrs William Reynolds and Edward Stevens. These two gentlemen are members of the Opposition who, upon hearing that Mr Seddon had prevailed upon Mr Thomas Kelly of Taranaki to vote against the franchise, changed their vote in our favour. They are to be congratulated for their morality. Thanks to them, the vote was successful and the Bill passed through the House of Representatives, twenty to eighteen."

Shouts of triumph and elation, and calls of 'shame on Mr Seddon' followed her explanation. Lucy was always astonished how forgiving and practical Mrs Daldy was, when she herself wanted to rage against the unfairness of it all. She struggled to come to terms with the lack of justice directed at women. Why should they always be so wronged? What was it about women that earned such disdain?

While her mind tussled with such questions, her heart remembered Richard treated her as something precious. Not as a chattel, but someone of value. She didn't believe Richard would renege on his word that she was an equal in his eyes. Could she use her position as his wife to further the cause for women? It might be possible if they won the franchise this time. She would think on it.

"To be fair," Mrs Daldy replied, raising her hand for quiet, "we always knew Mr Seddon was not entirely for us. He's long been known as strongly against prohibition, and the more our fellow franchise campaigners called for strict prohibition measures, the more weight was given to the Licensing Control Bill, and the more concerned he became about the franchise."

"But he was underhand," pointed out Mrs Collins.

"Possibly. Possibly not. He always promised us the Government would support women's franchise, and they have. We shall never know what was said to Mr Kelly to make him change his mind. All we know is that he did, and that would have been enough to tip the vote against us. However, let us not dwell on what may have been. The result is that the Bill has passed the House. Now we must wait for the Legislative Council to do the same."

Not everyone agreed with Mrs Daldy's charitable reasoning, and said so, but even they recognised that the Council had been the larger enemy and remained the stumbling block.

As the days passed, Lucy became more despondent, allowing her melancholy to overtake her enthusiasm. In her mind, all was lost.

27

A trip away

May 2022

The April school holiday trip meant Emma and Paige hadn't met for more than three weeks. The girl had texted a few times, one saying that Ryan was back earlier than expected and they were going well. She sounded keen, and excited to talk about her new discoveries. *As soon as you are back.*

Distracted by her internal conflict, Emma wasn't quite sure why she'd agreed to see Paige – although it was all part of tying up loose ends and putting her plan into action, but she felt detached, as if nothing mattered any more.

For early May, the weather was surprisingly warm. Staring out the French doors, watching the soft white clouds flow across the sky and hearing birds chirping in the garden, Emma listened, without interruption, to the girl's story.

"I'd never seen my Dad so … er … so, open, I suppose," said Paige, searching for the right words. "Vulnerable. He was hurting, and that's not like Dad. He's always so decisive and resolute."

None of it was helpful to Emma's task of tracing the women of the past, but she sensed it was a vital step in Paige's relationship with her father.

"We talked well into the night," continued Paige. "He drew me word pictures of my mum, recalling memories of her and me together. I just sat listening, scared to ask too many questions in case he shut down again and stopped talking. I was so young when she died I only have the odd fleeting feeling sometimes, but no memories. He let me see who she was as a mum."

While Emma listened to Paige recount some of the stories, she heard the wistful longing for all she'd missed from not having her mother in her life. In some ways, Emma drew parallels with her own mother. She'd been much older when her mother died, but they hadn't been close for years. At the time, the distance between them seemed right. Now, she wasn't so sure, and her resolve shifted. Could she do that to Rosie? She shook her head to clear the contrary thought. Of course Rosie would be better off without her, she rationalised. She was of no use to anyone.

"What surprised me most, though," said Paige, "was that Dad missed her too. I hadn't realised. He seemed so intent on his business, his associates, being surrounded by the right people, and having fun at parties, I'd always believed he was happy with the single, carefree life."

Paige's naivety was so obvious, Emma almost roared out loud. The girl had so much to learn about the complexity of relationships it was almost laughable. She had no idea what sort of front people could put up to safeguard themselves. *Like you are*, said a little voice in the back of her head. She brushed it aside.

Apart from the odd word of encouragement to show she was taking notice, Emma listened. Although her mind was on other things. Mostly on how she would find a way forward. Every time she was tempted to talk to Luke or Jess about her confused thoughts, as she'd promised, guilt stopped her. Their situation was all her fault. There was only one way she could see to prevent causing more pain.

"Anyway," said Paige, shifting her thoughts from the past into the present. "Something else happened that surprised me even more."

Emma watched the girl talking, but while her face and eyes were focused, her mind had again wandered to other things. She was startled by Paige's question.

"Emma, are you listening?"

"Yes, yes, of course. You were saying?"

"Dad. I thought we'd bonded in some way. I hoped we understood each other better. Which is why I was so shocked. I didn't know what to make of it. I still don't."

"Make of what?"

"David Frazer, the hard-nosed businessman announcing he's selling his fossil fuel shares to invest in clean energy."

Emma struggled to work out why Paige sounded so offended. "Isn't that what you wanted?"

"Except he's not doing it for any humanitarian or ethical reason. No, not my father. He's only in it for the money. Do you know what he said to me when I asked him why?" She didn't pause long enough for Emma to respond. "He said it made economic sense, as it was what people wanted. As long as he made money and could continue to provide us with the lifestyle we were used to, he'd happily make the right noises in the right places."

Paige was on her feet and pacing the room, too riled to sit still. "I couldn't believe I'd heard him correctly. After all I've said. After what Cameron said and – can you believe it? – he said Cam's ideas were fiscally sound whereas mine were emotional."

Emma could understand that reaction, the girl was so intense and passionate about the cause she so strongly believed in. The world needed people like her, but she'd need to learn to temper her arguments. Not everyone agreed or was as ardent.

"He's convinced nothing he does will make a scrap of difference to the planet either way, so why bother? I'm so angry. I don't know how to deal with it." She abruptly sat down again and stared fixedly at Emma as if she had the miracle answer. "What do I do?"

Emma chose her words carefully. "Don't take it personally. You've always known his views on money. But …" She paused, reshaping her thoughts. She didn't know this man beyond what Paige had told her, but she remembered Luke had liked him. "Are you sure about his motives? Have you considered it as his way of looking after you, of protecting you?"

"You're kidding me, right?" scoffed the young woman, not remotely interested in seeing a possible good side.

"No, I'm not. It might not be your way, but he knows money will buy you whatever you need in life. Sometimes even your health, or your child's. His child's."

Paige still looked unconvinced. "How did you come up with that rubbish?"

"Like I said before, by being a parent," Emma

answered, knowing her instinct to be correct. "Parents will do anything to safeguard their child." Was what she was contemplating going to safeguard Rosie? She had to stop this prevaricating; it wasn't helping.

She turned her thoughts back to Paige. "Try reaching him on that level. You made progress the night you asked him about your mum and the mums before her. Don't lose it all by fighting with him. If he doesn't believe he can do anything about climate change, then he won't. Antagonising him will only push him further away."

Emma wanted to say a lot more, but she was no counsellor. Neither was she in a position to give advice on people's motivations, but she had an idea. "Let me put it another way. You told me he missed your mum, that he felt he'd failed her and he'd promised to protect you, right?"

Paige nodded, her eyes flickering with memory.

"Does he invest in any health companies?"

A puzzled frown formed between Paige's brows. "Possibly. Cam said something about R & D portfolios. Why?"

Emma softened her voice. She didn't want to lecture, just plant seeds. "It sounds to me the reason money is important to him could be because of what happened in the past. If he thinks he failed your mum, does he blame himself for her death? Could he be spending money saving people rather than saving the planet?"

The expression on Paige's face changed. She was thunderstruck. "Are you suggesting my father might be a philanthropist?" She couldn't keep the disbelief from her voice. "Never in a million years."

Emma shrugged. "Ask him. You'll never know unless you ask. But that's enough home-grown wisdom for

267

one day," she said, pulling herself together. Charli had taught her the art of self-analysis, but right now she didn't like what she saw. "Now, after everything else, did your father tell you anything about the mums before yours?"

"Oh yes. That's what I came to tell you. You were right. The lady in the locket is Grandma Kate's mother. He thinks her name was Amy, but he's not sure. There were several in the family."

"Does he know anything about any protest activities?" Emma crossed her fingers for another clue.

"He says not, but I think he's lying."

* * * * *

Memories of the holiday quickly faded as Rosie skipped back to school and Luke cheerily returned to work. But Emma felt bereft. All she had was a feeling of failure and Paige's unresolved story to fill her days. Her fluctuating and inconsistent moods hindered her thinking. She had little enough to do, but even when she wasn't feeling wiped out, she had little interest in doing what needed to be done.

Luke and she were once again walking on eggshells around each other, trying not to say the wrong thing. Rosie was unsettled, tearful and sulky.

Overcome with the growing belief she was a drain on Luke and a worthless and ineffectual mother to Rose, she became more set in her view that the only way to solve the problem was to leave. To go somewhere until she was better or …

Did she think she was dying?

Her inner tussle intensified. She wished Charli was here. Someone she'd known for such a short time, and who had been the calming influence in her life. She'd understand what was going on with her. She'd guide her to making the right decision.

Looking back, Emma realised being the child of a somewhat unpredictable single mum had its flaws, but she'd mostly come through that unscathed, until later, much later. She was still angry with her mother for taking her own life. Angry at being cheated on by the first man she thought loved her, whom she had loved, at least to begin with. That was bad enough, but losing her first child was a trauma she would never truly recover from.

Each time, Emma blamed herself. If only she'd done something different. If only she'd known more about what was going on, she could have prevented it. If only … As she'd spun out of control, did some unforgivable things, said even more unforgivable words, she'd found Charli.

A memory flickered. She recalled a conversation they'd had. Charli had sent her off to do genealogy research. It had been the start of Emma's new career, and a way of coming to terms with the past and herself. Charli had hinted Emma's mother may have had undiagnosed and untreated depression. Charli understood depression. She had recognised the traits in Emma and led her to recovery. She'd saved her once before.

Thanks to Charli, she had Luke. The man who truly loved her, who'd given her Rose, who had given her the perfect life. So why did she now want to leave him?

To protect him, she answered vehemently, self-loathing rising. He didn't deserve to be punished for her state of mind. She didn't deserve him.

But every time she thought about the reality of leaving, fear stopped her.

The last thing Luke had said to her echoed in her brain. 'Get help, Ems. I beg you, get help.'

28

A dilemma

September 1893

The next day, Mrs Adams was of a different view. All was not lost. "Lucy, child. You are too decent for your own good. Nothing is that straightforward in life." She poured the tea and offered a biscuit.

Lucy shook her head. She was too upset to eat. "But if I hadn't disobeyed my father and gone out alone, I wouldn't be in this position," she argued, adding to her contrition. The more her father pressured her to set a date for their wedding, the more fearful Lucy became of Richard discovering her secret.

"Tut, tut," clicked the older woman. "Have you always so readily obeyed your father in all things at all times?"

Lucy blushed. "Not always. I've often challenged him and gone contrary to his wishes."

"Exactly my point. Now listen to me, my girl. I've not always been considered a lady, but my Sid didn't care. He made sure I was accepted in society by toadying up to them who needed something from him. Business is

271

business, he always used to say. Now I've got money, they are all over me and don't care where I came from."

"But, I don't see how …"

"Shush, girl. Listen. You admitted going out alone, in the rain. You said you'd fallen, which you did. You said you'd asked for my help, which I gave. What lie did you tell?"

"I didn't tell them about …"

"But did you lie about it?"

Uncertainly, Lucy shook her head.

But Mrs Adams hadn't finished. "Are there other things in your heart you have not told your father or anyone else about?"

This time Lucy nodded. "My dreams and hopes. I'm scared if I share them, they will not come true."

"And where do you keep these ideals?"

"In my journal. Why?"

"You'll see. Has anyone asked you about these private thoughts? The things you are hiding?"

Right then, Lucy saw the parallels in what Mrs Adams was suggesting. "I don't think anyone knows I keep a journal."

Mrs Adams seemed pleased. "And do you consider that to be lying?"

Lucy allowed herself a little reprieve. "No, I suppose I don't. They are my thoughts. My frustrations. If I choose to share them, I will, but I don't believe I have to."

Mrs Adams sighed in satisfaction and reached across the table, tapping her hand as she spoke. "You might have omitted to tell them certain details, but that is not the same as lying. You," she pointed, eyeballing Lucy, enunciating each word, "did not do anything wrong. Do you understand?"

Lucy nodded, too conflicted to contradict.

"Stop being so hard on yourself. We women do that, you know. We accept blame even when the fault is not ours. Do not let those minutes that man stole from you destroy the rest of your life. He's not worth it."

Lucy let her eyes wander around the now-familiar room. Since 'that day', she had come to understand the importance of having a woman in her life, something she hadn't even known she missed until now. Here she felt comforted, succoured even. Mrs Adams knew her secrets. There was no need to pretend or hide with her. She was someone Lucy could talk to about her innermost feelings. She knew what it was like to be a young woman, confused about much while yearning to be grown-up and estimable in her own right. Would that ever happen to her now?

As if reading her thoughts, Mrs Adams said, "You need to begin creating that life you've always dreamed of."

Lucy bit her lip. She had come here today with intent. She wanted to ask questions, but she was now overcome with embarrassment. How could she ever lead up to something so private?

Hesitantly, she asked, "Do you have children? A daughter, like me, maybe?"

"No, my dear, we were not blessed." Mrs Adams suddenly rose from the table and bustled about clearing the teacups and refilling the kettle. "But my Sid and I had each other, and that was all we needed."

"May I ask something very personal?" Lucy cast her eyes down, unable to look at her companion.

"There's no secrets between us. What do you want to

know?" Mrs Adams sat in her armchair and picked up her knitting, letting Lucy talk.

"I know you are saying I shouldn't allow myself to be weighed down by guilt for disobeying my father or that I withheld something since I didn't actually lie about it. Those are burdens I can put down. And I will try. But I can't undo …" Lucy sucked in her breath. Even thinking about it set her into a flutter. "I … I feel … One time, our carriage lurched and Richard toppled over me. I was so frightened. I panicked and screamed at him to get away. I couldn't bear him to touch me. Will that ever pass?"

"I can't guarantee it, but I do know that time lessens all suffering."

Lucy wondered what Mrs Adams had suffered in the past for her to sound so sure. She began to tell her about the moment with Richard in the parlour. "Sometimes Father leaves us to talk while he works in the study. I had just told Richard I wanted to delay the wedding. I didn't think I could ever … that I was ready … Thinking I was shivering with the cold, he led me to the fire, where he … um … kissed me."

Lucy looked up to see if Mrs Adams was shocked at her revelation, but she carried on knitting, saying nothing.

"All these months, I've only felt revulsion. Sickening and unbearable, hating myself but …" Lucy's voice dropped to a whisper. "That moment stirred up something I've not felt before. I didn't want it to stop."

She heard Mrs Adams chuckle and looked up at the smiling face turned towards her. "It's called love, my dear. Let me guess, you felt an unexplained longing, tingles like goose pimples, throbbing and aching in places you are too shy to mention." The woman raised a questioning eyebrow. Lucy blushed. "It is perfectly normal, child, and tells me you love this young man, and he loves you. That is something very precious. Don't throw it away."

Shocked, Lucy stammered. "How …?"

"How do I know what you experienced? Because it happened to me. Sid and I weren't blessed with children, but we were blessed with love. And love, good love, heals all wounds."

"Are you saying that it's …" Again Lucy was lost for words. She didn't know how to express her feelings.

"Acceptable? Normal? Not only that, it is natural, it is life-changing. It is unique. It binds you one with the other. And so much fun."

Mrs Adams laughed at the colour infusing Lucy's entire body as she went on to describe what Lucy could expect … and more. "Don't look so surprised." Her voice softened. "You are meant to enjoy life. The burden of guilt is laid upon women from an early age. We are taught that we are weak-willed, evil creatures, easily swayed by temptation." Mrs Adams's face darkened, the smile disappeared and a fierceness shone in her eyes. "Except when men do more than tempt. They abuse us. Betray us. Blame us. And throw us onto the trash heap."

Lucy didn't know how to respond. She had never heard a woman speak so before. Silence fell between them as Mrs Adams rose and stared out the window. She angrily wiped the bench and threw the cloth into the sink.

"Let me tell you a secret." She turned to look at Lucy with determination. She stood with her back against the benchtop, arms folded, calmer but tense. "I was younger than you. Far younger. My – no, he's not worthy of the title – the brute who forced himself upon my mother and produced me also decided I was fair game. I never told anyone. He was a respected, well-dressed church-going man, and a senior clerk. Who would believe me?" She paused, clenching her jaw. The pain as evident today as it had been at the time. "When he was caught out, he threw me onto the streets, shouting vile obscenities. I was sixteen."

She held her hand up to prevent Lucy interrupting. She took a deep breath before continuing. "So you see, I understand every thought and feeling you are struggling with. I understand the shame warring with injustice. You are faultless, yet you accept responsibility. I recognise your dilemma, which is why I'm telling you to grasp what is being offered with both hands."

Lucy covered her mouth. Never guessing for one moment that this well-dressed woman who appeared to be the epitome of a wealthy Victorian lady, carried such a secret.

"Did you tell your husband?" Lucy desperately needed to know the answer. It was the most difficult choice she had yet to make. The one that was eating her up.

Mrs Adams didn't answer the question directly. "I moved towns, more than once. No one asked any questions. I was a waif, a stray. Nobody cared as long as I did whatever work I could find, and kept out of the way."

Lucy listened in silence, hanging on every word, hoping with each pause and each stare into the past, that she would continue.

"Then I met Sid. When he found out I could read and write, he offered me a job in his grocery store, doing his books. He was nice. He had lovely eyes and an open heart. We used to talk sometimes. He would ask me what I wanted from life, strange stuff. Nobody had cared about what I wanted before. Nobody cared what women thought back then. They had their role and were expected to do it. But not him. He treated me differently right from the start."

Mrs Adams tilted her head up, looking beyond the ceiling to whatever she saw in her mind's eye. "Then things changed between us. We laughed a lot. I began to feel safe around him. I had never felt safe before. I trusted no one. I knew he was older than me but that didn't matter, not until the end. He was gentle, soothing, encouraging. One day he kissed me. Just like your young fellow kissed you."

The pauses were getting longer and Lucy became more pent up. She so wanted to hear Mrs Adams's story. To understand everything about what had happened so she could compare it to her situation. Was there hope for her after all?

"We lay together before we wed. I didn't have to tell him anything. He knew I was damaged. He knew I was filled with self-loathing, but there was a connection between us that transcended everything. I couldn't have children because of what had been done to me, but it didn't matter. Our love was all that mattered. Love is all that ever matters," she said wistfully.

She suddenly sprang back into life, bustling around the kitchen, putting the kettle on, gathering the bread and slicing it. "You should eat something. I've cold meat, and cheese and pickle."

Lucy didn't care what she ate. "Thank you. For trusting me with your secret. I would never have known."

Business-like now and to the point, Mrs Adams replied, "That's what happens when you are seen as respectable. My Sid, God rest his soul, sold up after we wed and moved us here. He set up another business. He was well liked and his business grew, he became a respected and an active member of the community, which made me respectable. We were invited to join their social circle and his influence grew. He prodded me to become who I am today. He left me too soon, but he healed my wounds. Let your young man heal yours."

29

Jess steps in

June 2022

As the weeks went by, Emma found Paige's continuous remarks about Ryan and the wonderment of young love touching. Nonplussed by her growing sentiment, she began to recall her fledgling romance with Luke. After Charli died, they'd viewed each other with a new perspective. No longer as threats or intruders, but as two people sharing common threads of grief and loss. They'd talked for hours, laughing over stories of Charli and her indomitable, if somewhat irascible nature. They'd fallen in love and their future seemed certain – until recently.

Not wanting to irritate Luke more than necessary, she stopped inviting Paige to her office. But with the rise in new Covid infections, she was cautious about going to crowded cafés, afraid to catch a second dose. Taking advantage of the pleasant day, Emma suggested meeting Paige at the beach. For early winter, it was surprisingly balmy.

"I have to pinch myself sometimes," said Paige as they sat under the shade of the trees, looking out across the almost deserted sand to the grey-green ocean beyond. "He's so clever, but he treats me as if I matter, as if my ideas matter. We don't always agree, but he never makes me feel like I'm silly or stupid or something."

"That's how it should be." Emma's voice was muted as her mind drifted. The beach seemed a good option, but now they were here, Emma realised she was simply prolonging the inevitable.

"Like the other day, we were chatting about Dad," the girl's voice floated past. "I was still fuming about his disregard of the science, but Ryan challenged my thinking. He said the fact that Dad had agreed to invest in clean energy was a win, regardless of his reasons. It was okay if money was his driver, as long as the beneficiary was the planet. The way he put it made sense, and I felt better after."

The sudden waves of exhaustion Emma had experienced had eased since their road trip, but the despondency that lingered left her as drained and confused as ever. If Paige noticed, she didn't appear concerned, and kept talking through the silence.

"I know you said the same thing in a different way, that I should give Dad a chance, so I'll try. Ryan's so optimistic about everything, I'm finding it harder to be so downhearted about things. I could listen to him talk for hours."

And on she went; about his eyes, his mouth, the way his fingers on her skin sent shivers down her spine. The way he made her laugh; how she longed to be with him every minute of the day. How they loved the same foods, shared the same taste in music, and wanted to travel.

As Paige talked, Emma relived those early days with Luke, allowing herself to fall in love again with the man he had been, the woman *she* had been. Travelling from place to place had never been on her radar. She'd moved around so much as a child, all she wanted was to stay put. Luke had wanted to establish himself in the industry first, not as a reminder of his father, but in his own right, before they ventured overseas. They still had plans to visit certain sights and countries when the time was right. What would happen to those plans now? Doubts settled in her mind as her heart reached out for the good times they'd shared, and for the life they had built.

"That sounds wonderful, Paige. I'm really happy for you."

But those days had gone. She battled to reconcile her selfish desire to be loved, to feel secure, with her obligation to protect the two people she loved the most.

Paige interrupted her self-absorption. "Have you found out anything more about my grandmothers?"

Another layer of guilt settled over her. She'd not even looked. She had her notes, and all her suspicions and calculations written up, but she'd done nothing for ages. "Sorry. No. I've been …" What was her excuse? "Busy." Hardly an excuse, and not even the truth.

Paige shrugged. "No worries. They aren't going anywhere."

Emma was flummoxed by the girl's sudden pragmatism. Maybe Ryan would bring out the best in her. She hoped so. Paige deserved so much more.

That niggling voice challenging Emma's every thought asked, *Why is Paige deserving while you are not?*

"How's Cameron?" asked Emma, attempting to divert her thoughts.

Paige laughed, a joyous tinkly laugh that spoke of hope. "There must be something in the water, cos he's good. We're good." She sounded amazed. "He brought his girlfriend, Nicole, to dinner the other day. First he's ever brought home, as such. He's always had girls hanging around, or a showpiece to bring to all of Dad's business dos, but never someone serious."

"And you think this might be serious?"

"Quite possibly. I liked her. She's bright and doesn't take Cam's cheek. She'll give as good as she gets."

"What's her line of work?"

"She's a planning consultant." Paige laughed again. "She wants to specialise in environmental protection, but she's got more quals to get first. Dad almost choked on his dinner. He'll think we're ganging up on him."

"Aren't you?"

"Not me. But reality will."

* * * * *

Later that afternoon, sitting in the armchair in her office Emma heard voices. It sounded like Jess dropping Rosie off after school. Before she'd had a chance to put away her notebook, listing all the pros and cons of her dilemma, and had stood up, Jess was in the room, shutting the door behind her. Emma quailed under her gaze.

"What's going on?" Jess demanded, leaning her back against the door.

"Nothing. Why?" She tried for nonchalant but sounded defiant.

"Don't give me nothing." Jess took a breath and lowered her voice. "It's not nothing, Ems. And it's been going on for too long. You promised you'd talk to me if there were issues. Well, I see issues, so talk."

Emma subsided into her chair, looking anywhere but at Jess as she tried to gather her thoughts. She wasn't ready to put it into words. She watched Jess pull a chair up in front of her, just like *she*'d done, in reverse, when her friend had been troubled.

"Let's start at the beginning, shall we?"

"Where's that exactly?" said Emma testily.

"I don't actually know. But let's start with when you had Covid."

Emma dismissed it as unimportant. "It wasn't that bad, I was just tired."

"Yep, and when did you stop being tired?"

She shrugged. "I'm okay now."

Jess was open-mouthed, but simply said, "Could've fooled me. And everyone else around you. But let me tell you what I see, before you start making excuses." She leant forward, elbows on knees, trying to get closer. "Late January, you caught Covid, isolated, and slept most of the time. You recovered, except you didn't. You kept on being tired. No, more than tired, exhausted. You pretended not to be, but we all knew. You complained of brain fog, you ran out of energy and spent a lot of time wrapped in your own little world. The Emma we all know and love disappeared. With me so far?"

Emma kept her head down, folding and unfolding the hem of her T-shirt. There was nothing she could say.

"You were moody and bad-tempered. You complained you had too much on your plate, but you've finished Ruby's story, declined any further clients, and Paige's history still isn't finished. I know, she rang me. She's worried there's something wrong, too."

Emma shook her head. "Nah, she's fine. I was talking to her this morning, she never said anything."

"Not to you, maybe. But I haven't finished. Let me see which came first, the visit to the doctor …" Jess was still ticking off the sequence on her fingers.

"Who had no idea about anything," snapped Emma.

"But then you fainted. Remember that? At the café. Scared the hell out of Paige, and all of us. You ended up in hospital, Ems, for Pete's sake."

"They said I was a bit run-down, that's all."

Jess sat centimetres away, willing her to see reason. "Really? The last conversation we had, you lost it. I told you Rose was upset, and you screamed at me. Well, let me tell you something, Rosie is now more than just upset and you're going to listen to me whether you like it or not."

Emma could tell Jess was pushed to her limit. She was trying to stay calm, but she'd always been the more 'heart-on-her-sleeve' of the two of them.

"Your husband is a saint. He's so loyal it'd be sickening if it wasn't so heart-warming and reassuring. I had to prise it out of him what you've been like. You should thank your lucky stars you have him."

Jess's words hit a chord. That was exactly what she'd been saying to herself: he was too good for her; she didn't deserve him; he'd be better off without her. Tears began to roll down her face. Jess grabbed the tissues off the desk and plonked them on her lap.

With a gentler voice, she continued. "Both the doctor

and the hospital said if your symptoms didn't improve you should go back to them. I know you haven't, despite all of Luke's pleading. Worse still, he says he can't reach you any more. It's like you've put up a barrier. You stare at him vacantly, letting his words wash over you. You're distant and you shut yourself away. Ems, you need help. Please, let me help."

Emma grabbed more tissues, mopped up her eyes and blew her nose, but still avoided looking at Jess. Everything Jess had said only served to confirm her worst fears and greatest doubts. "It's all my fault." She took a deep breath. "I'm not worthy of any of you."

"What on earth are you talking about? Of course you're worthy."

Emma shook her head again, her mouth in a tight line. She forced herself to glare at her friend, determined to say her piece. If she had doubts before, they had completely gone. She knew what she had to do to safeguard her family and friends.

"No I'm not. And that's why I've decided I'm leaving. I'm going away. Leaving you all to get on with your lives without me weighing you down."

Jess's face was like thunder. "Like hell you are!"

30

Prevarication

September 1893

Lucy remained in a quandary. Since her surprising conversation with Mrs Adams, who had presented her with more possibilities to consider, she knew she was avoiding the situation. She justified pushing it into the background because she considered there were more important events going on around her.

The toing and froing in Parliament seemed to go on forever. Day by day she read each and every report – anything to take her mind off the real issue – as more amendments were put and defeated. Appeals requesting the Bill be pulled were dismissed. New arguments, that in reality were a rewording of old arguments, were presented and repudiated. She tired of the same angry exchange of views, the same insulting and humiliating remarks, the same wasted energy.

Until the 8th of September.

"Don't get too excited, ladies," said Mrs Daldy while she and her inner cohort shared tea. "While the third reading of the Bill was passed through the

Legislative Council – thanks be the Lord – it is still to be assented."

"But surely, that is just a formality, isn't it?" asked Lucy, followed by similar mutterings.

"I pray you are right. But we have been disappointed so often, I cannot allow myself to celebrate until that assent is received. And …" Mrs Daldy's voice trembled, the strain of the last months, if not years, taking its toll. "If, and I do emphasise *if*, so you may not be further disappointed. It may well not happen before this election, which means the opportunity for us to exercise our vote will be delayed for several years. And who knows what may happen in those intervening years."

Milly clutched Lucy's hand. "Grandma is putting up such a brave face, but she is exhausted. I don't know how many more setbacks she can take."

"Milly, dear. She knows she has our support. She will hold up, I'm sure." Lucy hoped to offer comfort to her friend, but she understood how continued failure drained a person's energy. "Father assures me assent will be a matter of course." She kept the news about renewed counter-efforts to herself. Every day brought new aggressions, further doubts and increased efforts designed to defeat them.

Lucy struggled to maintain her equilibrium, pretending that all was well. At the breakfast table, where she and her father started their day and talked more freely, he asked if she was well.

"I'm just so exhausted by all the setbacks, Father. But I am well within myself."

He had stared at her with a puzzled frown but didn't say anything further. She was glad Milly had become her almost constant companion of late, enabling her to push her dark thoughts away.

Four days later, Lucy's heart lifted once again. A deputation from the Wellington Women's Franchise League had presented white camellias with a note of appreciation to each of the 20 members of the House of Representatives who had voted in favour of women gaining the vote.

"What a lovely touch," she said. "Beautiful white camellias, a symbol of purity, of gentleness and womanhood. Don't you just love them?" She spoke the words without thinking, but no sooner were they out of her mouth than she thought how unfitting she was to wear the symbol herself.

"Yes, I do. And did you hear," asked Milly, nodding in agreement, "the Auckland ladies are planning to attend the arrival of representatives returning from Wellington to present them with more gifts of camellias to extend their thanks?"

"I did. I wouldn't miss it for the world."

Not to be outdone, a matter of days later the Wellington anti-Women's Franchise League presented a basket of red camellias tied with red ribbon to those men who had voted against the franchise to wear in their coat buttonholes.

Lucy was dumbfounded, and disillusioned that such a league existed. "Will the hostility never end?" she moaned to Milly and all who would listen to her.

The following day, they were met with the news that errors had been discovered, and that misplaced and missing words had put the Bill in jeopardy. On top of that, as Lucy had suspected, a 'no wine, no women' slogan had appeared in the newspapers. It strongly suggested that the Licensing Control Bill and the Electoral Bill had became so entwined that one bill was reliant on the other.

"I can't stand it any longer," said Milly. "My nerves are on edge. Why is it taking so long for assent to be secured?"

Lucy's nerves were at breaking point, too. "I can only tell you what I've read, which you yourself have read. There's a number of bills being debated and passed that Parliament wants to put through at the same time for signing. It's not about the franchise."

The days passed, energy-sapping days. Women met in groups, at meetings, in the street, after church, in houses, decrying the delay, showing unity and offering encouragement and support to each other.

"Have faith," they said as they put forward ideas of renewed action and handed out camellias.

Have faith. The words echoed inside her head. *Have faith.*

* * * * *

"At last!" whooped Lucy, as she and Milly held hands, jumping for joy.

On Tuesday 19th September, The Electoral Act, 1893 was assented and New Zealand women became the first in the world officially granted the franchise.

"Finally," repeated Lucy. "We've won!" Mrs Adams had been right; all was not lost after all.

Similar expressions of joy, from the polite and restrained, to the relieved and ecstatic, were exhibited in drawing rooms up and down the country. Little else made the newspaper headlines. Women gathered wherever they could to celebrate together. Meetings were called, prayers were given, speeches were made. The leaders of the movement from the most senior to the lowliest were acknowledged. Sir John Hall, Sir George Grey and others who had led the charge were honoured. Jubilation filled their hearts.

But their work had not finished. The very next day, even the newspapers were beseeching women on all fronts, with every ounce of strength and energy and fortitude they had thus far displayed, to renew their campaign to register.

Mrs Daldy gathered her team. "Our task now is to ensure the women of this country are registered and ready. To fulfil our responsibility to the cause, we must now encourage every woman to put her name down on the electoral roll."

Blocking her mind to her personal difficulties, Lucy threw herself into the next task. There was no time to lose. The election date had been announced for 28th November. A short ten weeks in which to gather enrolments.

Day after day, wanting to be around other women, celebrating their success and sharing their sense of oneness with others, Lucy and Milly attended all the meetings that had been called. They collected the new registration forms and delivered the papers to shopkeepers, churches and numerous other establishments where women could enrol. The newspapers urged women to record their names at the post office, at the city council offices or any other place where they could fill in the forms, constantly emphasising the urgency, due to the time limit imposed.

If the girls were surprised at the level of activity, they had no time to discuss it. Electioneering had started in earnest. Men who intended to stand again for Parliament singled out those most likely to vote for them. The women's vote was particularly sought after.

During the day, Lucy kept herself too busy to think. It was the night-time, when she lay alone in her bed, that her thoughts crashed around her. She couldn't put it off any longer. A decision was needed.

* * * * *

"Lucy, my dearest darling Lucy. I am a patient man. I have shown great restraint and gone along with your wishes, but the vote is won, my love. You have won. Now, will you do me the honour of marrying me?" His eyes burned with desire and wishfulness across the distance between them in the parlour.

Quickly, before she changed her mind, again, she agreed. "Yes, Richard, I will marry you."

He reached out to take her in his arms, but she stepped back, with a hand up to stay him. "But first, there is something you should know. I am … shall we say," she swallowed the lump in her throat, "let me say, I do not believe I warrant the esteem you shower me with. I am an imperfect being."

"What are talking about?" A frown marred his elegant face. "No one is perfect. We all have flaws. But I know yours." He winked giving her a cheeky grin. "And I'd like to get to know them better."

When Lucy made no attempt to join in his light-hearted teasing, he modified his approach. "What makes you think you are so imperfect? Or that I am not?"

Lucy ignored the leading question. "Please, Richard, don't ask me for details. Just know that I love you and I am asking you to love me in return."

"I have always loved you, Lucy. Have you ever doubted that?"

He took a step towards her, but she turned and moved to the other side of the room. She couldn't welcome his embrace until she had said what she needed to say.

She took a deep breath to calm her nerves. "I am asking you to have faith in me. There is something I can never share with you. If you are prepared to live with the knowledge that I cannot be completely honest with you about this one thing, then yes, I will marry you. If not, then we must part. The burden is mine, not yours. I will be true to you in all ways except this."

He looked bewildered and completely at a loss. "I don't understand. A secret? Whose secret?"

"I can't answer that. Just accept I am not everything you would wish for in a wife."

"Don't be ridiculous. You are wonderful. Beautiful, kind, sometimes spirited, but someone who believes in doing what is best. We will be a great team." He paused, clearly perplexed. "Is there someone else?"

Tears filled Lucy's eyes. She shook her head vehemently. "No," she promised. "And never will be. I love only you." She saw the relief in his face before the next thought crossed his mind.

"Does anyone else know this secret?"

She hedged, deciding if she could at least confess that part. "One other. Mrs Adams."

She saw him register the interrelationship.

"Do you not trust me? Is that the problem."

"Of course not," she hurried to reassure him. "I trust you with my life. From this day forward, I promise I will share everything with you. It is you who needs to trust me."

Hands folded in front of her, resting modestly against her skirt, she waited, watching him looking at her, his mind reflected in the turmoil in his eyes.

When he did not immediately answer, Lucy added, "Mrs Adams has become a staunch friend and will remain so until the day we are parted. She is the embodiment of the mother and grandmother I never knew, and I can never divulge what we discuss."

She watched him consider what she had said. She hadn't tried to conceal she had something to hide, she had simply asked him to trust her. She held herself taut, controlling the fluttering and trepidation that threatened to undo her.

What he said next would determine her future.

31

When there is hope

June 2022

"Come with me." Jess was as mad as Emma had seen her. She grabbed Emma's wrist, dragged her from her chair, through the kitchen, out the front door and pushed her into the car.

One part of her rebelled. It was none of Jess's business. Another part surrendered. She didn't know which way to turn. The constant fear of not being in control had spiralled until she no longer had control.

Emma sat in the passenger seat feeling numb.

"We are going to sort this if it's the last thing we do," stated Jess, driving through the streets.

Emma had no idea where they were headed, but it was clear Jess did.

Shortly after, Jess pulled up in a car park and turned towards Emma. Her voice softened, the anger gone. "I didn't mean it to happen this way. I wanted to tell you more gently and kindly what we've done, completely without your permission, and persuade you around to our way of thinking."

"What is this place?" asked Emma, fear etching her features, her hands gripped tightly in her lap.

"Somewhere I hope you'll find someone who can help you. Will you at least give it a go? For my sake. For Luke's and Rosie's?"

Emma looked at Jess, seeing concern and love. She nodded.

Together, they went inside. Emma looked back at Jess sitting in the waiting-room chair, next to the obligatory palm in a pot, as she followed the psychologist into her office.

"I can't explain these thoughts," she said to the genial woman before her. "I was just tired. So very tired that I couldn't think straight. I began to worry there was something seriously wrong with me."

"… And because no one could identify anything specific, you searched for information online. Not a wise thing to do."

Emma nodded, accepting the quiet reprimand. "I became convinced I had a brain tumour, or a chronic illness or … something that would mean I was no longer the person I used to be. I couldn't bear the thought. I had no idea how to handle it and, and I didn't want to be a burden on Luke and Rosie, so I thought …" She couldn't put her finger on what she thought, only that running away seemed her only solution.

"I can tell you what you thought, and why. The only way to cope with the unknown is to deny it, to run away from it, but you were held back by logic. Leaving your family didn't make sense. So you began to blame yourself. Believing you were making their lives miserable so you had to punish yourself to save them."

Emma stared at the woman who had put months of fear into a few words.

"It's not uncommon, and what you're feeling is quite normal in these circumstances. But let me tell you, you have nothing to worry about," the counsellor reassured.

Hope began to flare inside Emma, where dread had resided for so long. She listened to the woman, clinging to her every word, as she explained what Emma was experiencing. She wasn't dying. She wasn't suffering from an incurable illness. "And I'll recover?"

The woman smiled. "You should. How long the medication I'm about to prescribe will take to settle in and reduce your anxiety, I can't be certain. But we'll keep an eye on you."

The counsellor escorted her out to the waiting room where a worried Jess glanced between the two, seeking reassurance.

Emma felt as if a great load had been lifted off her shoulders and all she wanted to do was tell Luke. "Can we go home now?"

The welcome home was better than she expected. Luke and Jess were beaming. The three of them sat in the lounge, where the late-afternoon sun still streaked across the floor. Rose and Olivia were happily ensconced in Rosie's bedroom 'doing whatever young girls do', according to Luke. A vase of flowers had appeared on the coffee table, and Luke presented her with a box of chocolates and a pampering voucher at a nearby spa.

As they munched on the chocolates, he and Jess confessed how they'd cooked up the plan to get help for her, setting up several appointments with a psychologist in advance, hoping to persuade Emma to seek help.

They'd provided the clinician with a potted history of Emma's life, which is why she knew how to approach their first meeting.

"We only want what's best for you, sweetheart," said Luke, apologising for not telling her beforehand. "I hope you see that."

"Yes, sorry for going behind your back," agreed Jess, "but we couldn't see any other way of getting you to agree."

The diagnosis came that she was suffering from severe depression, triggered by long Covid. The stress of being ill, combined with exhaustion, had sparked a psychological response and set off a chain reaction that recalled all her past traumas, and her body had shut down to protect her.

"Including all that angst my family tree caused you," said Jess. "Simple explanation, when you know. And I'm sorry I added to it."

"But you're not out of the woods yet," Luke reminded them. "This level of anxiety doesn't just go away, but now we know what the problem is, we can tackle it together."

He sat beside her on the couch and wrapped his arm around her. "Are you listening to me, Ems? We do this together. No more shutting yourself away. No more dreaming up hare-brained schemes. No more self-blame. None of it is your fault. Do you hear me?"

Emma could only nod. Her eyes filled with tears of love and exhaustion, of relief and forgiveness. "Thank you," she whispered. "Thank you for caring."

Within a few days, now that the terrifying weight had been lifted and with the help of the medication, Emma began to feel more like her normal self. She agreed to follow the self-help suggestions about routine, diet and exercise and allow herself time to heal. It would take time.

But it wasn't only time that would heal her, it was love. Luke's love.

* * * * *

"You look brighter," said Paige rushing through the French doors into the warmth of Emma's library, stripping off her wet-weather gear as she came.

Hurrying her inside, Emma took her wet coat to hang up on the antique coat hooks on the back of the door and assured her she was feeling better.

"I'm glad," said Paige. "You had me worried."

Emma smiled inwardly. She'd had herself worried, let alone everyone around her.

"Thanks. Me too. And now I'm looking forward to finally solving your puzzle."

Emma had persuaded Luke she enjoyed having Paige around and wanted to work on the girl's history. She couldn't just stop her life and sit around waiting to feel better. She'd already done that and it hadn't helped. She needed the stimulus.

"What news do you have?" asked Emma, settling in her chair while Paige curled up in the wingback.

"Nothing really. I'm sure Dad's hiding something. He evaded all my questions about what he meant by my grandmothers being troublemakers. He told me they were 'women like you who ask too many questions'. I know he was teasing, but he still wouldn't tell me anything. I know he doesn't like me nosying into his business dealings. Maybe men have always thought that about their wives and daughters. Poor feeble creatures that we are, can't cope with the difficult things in life."

"Possibly," agreed Emma, ignoring the sarcasm and thinking exactly the opposite. Men who treated their women as second-class citizens either had something to hide or serious ego issues, in her opinion. None of which sounded like Dave Frazer. There had to be another reason. Changing the subject, she asked, "What's your views on women who go against the norm?"

"How'dya mean?"

"Like, women who don't marry, illegitimate children, same-sex relationships, women doing men's work. That sort of thing."

Paige hitched her shoulder. "Who cares? We can do whatever we like. It's our bodies, our lives. Why?"

"Can we, though? What about all the racism and sexism we hear about from the workplace to home, and within certain religions, and in other countries? Or how the disabled are shut out?" Emma paused briefly, realising she'd nearly become a victim of categorisation herself. Another woman with an unseen disability because of an illness few understood. "Can we do as we like? Or are we all bound by certain covert rules of behaviour? Is it different in our country than others? Do women of colour fare better or worse than us?"

Emma sparked a forthright response in Paige, who had loads of opinions and wanted to express them all. For a time, they debated the political upheavals in the States, the war in Ukraine, the religious and cultural struggles of the Middle East, the numerous refugees fleeing their own country to seek a better life in another, touching briefly on the #MeToo and #BlackLivesMatter protests.

Emma thoroughly enjoyed the conversation with an intelligent and well-informed young woman. Not that they were going to solve the world's problems in one conversation. Emma was simply trying to gauge Paige's belief system and how she – or her father, for that matter – would respond to what she was about to tell them.

"So, *if* I discover something about your grandmothers, secrets they kept because it broke the mores of society as they knew them, how upset would you or your father get?"

She thought for a moment before answering. "I have no idea. But if you're asking me, then I'd love to know about the secrets of the past. I think it would be fascinating and show what sort of people they were. But Dad? Hmm. I think he's one of those in the 'need-to-know' school of thought."

As Emma had expected. Now she was in a predicament. She had information Paige wanted, but if she told Paige, then her father would not be happy and it could cause more issues between them.

"Tell me more about the badges," asked Paige. "Can I see them?"

"Of course. They're yours." Emma opened a drawer and withdrew the trinket box and handed it to Paige. She had long since removed the tags. She had it all recorded in writing and in photographs. "Do you want to take them home with you?"

"Not in this weather. But someday. When you've finished with them."

Emma watched the girl finger through the various

badges, reading the words, holding older ones up to the light. "What are these?" she said, holding the two cravat pins Emma had dislodged.

"I have no idea how they fit or who they belonged to. They are the only men's jewellery items in the box."

"Can you find out?"

Emma tilted her head. "Possibly, if I can trace the tree back far enough to find the women's married names. They might line up with the husband's initials."

Paige picked up the Centennial Suffrage Medal. "Tell me about the Suffrage Petition."

"What do you want to know?"

"I looked it up on line and there's a picture of it. It must be quite impressive. Especially in its day."

"I'd have to agree with you," said Emma, going on to describe what she'd seen at the museum, and how she'd felt reading some of the signatures. "You should go. See it for yourself. Most, if not all, of the 1891 and 1892 petitions appear to have been lost. They say 32,000 people signed the petition in total. I read in Papers Past it could have been 35,000, but they only have 25,000 on display. Sheets are missing. Of those signatures some are Māori and Chinese women, and a great number of men."

"Cool."

Sometimes Emma struggled with the offhand, one-word answers and shrugs the girl offered, but she'd learnt Paige was genuine and interested in everything she had to say.

"That election was significant in more ways than one. The landslide victory was the start of a long period in office for Richard Seddon. He oversaw the beginnings of our welfare system with the introduction of the old age pension shortly after."

Paige nodded. "I've been thinking again about what you told me about my Grandma Kate. And Mum, for that matter. So, if I've remembered right, Mum could have been an anti nuclear protester. Apart from that badge Dad gave me, he neither confirms nor denies. He avoids. Instead, he tells me about how she played with me and Cameron and how lovely she was. I'm sure she was, but what did she believe in? What was she passionate about?"

"We may be wrong with the assumption about her being involved in protests," Emma said, hoping not to raise Paige's hopes or create more issues with her father. "She might have voiced concerns but not joined a protest. Her passion in life could have been her children. Being a mum is important." She felt the flush of guilt at what she'd nearly done to Rose. Now she understood her condition better, she was learning to blame the illness rather than herself.

"Either way, and I will get it out of Dad eventually, but you said her mum had been killed in a car accident, right? And her grandmother – who we call Grandma Kate – raised Mum as her own."

Emma nodded as the girl racked her brain for the links.

"But didn't you say Mum's mum was likely to have been a feminist? Part of the feminism protests of the time. I did what you said and read up about them. I never knew anything about it. The freedoms we have today are all a result of past fights for women's rights – in equality, in finance, health, everything, aren't they?"

"Decade by decade, generation by generation, we always want our children to have a better life than we had. It's natural," said Emma.

"Okay, so if we go back and look at Grandma Kate and her generation, you said she was anti-war."

"I believe so, Paige, But none of it is proven. All I've done is look at the badges in that lovely trinket box and fitted them to a generational timeline. Yes, your mother lived through the time of anti-nuclear protests, and her mother through the feminist movement period, and her mother through the post-war years. They are all assumptions, based on unanswered questions around why they had so many protest movement badges in that box."

Paige was letting her enthusiasm run away with her again. Emma could see it in her eyes. She was leaning forward, hands resting on her knees, reeling off a timeline that played in her head. "I know that, but it all makes sense, doesn't it? If my mum was a protester and so was her mum and her mum before that, then it makes sense that the mums before them might have been as well. Each mum teaching her daughter about doing what's right and fighting for what they believed in. They could be the line of troublemakers Dad talked about."

"That's my thoughts. *But* …" she emphasised, as Paige began to interrupt, "before you get too carried away, we still need to check our facts."

"How do we do that?"

"Research. Read old papers, look for their names, find them in police files, or on …" Emma didn't get to finish her sentence.

"The Suffrage Petition," squealed Paige. "One of them was a suffragette. I'm sure of it. Oh please, Emma, can you find her?"

"Are you sure it's not going to cause more problems with your father?"

"I don't care. It's my history not his."

Emma frowned at that comment. "That's not fair, Paige. Your relationship with your dad is very important, far more than digging in the past. Don't spoil it. He must have his reasons for keeping secrets. Maybe in time he'll tell you, when he thinks you're ready. The past will always be there, you can go back to it. The now is more important than back then."

Paige shook her head. "But it's something to do with back then that's caused all the problems. I'm sure of it."

32

An historic day

November 1893

The weeks had flown by in a whirl of feverish anticipation since the Act was passed. With Election Day fast approaching, it was becoming clearer that their efforts had paid off. Well over 100,000 women throughout the land had registered to vote.

"Isn't it wonderful," she enthused to all and anyone who would listen to her catchphrase. But that momentous day hadn't only been about the passing of the Act. It had determined her future.

Thinking back, Lucy had not realised how much she risked by putting her appeal forward, or how pent up she had been while she waited for Richard's decision. Not until he had dismissed her concerns with a wave of his hand. She'd released her breath like a balloon bursting, her greatest fears vanquished.

"I trust you," he had said, and taken her in his arms, kissing her thoroughly, and kindled the feelings of love that set her heart fluttering.

While Lucy was still, at times, beset with doubts as

to whether what she was doing was morally right, Mrs Adams had insisted that true love healed all wounds and Lucy should put her misgivings aside. She'd never met anyone as free-thinking or as concerned solely with women's welfare as Mrs Adams. She found her refreshing and, more importantly, reassuring.

Since then, Lucy had become engrossed in what the candidates for the new Parliament had to say. Until now, she had never fully appreciated how important it was to know what each politician stood for, what policies they believed in, and what benefit she might receive. Or how such information was paramount to her decision on who to vote for. Despite her concerns about the tepid support Mr Seddon had given the franchise, she found little fault in his progressive social reforms for the future. He was convincing in his arguments that he was a man of the people and charismatic in his dealings.

During this time, Milly and she became inseparable. They never saw Hope any longer. They had read about the lavish wedding they'd not been invited to, and about the gifts and plans for the lengthy honeymoon involving significant overseas travel with detachment. After seeing the guest list, neither showed any surprise that they no longer met the standard of acceptance.

"I'm actually glad it worked out this way," said Milly. "I will never have the financial riches that she now has, nor could I compete with her style."

"You should never have to compete or keep up," protested Lucy. "You should be accepted for who you are. And you are my friend for life."

The girls hugged and giggled and talked their way through the daily routine, until Lucy could no longer hold back the news. "Richard and I have set the date for our wedding."

Milly instantly bounced with joy at the news, knowing nothing about Lucy's struggles – only her journal knew the truth.

"That's wonderful news, Lucy. I'm delighted."

"And will you be my bridesmaid?"

"Oh, yes, please."

And so it was decided.

Lucy had begged and cajoled Richard into delaying the ceremony until after election day. 'Please, Richard, the ladies have such a short time in which to galvanise women to register now so they are eligible to vote. We will have a lifetime together; let me have these few weeks.' She had another ace up her sleeve she had not realised until recently. 'This means so much to me. I signed the petition as Lucy Young, I worked for the cause as Lucy Young, I have already registered as Miss L Young. As it is, there may not be time to legally change my name to Mrs Richard Harris. Dear Richard, it would break my heart to lose the opportunity.'

She loved him all the more for accepting her argument and conceding, sure she was making the right decision.

Amongst all the political hubbub, she now had to find time for the hustle and bustle of wedding arrangements. Her first stumbling block was her father. "No, Father, please," she begged. "Do not make me have a full-scale society wedding. I would much prefer we married quietly in the church we always attend, and host a small breakfast for those friends and family who will continue to be a valuable part of our daily lives."

"And do you not consider our important customers valuable or part of our daily lives when they provide us with the lifestyle you are accustomed to?" He was doing his best to restrain his increasing frustration. She had prevaricated, delayed, argued and changed her mind so often throughout the year, he had lost patience with her. "Lucy. Let me make myself plain. You will accept the guest list that your future father-in-law and I have put together without argument. Do you understand?"

She had, however, won the battle over the size of the bridal party. Only Milly would attend her. No flower girls, pageboys and other attendants, even if they were the sons and daughters of those all important clients. Richard, in turn, would only need a best man to stand up with him.

"Very well," her father conceded eventually.

"My only other request is that Mrs Adams be included as part of the family group." Lucy stood her ground.

When her father had hesitated, she pushed her point. "Richard's family is larger than ours. His mother and grandmother will be there. I have neither. Please, Father, allow me this indulgence. She has become a good friend to me." Lucy flashed her most charming smile, pleading with puppy-dog eyes. "I'm sure Grandmother Stone and Mrs Adams will get on well, and it is such a small request amongst everything else."

"If that is what you wish."

Lucy almost knocked him over as she threw herself at him and wrapped her arms around his neck. "Thank you, Father. Thank you."

"Calm yourself, Lucy," he said as he untangled her

arms. "You are about to become a married woman, please behave like one."

Suddenly demure, but unable to hide her high spirits, she smoothed her gown into place and bobbed in a quick curtsey. "Yes, Father," she grinned.

Aloysius Young laughed. "I could never curb your spirit, could I?"

For a brief moment, Lucy wondered whether her spirits were fully restored or would the self-deprecation return. *Too late for that*, she scolded herself, recalling Mrs Adams's words.

* * * * *

On Tuesday the 28th of November 1893, Richard and her father escorted Lucy to the voting booth. Contrary to the many concerns voiced during the campaign that women would be hassled by opponents and subjected to conditions to which they were unused, the day was one of good humour and propriety. Lucy thoroughly enjoyed herself.

"Good morning," she said to several ladies who had come to cast their vote, dressed in their best and most colourful outfits. Many carried parasols to ward off the sun until the breeze picked up later.

"Isn't this wonderful," Lucy stated, bubbling with joy, not expecting a response from her father or Richard as the women nodded their heads in agreement.

Another horse and carriage pulled up to deliver a group of gaily dressed ladies to the booth, chattering non-stop to each other. Many of the working women came on foot, their shawls wrapped tightly around them and a hat pinned to their unruly hair. Some came by bicycle. The streets were full and the atmosphere one of good humour.

"I'm so happy," she smiled.

After a lot of consideration, Lucy decided she would vote for Sir George Grey, even though he was standing as an Independent. He deserved a return to Parliament as a thanks for all the support the Auckland Women's Franchise League had received. Although she was torn. The Liberal candidate was Mr John Shera, and she acknowledged that his amendment to include Māori women in the franchise had tipped the scales. Still, it couldn't be helped.

On the way out, someone yelled out, "Who'dya vote for?"

A reporter, she assumed.

She smiled. "That is for me to know. My vote is my secret."

The moment she and 90,000 other women made their choice and the vote was duly placed in the box was a turning point in the history of the world as the first country to grant women's franchise, and a privilege she would never take for granted.

Later, she would record the small part she had played in changing the lives of women in her journal. She would never forget how her heart had swelled with pride at that moment in time.

* * * * *

Three days later, following a landslide victory for Premier Seddon's Liberal government, her father was once again escorting her to another significant event in her life. One that would offer her opportunities beyond her dreams.

To appease Richard's female relatives, the likes of Mrs Bush and dear Mrs Adams, not to mention Milly, who had all expressed an opinion, Lucy chose a simplified version of the fashionable wedding gown without all the overlarge frills, hoops and petticoats. The cream silk draped beautifully from a fitted waist. Long sleeves of lace and ruffles graced the bodice, and a full-length veil, held by a clip of pearls, fell to the floor with no train. At her throat was pinned the ruby mounted on a simple gold bar, her first gift from Richard.

The pale-green gown flattered Milly who whispered words of encouragement throughout the dressing process, adjusting strands of hair to hide the barely noticeable scar at her temple. Finally, after handing Lucy a large bouquet of early summer flowers and trailing greenery, Milly helped her into the carriage. Her father sat beside her on the magnificent summer's morning while Lucy recalled the moment he had fastened her newest and most-valued possession around her neck.

"You are too kind, Father," she'd whispered, her eyes shining with so many emotions she couldn't identify half of them. She stared into the mirror and fingered the gold locket hanging from a rope chain that now nestled amongst the lace frills. She turned to see him looking at her with such love she almost cried.

"I am so proud of you, Lucy, my dear. You will do great things in your life. I am sure of it. You make an old man overjoyed with happiness."

Those were the most effusive words she had heard

her father speak. She hugged him tightly, promising she would care for him forever.

Lucy made her way down the aisle towards Richard, her hand resting on her father's arm and accompanied by Milly who shone with gladness. The moment had come.

Lucy's face ached from smiling throughout the noisy brouhaha of the wedding breakfast surrounded by so many people wishing Young and Harris a great future. It never ceased to amaze her that neither Richard nor her father could understand her annoyance at being a symbol of partnership that had nothing to do with her marriage. But for her father's sake, and the couple of hours it took, she smiled, nodded and was extremely polite to all the simpering.

Later that evening, she and Richard and her father sat in the parlour. The mood was relaxed and convivial, and Lucy content. The men toasted each other with a glass of whisky and chatted about the events of the day and business. She and Richard had decided to delay their honeymoon until after the New Year, as he was expected to assist in the rush up to the big Christmas sales. Unwilling to move into her parents-in-law's home while Richard sought permanent accommodation, they had decided to reside at her father's house in the interim.

"I will wish you gentleman a good night," she said as darkness fell, choosing to prepare herself for bed and the night ahead alone. "Goodnight, dear Father. Thank you for everything." She kissed him on the forehead.

It seemed no time at all, even though it was approaching midnight, before a gentle knock signalled Richard's intent. "May I come in?"

Sitting at her dressing table, brushing her hair with contented strokes, she suddenly froze and swallowed hard. The time she had feared had arrived. She would be put to the test and she prayed she would not fail.

She cleared her throat. "You may."

The lamp softly lit her features, as she stood in front of the dressing table, her hair over one shoulder. He entered the room to see her silhouette outlined under her fine muslin nightgown. His face was infused with awe, and he stood staring at her for long moments. Slowly, he took a step towards her and reached out a hand. She touched the tip of his fingers and found herself wrapped in his tight embrace. Whispers of love and desire and hope filled her ears, as his kisses raised sensations she hoped would blot out the past. They clung together in the middle of the room. Time passed, seconds, minutes, aeons, lost in yearning.

A loud noise rang out, startling them. She had no idea what it could be, but at the speed Richard left the room, she suspected he did. Following closely behind, she raced down the stairs and stopped abruptly three steps from the bottom. Her hand went to her mouth, her eyes stared and her hammering heart filled her throat while her mind screamed *No!*

Her father lay on his back, his right hand flung out beside him, facing upward, while one leg was folded under the other. He looked as if he could be asleep in the soft light from the lamp on the hall table, apart from the gaping hole in his throat. His vacant eyes stared at the ceiling. Dark crimson blood seeped from the wound and soaked into the carpet runner beneath him.

"Go back!" insisted Richard, trying to turn her around, to not look. "Go upstairs, Lucy. I beg you."

But there was no way she was going anywhere. Not while her father lay in the hallway, the front door wide open, the pitch of night beyond offering no explanation.

"Father!" she screamed. "Father?"

With two leaps she was kneeling on the floor beside him, cradling his head on her lap, his blood covering her hands and soaking into her nightgown as she cried, beseeching him to answer, begging the Lord not to take him. Not now, not today.

Richard tried and failed to comfort her, wanting to reassure her that he was there to care for her, to protect her. She wailed and shook her head, pushing him away, denying everything except what lay in front of her.

Her father was dead.

33

A line of troublemakers

August 2022

As each week went by, Emma could scarcely believe how much more alive and like her old self again she felt, despite the gloomy wet weather that usually wore her down. The relentless rain had continued for weeks, and the ground was sodden.

She knew the meds had made the difference to her moods and she was grateful. The doctor had arranged for more tests to be done to rule out any other possible causes, but both she and the counsellor felt convinced anxiety was the root cause rather than any of the chronic illnesses that often lay undetected and misunderstood. Emma could live with that. Anything was better than long Covid, which she'd since read was being investigated as a form of the debilitating and incurable chronic fatigue syndrome. Emma counted herself lucky.

Until she felt able to take on clients again, she decided to start a blog on her website. She wanted to write about the lives of women of the past, highlighting the stresses and strains they lived under, the lack of rights, the difficult choices they had to make, the trauma of loss. And how, in days gone by, uncharacteristic behaviour like hers, today diagnosed as a medical condition, would have landed many women in the asylum as uncontrollable mad women, who were locked up for years. She also wanted to investigate the possibility of writing more life stories of the signatories to the suffrage petition. So many were unknown and forgotten. She would like to give them life if she could. It would not be an easy task.

She put away her notebooks, not ready to share her ideas, and opened up Paige's Ancestry page. She'd be here soon, and Emma had a lot to tell her.

"Hi, Ems," said Paige as she bounced in through the door shortly after nine, stripping off her wet-weather gear. "How's things?"

Emma grinned. The girl had made herself at home and part of the family. How – or when – she'd befriended Rose, Emma wasn't sure; sometime around the time she'd landed in hospital, she thought. Either way, the dynamics had shifted a lot since then. Rose was back to her usual self; Luke was happy with that and credited Paige with much of it, and Paige said she loved having a little sister. She was also less mercurial, letting sense overrule emotion, mostly.

"Great," said Emma. "And raring to go. Shall we recap?"

Paige pulled up a chair next to her so she could look at the screen.

"So here *you* are. Generation 1> **Amelia Paige FRAZER,** born 2003. Then your mother, generation 2> **Lucy Kathryn WILSON**, born in 1975, married David Fish FRAZER in 1997 and died in 2006."

Emma didn't say anything sympathetic or try to dress up the facts. Paige's mother was gone and nothing would change that, and there were other fascinating facts still to be revealed.

"Then her mother, your grandmother. Generation 3> **Amelia Lucy,** better known as Amy. We know she died in 1977 in a car accident. What I haven't been able to find is a marriage certificate."

"Do we know who my mum's dad was?"

Emma shook her head. "No. I did try, but she didn't list a father on your mother's birth certificate, so we have no way of knowing, unless you wanted to go all out and do a DNA test and hope he comes up on the database."

"Nah. It's not that important." Then she paused. "I'll think about it. I might want to know one day. But it's the mums I want to know about right now."

Emma continued. "Next is Generation 4> **Kathryn Lucy MILLS**, known as Kate. Your great-grandmother."

"Grandma Kate, right? Who I thought was Mum's mother but was really her grandmother."

"Yes. She married Michael John Wilson in December 1945. Amy – your grandmother – was born nine months later."

"And Grandma Kate died a few weeks after my mum. I know that much," said Paige. "Hang on a minute, I've just twigged. My Grandmama Amy wasn't married when she had Mum."

"That's right. But thanks to changing social attitudes and law reforms in the late '60s, she wouldn't have been stigmatised with awful names to the same degree as earlier generations."

"I should think not, too! That was cruel."

Emma clicked a couple more links. "Believe it or not, once you get back far enough, online records are easy to find. After I found Grandma Kate's marriage in the newspapers, it was easy to find her parents. Generation 5. Your two-times great-grandmother, **Amey Kate HARRIS,** born 1897."

"That's super cool."

Emma felt a surge of satisfaction. The girl was as rapt as she about finding her ancestors. "Amey Harris would have been about 18 when World War One started. It took me a while to find the details, but eventually I found a newspaper article saying her fiancé had been killed early on in the war. The Harris family were quite well known then. I later found a marriage to a Robert Mills in 1920, long after the war had finished."

Paige sat glued to the screen not saying anything, so Emma continued her explanation.

"This I can't be certain about, but again, it's all about the badges. In 1931, the Peace movement in Geneva sought international disarmament. Here in Auckland, members of WILPF collected close to 42,000 signatures and held a disarmament meeting at the Auckland Town Hall. I'd take a bet your Great-great-grandma Amey was there. Because …"

Paige suddenly turned to face Emma, looking astounded. "Whoa. Wait up. Have you written all this down? I don't think I can quite keep up."

Emma chuckled. "Yes. It's all here."

She flicked a sheaf of papers sitting on the other side of her desk. "See?" and flipped a page over to show the same chart that was on the screen and showed Paige a USB stick. "You'll get used to it. Once you get the names in order – and the reason for the names – but I'll get to that shortly, then it'll all make sense."

A heavy downpour sounded on the roof. "Wow," said Emma looking out the French doors to see puddles forming in the lawn. "I hope this lets up soon or there'll be flooding in low-lying parts."

"It's been a nightmare getting around lately," agreed Paige, turning her attention back to the screen. "Why do you think this Amey was at that anti-war meeting?"

"Because when I put the tree together, not only had she lost her fiancé, but she also lost a brother to the same war. Is it any wonder she became anti-war? Amey had one child, your Grandma Kate, but your great-great-grandma never met her namesake, Kate's child Amelia. The death certificate says she died of heart failure. She was forty-nine."

"Oh, that's sad." Unexpectedly emotional, Paige wiped her eyes on her sleeve.

"Even more sad, as I discovered she was already a widow. Her husband and her younger brother were killed in World War Two," said Emma.

"She lost a fiancé, two brothers and a husband to war!" Paige looked stunned. "That's terrible."

Wanting to cheer things up a bit, Emma sympathised, "It is. But these things happen, and we can't change the past; all we can do is celebrate it and be happy to know who our ancestors were and what they achieved in life. It's their legacy, their blood you carry."

Hoping one more discovery would give Paige what she'd been seeking, Emma said, "Last but not least, as this is as far back as I've searched." She waved her hand around. "Ta-da … My grand discovery, which I'd suspected for some time, is, I believe, that the trinket box belonged to your three-times great-grandmother, Generation 6> **Lucy Young**, born in 1872 and ..." Emma paused, delaying the surprise, one she hoped would excite Paige as much as it had her.

"Stop teasing. And what?"

"Your Lucy Young was a suffragist with a long and beautiful story."

"That's dope!" said Paige in awe, switching to slang she usually avoided when talking with Emma. "Go on. What else? How do you know?"

"The badges, the jewellery." Emma opened up the photos of the three women again and showed Paige the Photoshopped version of the oldest and smallest image they had of a young woman holding a baby. "It's not perfect, but see the brooch? That's in the box. The box has an 'L' on it. She's also wearing that locket and chain. But it's the naming pattern that gives it away."

"No way! How?"

Emma handed Paige a printed ancestor table, knowing she'd find it easier to understand written down. "Let's start here."

"Lucy Young married Richard Harris a few days after the election in November 1893. Her father was Aloysius Young. He died the same day."

"What? How dreadful. What happened?"

"I'm not sure yet, I need to do more research, but what's significant about their names is the initials RH and AY."

Paige looked puzzled for a moment until she remembered, "Those were the initials on the cravat pins in the trinket box, weren't they?" She jigged in the chair with excitement. "It's all falling into place. Thank you, Ems. Thank you," she breathed, suddenly giving Emma a hug.

"Great, isn't it, but let me finish. Lucy named her daughter Amey – with an E, just like Amey Daldy, president of the 1893 Auckland Women's Franchise League. Middle name Kate – wild guess. Probably after Kate Sheppard," said Emma going through each point line by line. "I've attached the Peace League badges from the 1920s and '30s to Amey's activism."

She promised to explain more about each of the badges to Paige one by one, but not now.

"Amey named her daughter Kathryn Lucy – a fuller version of her middle name and her mother's name – better known as Grandma Kate, your great-grandmother.

"I think she was also a Peace League member in the 1950s, and more than likely a Quaker, but I can't prove it. She named her daughter – your grandmother, Amelia Lucy, known as Amy – after her mother and grandmother. There's little doubt that Amy was a feminist in the '70s, a women's libber, as they were known. She named her daughter – your mother – Lucy Kate, who became anti nuclear in the '90s."

Emma came to the end of the generation list. "I'm certain that's the right line – and your so-called 'line of troublemakers' who got themselves involved in any number of movements aiming to gain rights for women and improve society as a whole."

"I love it. This is better than I ever hoped." Paige ran her eyes down the list of acronyms from the WCTU, the WILPF, NCW, to NOW, and others. "What's this one?"

Emma looked at where her finger pointed to the SPWC. "I had trouble identifying that one to start with. There's a much larger story attached to it that I'd like to leave until later, so I can put it altogether in one place."

"Okay," agreed Paige. "What else?"

"This." She handed Paige a photograph. "I found the signature of an L Young on the online suffrage petition. You can go see it yourself at the National Library sometime."

Overcome, Paige's eyes pooled with tears. "Who do you think this is holding the baby?" she asked, pointing to the oldest photo.

"I'd say that was Lucy Young Harris holding Amey, whose photo is in that locket."

Paige sat staring at the photo, up at Emma and back to the photos, elated but speechless.

"The rest of her story is quite remarkable. It's a legacy you'll be proud of."

Paige's phone beeped. She looked at the message and Emma saw her face drop. "Sorry. It'll have to wait. Gotta go."

* * * * *

The unrelenting rain continued as Emma read Paige's stream of texts explaining why she'd rushed out in such a hurry.

My bike's outside yours. R picked me up.

Heading to his grandparents.

It's pouring. Really bad.

Roads r a mess.

Lots of flooding. We're ok but it's hard to see where we're going.

An hour later, Emma understood the reason.

Ems. It's awful. His GPs house is a disaster zone.

Can I do anything to help? texted Emma.

Anxious minutes passed before Paige answered. Emma assumed Paige and Ryan were talking. *Phone my Dad at this number. Need rubbish skip digger & manpower. And spades & brooms.*

A minute or two later came more requests.

Got any wet-weather gear? Need gumboots. Can you come? Bring water and food pls.

Paige sent Emma the address. *Be careful. Don't want you getting trapped.*

Emma phoned Dave Frazer.

"Is she all right?" was his first question. Emma liked that he thought of his daughter first even as she rattled off the list of requests.

"She assures me she is, but the place is completely flooded, from what I can gather. The grandparents can't manage on their own, and Ryan's parents live on a farm in the Waikato. It'll take them a while to get there. Can you help?"

"Of course. I'll set it all up and meet you out there."

With adrenaline surging, Emma began to gather what supplies she thought would be needed. She quickly made some sandwiches, filled as many water containers as she could find, pulled out some frozen meals she'd stacked in the freezer and set them to defrost as she hunted for coats and gumboots, and told Luke what she planned to do.

"I'm coming with you," he stated categorically as they packed his SUV with supplies and tools.

While she'd never admit it, she was glad. She was a confident driver but was happy Luke would drive in the rain while she navigated and was free to text. Two were always better in an emergency.

She'd texted Jess: *Explain later. Paige needs help. Can you keep Rosie.*

She received a thumbs up in reply, pushed the phone into her pocket and climbed in the SUV. "It must have been an isolated downpour to cause flooding," she said as they drove. "We've not seen that much rain."

"It's been wet for days, so a heavy downpour could easily overflow our outdated systems."

Emma's heart thumped in time with the swish of the windscreen wipers Luke had set to fast as they made their way through the increasing rain. Thank goodness it was daylight.

Converging within minutes of each other Emma, Luke and Dave were soon standing in the grandparents' temporary motel room. Ryan towered over his diminutive grandmother as she wrapped her arms around him, delighted to see him but in distress at what had happened.

"It's okay, Nan. We'll see you right," he reassured her as introductions were made. "See, we've brought in the cavalry."

Emma watched Paige's body language. It might not have been the family meeting she thought might happen one day, as she was introduced to his parents, who had arrived sooner than expected, and sympathised with his grandparents as they welcomed her, but it was good to see Ryan in his environment.

Dave sidled towards Paige. "Are you okay? I was worried about you."

She nodded, smiling. "Yeah. We're all safe, that's what

matters, but it's not good news about their house. You should see it. I'm going to stay and help with the clean-out."

"I'll stay too," he winked and turned to Nan and Grandpop. "We're here to help, but can you tell us what happened first?"

The lunch Emma had packed turned out to be the perfect solution. Tea was made and they sat wherever there was space to hear the story Grandpop related.

During the night, the floodwaters had come in one door before sweeping out the other, leaving behind a layer of mud and the smell of sewage. The rain had been falling unabated for days, drains were overflowing, and flooding made many roads slippery, if not dangerous. But the sudden deluge had pushed the infrastructure to its limits.

The once-landscaped bank behind the house looked more like a waterfall as stormwater from the road above rushed down their driveway and through their home. The nearby creek had become a river, bursting its banks, and the entire area was awash. Emergency services were out in force, and contractors were desperately trying to clear the numerous slips and blockages, while volunteers combined strengths to help the displaced.

Evacuated from the home they'd retired to a long time ago, it appeared they had lost everything, but Emma could see how stoic and resigned they were. They were alive. They had each other, and people were there to help them.

"We've seen floods before, young lady," explained Grandpop, directing his words towards Paige. "But this time … I'm not so sure what we'll do." He shook his head sadly, taking his wife's hand. "But we'll survive."

"I'm sure you will," she murmured in reply, even if no one had a clue what the council could, or would, do to fix the problems. Or when.

"People have been complaining for decades and we've not done a damn thing about it," continued Grandpop. "Every year the rains get heavier and the winds stronger. The floods are getting deeper and faster, bringing more rubbish with them. Forestry slash is causing enormous damage. And nothing is done." He paused, clearly distressed. "This is the worst I've seen – and I've seen some bad floods in my time, but never like this."

Nobody knew what to say to console the old man. All they could do was listen.

"Right then," said Dave, looking out the window. "Rain's stopped. We should get started. The equipment I ordered should be there by now."

Fortunately, his grandparents' home, on a sunny, north-facing property overlooking the ocean, was considered safe by Civil Defence, if not liveable, and they could re-enter. Leaving his mum with her parents, Ryan, his dad, Paige, Dave, Emma and Luke went to the house. Work had already begun.

The digger was busy piling up the tangle of silt and tree mess from the driveway and clearing a path to the garage and front door.

Ryan and Paige paired up, the three men set about the heavy lifting while Emma started emptying cupboards. The group began to sweep out the remaining watery sludge, ripped up carpets, tossed out furniture and got rid of damaged kitchen appliances and food before it rotted, tossing most of it into the skip that had just been delivered.

"How did you pull that off so quickly?" asked Luke as he and Dave lifted the sofa over the edge.

Dave looked uncomfortable. "Simply a case of knowing the right people, I guess." He didn't elaborate.

As Emma moved through the house, rescuing what she could, her heart broke for the elderly couple and the others like them who had lost nearly everything.

Paige and Ryan collected the boxes of precious photos, mementos and whatever else his grandparents had stored safely on higher shelves.

"Nan said she didn't care about the other things," he said, passing Paige another box. "They have insurance. It's the family things that matter."

They even managed to rescue some clothes, but most were too contaminated and nothing that touched the floor was salvageable.

Emma gathered a few drink bottles together and wandered around to where the three men were working. "Don't get dehydrated," she warned, handing them each a bottle.

"Thanks, Ems," said Luke, taking a swig. "We're making good progress."

Dave raised his bottle in salute. "Paige talks about you all the time. It's good to meet you face to face. Thanks for looking after my girl."

"She's a delight," acknowledged Emma. "I love her youthful exuberance. I hope she never loses her sense of purpose."

"She won't. Not with all the women before her in her make-up."

Emma filed that comment away to add to her dossier on the women of the past.

Next she found Ryan and Paige toiling side by side in another room and gave them a bottle of water each. The girl's earnest face shone with love and admiration for the generous-hearted young man who had dropped everything to help his grandparents. She hoped Paige would see the alternative set of family dynamics in action and would take this new wisdom home with her. Dave was a far better person than she'd depicted.

Ryan laughed as he leant against the wall, swallowing a drink of water. He grinned at Paige. "I love the way your nose crinkles at anything stinky."

Paige half-heartedly threw a wet cushion in his direction and grinned back. "What, like you?"

He grabbed her and she wriggled as he tried to tickle her, before he kissed her and she melted. They were good together, thought Emma as they laughed some more. She left them to carry on.

"I don't quite know where to turn next," Paige said to Emma a short time later as she rinsed her hands in the bucket of water on the kitchen bench. "We've ditched so much and the place still looks like a disaster. It's really upsetting and it's not even my place."

"I know what you mean. It'll take months, if not years, to fix all this," said Emma. "They won't be living here for a long while, if ever."

"That's so sad. They are not young any more. How will they start all over again?" She went to stand by the ranchsliders looking out over what once was their garden and the view beyond, watching the clean-up outside continue.

"Penny for them," grinned Ryan coming up behind her. He wiped his brow leaving a muddy mark.

She smiled at him lovingly. "I was just thinking. I'm more determined than ever that we have to do more to save the planet. We have to come up with better ways, better systems, so this sort of thing doesn't happen. It's not fair."

"I applaud your intentions, but I doubt you can change the weather," said Emma, listening in.

"Maybe not, Mrs Grainger," said Ryan, "but we can learn from Mother Nature. Right now, our practices are making things worse. With our population growing as it is, we need a total rethink on our infrastructure systems. We must have clean water and food to survive."

Emma didn't want to get into a debate with an environmental scientist about what was best, given her scant knowledge. She turned her attention to Paige. "You told me when we first met that you came from a long line of troublemakers and you wanted to make a difference. Have you decided how best you can do that?"

Paige turned towards her, perplexed. "Not exactly. Not yet. But after listening to Grandpop's story, we have to do more than we are. We can't turn back the clock, but we can change the future."

"That sounds like a start," said Emma, smiling. "One bite at a time, remember."

But Paige was on a roll now and reeling off her thoughts. "We have to learn to adapt. If we used less and reduced our individual footprint, we'd be in a much better state. Do you realise ours is the sixth highest footprint per person in the world? In clean, green New Zealand for *phss'* sake. It's as if no one cares."

Ryan put his arms around her and kissed her nose. "You are such a firebrand. I'm not sure I'll be able to keep up with you. But I agree. It's action time. No more slogans. No more promises. You and I are going to change the world – together."

Emma felt out of place eavesdropping on their very public declaration but couldn't see a way out without breaking the moment.

Paige threw her arms around Ryan's neck. "Together. Yes." But she was riled up now. "I can't do much of anything on my own. It's got to be something everyone does together. Why isn't that obvious? I don't understand the lack of will."

"Isn't it more about the enormous cost?" asked Emma.

"Yes, but I still don't understand why so few are willing to put up the money to make the necessary changes?"

"Your dad seems ready to put up some money. Helping us out like this will have cost a fair packet," said Ryan, nodding his head in Dave's direction outside. "But did you know he's also promised to see them good with the rebuild – or resettlement if that's what Nan and Grandpop want."

Paige turned to watch her father, mud covering his gumboots, his clothes equally caked, with a serious look. "He has, hasn't he? I'm thinking he's not such a bad stick after all."

34

Despair

December 1893 – March 1894

For weeks after, Lucy felt numb and drained of all feeling. She wanted to rant and scream and rage but had neither the energy nor the will. She could not weep. She could not speak. Words billowed around her. Questions were asked that had no answers. Other than the fact that her father was dead, there was no evidence. Nothing to show what had happened. No one knew why. No one knew who.

She withdrew within herself, shunning all sympathy, shunning everyone – including Richard. She had no doubts that her father was punished for her misdeeds.

In her mind, she relived the nightmare. Imagined the feeling of alarm and terror her father must have experienced. The last thing he saw was the muzzle of a gun. His life was over in seconds, he was never to experience pain or longing or fear ever again. Her life of pain and longing had only just begun.

She had bathed his body and prepared him for the expected and very public funeral she did not want. She proceeded through the motions and rituals in silence, present but not participating.

"Lucy." Richard spoke quietly, touching her arm gently. He didn't want to startle her. "Can we not share our grief and mourn his loss together? You might find greater solace. I know it would help me." He attempted to take her in his arms and break the terrible grip of despair that cloaked her.

"Don't touch me, Richard." She pulled away, flinching. "I don't deserve solace."

"Stop punishing yourself like this, Lucy, my love. Let me help you." When she didn't reply he added, "You must make some decisions soon."

The will had been read. It was all hers. Everything her father owned. Everything that was of note and value. Hers. The near-decade-old Married Women's Property Act gave her rights. She should rejoice. She was a woman of means, a woman of stature.

Lucy looked at him blankly.

"I can advise you," said her husband, still in name only. "But you must decide. You must sign the papers."

At her insistence, they had maintained separate rooms since 'that night' when a new reality had changed her life irrevocably. She refused to be consoled, never mind how hard he tried.

Sign? Sign what? "I'm not ready, Richard."

* * * * *

A summer of warmth and sunshine softly crept in, the festive season of joy and celebration passed, a new year began and Lucy continued to grieve.

Only Mrs Adams could reach her. Matchless in her approach, she had a way about her that freed Lucy from her insentient state. "You must move on, my dear," she said gently.

"But how? It's all my fault," insisted Lucy, irrationally blaming herself for her father's death, while reciting all her perceived sins. "If I hadn't disobeyed him. If I hadn't gone out that day. If …" she sobbed inconsolably. "He paid for my misdeeds with his life. Why would God punish him and not me?"

Over the compulsory pot of tea, Mrs Adams took her protégée to task. "Rubbish. It has nothing to do with you or God. You must stop this, Lucy, my dear. Mourning is one thing, but this uncharacteristic behaviour will land you in trouble, if not the asylum."

Fear etched her features as she stared back at Mrs Adams. "It is probably no more than I deserve," she stammered.

"Don't be ridiculous. Pull yourself together now, and be sensible. Nothing you did brought this about. It was a random deed by a random assailant. You must think ahead. You are now a rich woman. You own your father's house and his business, and you have a husband. Someone who loves you and is patiently waiting for his bride to reconcile her loss and re-engage with him. Am I right?"

Lucy could only nod. Her head ached and she couldn't think straight.

"While you must be seen to respect your father and mourn his loss, you should allow your guiltless husband to love you. There is nothing stopping you making decisions about the future, either. Take charge before someone starts to make your decisions for you."

Lucy looked at her friend for reassurance. "I fear some decisions are greater than I have ever considered before. How will I know I am making the right one?"

Mrs Adams scoffed. "You may not to begin with, but let me tell you, men often don't know what they are doing either. It comes with experience. You are a wife now. In some matters, your opinion will hold sway; in others, you may have to mutually agree on many important decisions. But don't lose control because you are afraid of making a mistake." Lucy looked unconvinced as Mrs Adams kept prodding her. "Begin with, where will you live? In your father's house? Your house now. Or in one that your husband purchases? Where will you be happiest? Where will he be happier?"

"I can't imagine being happy ever again."

"I understand how you feel, but let me assure you the abject pain you are suffering will ease. Better memories will return, you'll be warmed by the good times shared. It will come to you, in time. But you have to help the process by letting your husband into your life, accepting it will never return to the way it was and you have to make the most of it."

The pair went through the ritual of emptying and refilling the teacups. Lucy nibbled at a piece of fruit cake and pushed it away. Mrs Adams proffered options in the background while Lucy tried to pinpoint which of those she felt capable of carrying out. If any.

Something in her change of tone, or the words she used, drew Lucy from her stupor. "You have a responsibility to your father to use your money wisely. You cannot let his business fail, nor his life's work be for naught. Neither should you ignore the plight of those less fortunate than yourself. Put yourself in their shoes and do something to ease their suffering. Believe me, it will also relieve yours."

A sudden lightness filled Lucy's body where pain had resided. She remembered then all that Mrs Adams told her about her association with women's groups and organisations designed to lift the lot of those who had less. Such projects had helped her recover from the loss of her Sid. The love of her life. She had no children to pass her wealth on to, so she used it to benefit those in need and was rewarded in untold ways.

Could she do the same? Would work, mental and physical work, and philanthropy fill the void her father had left behind?

She'd think on it.

From then on, her mind couldn't rest. In a flurry of activity, she consulted the lawyer who proceeded to tell her what she should not do as a woman. "It is unseemly, Mrs Harris, quite unladylike, but, you are correct, there is no law stopping you. You may put yourself in charge of all your finances and set up a trust in perpetuity for the benefit of others if you so wish."

She talked with Richard, who knew better than to say she couldn't, but offered suggestions that were probably more acceptable to the businessmen he and her father had dealt with.

"Not forgetting my father," Richard reminded her, "who is rather more set in his ways than your father ever was."

Most of her wisdom came from Mrs Adams.

She talked with the ladies of the Benevolent Society and similar welfare agencies about the soirées and concerts they held to raise funds, and how welcome donations were in providing the commodities most needed to those without. But the one organisation which moved her the most was the recently formed Society for the Protection of Women and Children, the SPWC, founded thanks to the efforts of Henry Wilding, a devout man with great dignity and persuasion, to safeguard the vulnerable from boorish men.

If Lucy thought it odd that a man should feel it necessary to protect women from other men, she never considered it a barrier. If anything, she believed the opposite. She thanked the Lord for such men, who saw women as deserving and children as victims. Like her father. Like her husband.

With that part of her self-imposed obligations falling into place, Lucy turned her attention to her own situation and that of her marriage to Richard. "I must apologise, I feel, for my detachment of late," she began awkwardly. "I have not been the most attentive of brides."

They had continued to live in her father's house – her house, she had to keep reminding herself – but had maintained their distance. Richard, generously, divided his time between his father's increasing demands and checking on the manager overseeing Young Importers, the business she had sorely neglected.

"My darling, Lucy. I never expected anything different of you. I know the fearsome loss you have suffered. One that only time, and I hope, my love, can alleviate."

Lucy looked at him, more fondly than she had done for some time, realising much of what Mrs Adams had said was more true that she'd given credence to. His solicitude was exemplary and his patience laudable, even under the circumstances. Far more than she deserved. Many a man would not have been so tolerant and long-suffering. Something inside her shifted.

"It is also my hope." She put her hand to the face that offered her a lifetime of devotion and optimism. "I must thank you for your forbearance. I have not been easy to live with, I know. But it is time for us to move forward in life, or so I've been told." Even though her year of mourning was nowhere near finished, the business needed her, Richard needed her.

Richard sighed, took her hand in both his and gazed into her eyes with desire. "I am your willing slave. Tell me what it is you wish."

How had she overlooked this man for so long? His constancy gave her strength, but as Mrs Adams repeatedly reminded her, marriage was a partnership of two people, and one must not take the other for granted. *As you have, missie,* said the voice in her head.

"I do have ideas, Richard, but I would not venture to suggest they are without flaw. But I hope you will listen to them. As we spoke about in those early days. That we would respect each other, listen to each other, and agree on the best way forward, together. Can we still do that, Richard?"

"I'm beginning to think I have reason for concern. You sound so serious. Surely nothing can be that terrible?"

"No, not terrible, but a little unconventional maybe."

"Since when have I ever expected convention from you?" He laughed, his eyes twinkled and she remembered why she loved him. "What do you have in mind?"

Briskly outlining her thoughts, she hung on his reply.

For long moments, he remained silent, while she became more keyed up, fearful he would decry each and every one. She watched him pace before the fireplace, stop, put his hand to his chin, pace again, until finally he turned towards her. "My father will have a fit," he began, her stomach churning with disappointment, "but I believe you may just have hit upon something quite grand."

She leapt to her feet and threw her arms around his neck, her optimism for the future restored. They would continue to live in the home she'd grown up in and loved and, if it went according to plan, dreams would be fulfilled.

Instinctively he pulled her to him and held her tightly, waiting, expecting her to withdraw. When she didn't, he closed his eyes and whispered in her ear, slowly moving his lips towards hers. She felt heat rising as dormant, but not forgotten, sensations swamped them both. Enveloped in his arms, and thoroughly caressed by his kisses, she was carried upstairs.

The night she had feared so many weeks ago now fulfilled her in every way. And a new understanding fell into place. She had not been penetrated before. The drunken sod had merely released his seed over her, to be washed away. Overjoyed, forgiveness came in a flash, passion overcame caution and details Mrs Adams had shared, that had once shocked her, now came to fulfilment.

Within weeks, arrangements had been made. The Lucy Trust for Women had been set up. Young and Harris Enterprises was created, combining the importing aspects of one with the warehouse practices of the other under one roof. Richard Harris became the proprietor and director of the business known as Lewis's Department Store, one to rival any in the country.

The search was on for the right building.

Months later, after a lot of huffing and puffing, Harry Harris decided the store held far greater prestige than the old warehouse. He was soon prevailed upon to take up the role of the charming host who would lead the customers to the perfect merchandise for their needs.

"That was a brilliant idea of yours, my love," said Richard proudly, having watched his father preen, happily greeting each customer and handing them over to the relevant salesperson or in some cases, if the client was important enough, to attend to them himself.

"He feels important, and that's what counts. But it's you who runs the business, my dearest. You who are its torchbearer."

"And you, my darling Lucy, are the flagbearer for the downtrodden. You have already made a huge difference to the lives of many."

"Not really," she demurred. "I stay in the background, but I am forever thankful to you for trusting me, for being my champion, so I can champion others."

"Your clever streamlining of the finances enabled all that. That is your father's legacy. The Lucy Trust is your legacy."

She smiled shyly, taking his hand and placing it over her stomach. "In a few months, this will be your legacy."

His kiss said it all.

35

Resolutions

A couple of weeks after the flood, Paige persuaded Dave to invite Emma into the discussion to complete the story of the search for her ancestors. They sat overlooking the balcony with beautiful views of the harbour, soaking up the early summer sun reaching into the living area. Mocktails of varying flavours, and nibbles, helped relieve the seriousness of the discussion. Emma sat back in the luxurious white-leather armchair and listened …

Dave had more than come around, he'd positively joined the research party.

When Paige had gone home with all the names and dates and stories and badges and, 'Oh, everything,' she'd trilled, excited as a child with her first basket of toys, he was taken aback. For so long, he'd tried to shield Paige from the past.

'Why?' she'd demanded.

Bit by bit, the truth had emerged. Slowly, in stages, out of sequence and mixed in with tears and laughter, but finally, they had connected and the truth came out. He hadn't known all the details but admitted to knowing more than he'd let on. The five women Emma had unveiled – Lucy, Amey, Kate, Amy, and Lucy – had all been feminist activists, demanding rights for women, better laws for women, better laws for society and the protection of the planet. They had each in turn managed The Lucy Trust as per the dictates set down in the original deeds.

They had also toiled endlessly and died young, except Grandma Kate. He'd known her story too, and about the death of her daughter, and raising her granddaughter, but she never revealed who the father was. Whether she knew or not, they would never know.

"After losing your mum," he'd explained, talking directly to Paige, "I was terrified of losing you. The parallels scared me. They had all invested so much of their time and energy and health into achieving what they believed in, they sacrificed themselves in the process. I couldn't risk you doing the same thing. I couldn't save your mum. I couldn't protect her, but I promised to care for you, to protect you. I did my best. I'm doing my best."

"And I'm grateful, Dad. I really am. And I appreciate what you did for Ryan's grandparents. That was very generous and kind, but now do you see why I think it's so imperative we tackle climate change? Why don't you care about it?"

She'd been tough on him, berating him for not accepting the science, not committing to making a difference. He'd kept his temper, even though Emma could see he was being pushed to the limit.

"I do care, Paige. Very much. I want clean water and more native plantings just as much as you. I want to see people properly housed and an end to all the devastating flooding. I want people to live long and healthy lives. I just see different ways of doing things from you. Like your mother and grandmothers. They had their ways, and I have mine." His voice croaked at the end.

"But you invest in oil!"

"You got that one wrong, sweetheart," he said with a sigh, pushing his hair back from his forehead in frustration, trying to hide his emotions. "I invest in R & D. I always have. Researching new ideas and better systems. And developing cleaner, more sophisticated products and equipment. We do need to be more innovative in the way we do things. Some are very close to completion. I believe these innovations will be the way forward and hopefully solve, or at least mitigate, many of the current issues. But to get to that point, sometimes you have to join the devil to beat him." He grinned sheepishly.

Luke had said he'd liked Dave, and Emma could see why. She had seen it for herself while they were cleaning up Ryan's grandparents' place. He was a decent and trustworthy man. Emma remembered a feeling she'd had while she'd been in hospital all those months ago. "Do you invest in the health sector?"

She'd never seen a grown man look so embarrassed and awkward by such a simple question, as if he'd been caught out doing something wrong.

"I do what I can," he muttered, diverting the conversation as he poured more drinks, condensation glistening on the glasses.

Picking up his briefcase, he withdrew an old leather-bound notebook. Emma instinctively knew it was older than anything she'd seen before. "I think you should have this," he said to Paige. "I'd forgotten about it till you found that trinket box. How it got left out I have no idea."

"What is it?" She took the journal from him, carefully turning the pages, overawed by the significance of history, of family, of herself wrapped up inside the pages.

"Part of your mother's legacy. Grandma Kate wanted you to have it on your 21st birthday. I promised I'd look after it until then. I kept everything locked in a safety box at the bank. Or I thought I did," he smiled ruefully.

"The trinket box is what gave me all the clues," said Emma. "The badges mostly, but then discovering the hidden newspaper clipping and the two cravat pins."

"You're a clever woman to have discovered so much with so little," replied Dave.

Emma shrugged off the compliment. It was her job.

"To be clear," he continued, grinning at Emma, "I am in no way related to that Mr Fish of Dunedin. Nor would I want to be, from what I've heard. For the record, you were right, it is a name handed down through a maternal line to the sons, just not from that one. I've never liked it and only use it when I have to. I'm the last. I refused to pass it down to my son."

"Much to Cam's relief," laughed Paige.

Emma allowed herself a quiet smile. She'd guessed correctly, just not the right ancestor. Maternal lines might be notoriously difficult to trace but women who carried their maiden names forward had great insight. Now she was itching to get her hands on that notebook.

"Oh, Ems, you must read this. It's Lucy's story right from the beginning when she was twenty-one."

* * * * *

343

And read it she had. A journal passed down, generation to generation, each adding their own story, as she'd soon discovered after Paige delved into what else was in that safety deposit box. Dave apologised for keeping secrets, for not telling her about the business and for trying to stop her doing something she believed in. His reasons were genuine, if a little overprotective of a modern, intelligent young woman.

"Grandma Kate came from a different world, with a different understanding of women's roles in life," he explained. He had just lost his wife and the mother of his two children. She had lost her granddaughter, the daughter of her beloved daughter, both of whom had died too soon. She had wanted to protect their legacy, to preserve their story. "I was in no state to make decisions about the past."

Grandma Kate had taken control, telling him how she wanted matters handled. At her behest, he locked away the family history and heirlooms until the girl was of age. Two months later, she died of a heart attack.

"I didn't intend to keep it from you, sweetheart. I just pushed it away. You have to understand, your mum meant the world to me, and I've missed her ever since. Those things were reminders I didn't need."

Emma empathised with the man who had just laid his heart on his sleeve for his daughter. She understood how, with no one to maintain the stories of the past, they melded into his pain and heartache, and talking about them hurt too much.

With it all out in the open now, Paige had found the foundations for who she was. "Thank you, Dad. For telling me my story. I love you."

Epilogue

As she put the final touches in place, Emma hoped she'd written Lucy Young's story as she wanted it remembered.

She and Richard Harris had made a great success of Lewis's Department Store but it died with him as loss and tragedy undermined his purpose. Their firstborn son, Lewis, named after Lucy's late father Aloysius, had met an early death during World War One. She'd have been proud of both husband and son if she'd lived to see it all.

Lucy, who had dedicated her life to the cause of women, whose philanthropy had provided care and welfare to countless numbers, who had advocated alongside the Society for the Protection of Women and Children – the SPWC, the one Emma had struggled to identify – for better conditions for women, had lost her life bearing their third child, a son, Lucas in 1913. She was forty-one.

She had worked tirelessly. During the 1890s, the SPWC had successfully campaigned to raise the age of consent from fourteen to sixteen, to make incest a criminal offence, and for harsher penalties for cruelty and neglect. In 1906, a separate court system for juvenile offenders was introduced – a major achievement for Lucy and the Auckland society.

Lucy and Richard's second child, Amey, named after Amey Daldy as Emma had suspected, became a surrogate mother to her brothers from an early age – long before she became a war-time nurse and anti-war campaigner with the International League for Peace and Freedom, collecting signatures just as her mother Lucy had done. She married late, bore her child at a time when she would have been considered too old, and died while her daughter was still in her teens. Another sad loss to the world.

Amey's daughter, Grandma Kate, had similarly worked with the Peace League in the 1950s and had passed on the family passion for defending women's rights to her feminist daughter, Amy. Amy's devastating death would have destroyed a weaker being, but the reason, Emma believed, that Kate had lived longer was because her cause had been her daughter's child, the new Lucy, until she too was lost to her.

According to the newspaper report, the authorities never discovered who killed Aloysius Young, or why. A burglary gone wrong was the official theory and the case slid from the front pages. To Lucy, the mystery remained a bitter canker, but the tragedy gave his daughter the means to become the patron of The Lucy Trust for Women that continued until this day.

* * * * *

Not to be undone and certainly never forgotten, Paige bounced in and out of Emma's world as often as Jess

346

these days. She had changed a lot since they'd first met at the start of the year. She sounded wiser, more perceptive, more patient, and her attitude to her father and her home life had completely turned around.

"Isn't it wonderful," said Paige. "Dad's such a good stick. He's given me all of Mum's stuff before my birthday. He says I've earned it. There's more bits of jewellery, but nothing like the locket and brooch that led us to my grandmothers, but I love it all the same since it belonged to Mum."

She'd also discovered her father was not only a benefactor, but he supported many causes dedicated to women. "He said Mum inspired him so much he'd promised he would not let her work die with her. He took over the trust set up by Great-grandmama Lucy and expanded on it. He's given squillions to women's health."

Emma was delighted to see the girl become a champion of her father at last. Life was looking up.

"I've seen what's possible," Paige said another day. "I've seen optimism and steadfastness. I've seen love in action. I want that in my life, too."

"I'm glad to hear it. But what brought that about?"

"Dad really likes Ryan; says he'll be the making of me. Cheeky old man," she teased, clearly delighted. "Oh, and Cameron and Nicole are engaged."

"That's wonderful news. I'm so happy to hear your family is united thanks to your persistence in finding out about your past."

Paige's eyes opened wide at the thought. "Yeah, it *was* that, wasn't it?"

"That. And seeing what can be achieved when families pull together."

Paige nodded furiously. "And understanding how each generation fought for justice. Just like we're doing today."

"So, what other news in the Frazer household?"

"Dad says he's adding a charitable arm to their business focused on adapting to climate change using sustainable practices, and Cam and Nicole are developing a new environmental management infrastructure plan. Isn't it wonderful?"

"And you?"

"Me." Her eyes gleamed. "I'm going to join the business, and when I've finished my degree I'll manage the charity and, in time, The Lucy Trust. By then we'll have more technological R & D underway and I'll be halfway to achieving my goal. I want to continue their legacy."

"I like the sound of that. And Ryan?" asked Emma, wondering how he'd fit into the picture.

"Him too," grinned Paige. "There's room for everyone. His approach will be different, but his enviro science expertise will be a bonus. He'll probably work in the field as well."

* * * * *

The story was told, and Emma felt a sense of relief, and profound respect and awe for the women in Paige's life. The girl was immensely proud of her long line of so-called 'troublemakers'. A legacy she would never forget, and which would continue for generations to come if she had any say in the matter.

Emma was still editing as Luke stuck his head around the door. "Finished?"

She looked at her closing words and decided she was happy. "I have."

"Then let's celebrate." Luke grinned, holding out his hand, and wrapped her in his embrace. She returned his kiss with longing.

A satisfied client was a huge reward, but true fulfilment came with personal happiness – and she was as happy as anyone could be. Her health was back on track, she and Luke were closer than ever and Rose was their joy. Their future looked bright.

Lucy's Mrs Adams had been right … true love heals all wounds.

Now, after completing Lucy Young's wonderful story, Emma felt ready to tackle the next phase in her career.

* * * * * * * *

Family Tree

Aloysius YOUNG (1842–1893)

Lucy YOUNG (1872–1913) m. Richard HARRIS (1869–1943)

Lewis (1895–1916) – **Amey Kate** (1897–1946) – Lucas (1913–1942)
m. Robert Mills

Kathryn Lucy MILLS *aka Grandma Kate* (1921–2006)
m. Michael WILSON

Amelia Lucy WILSON *aka Amy* (1946–1977)

Lucy Kathryn WILSON (1975–2006)
m. David Fish Frazer

Paige Amelia FRAZER (2003–)

Thank You

If you enjoyed this book, then you should enjoy the two other stories in the series. Or branch out and discover other unforgettable family heritage stories inspired by immigrants seeking a better life in a foreign land.

THE ART OF SECRETS SERIES
dual-timeline stories about discovering your roots.

Book 1 The Art of Secrets
Book 2 Elinor
Book 3 Lucy

THE NEW ZEALAND IMMIGRANT COLLECTION
suspenseful family saga fiction about overcoming the odds.

The Cornish Knot
Portrait of a Man

Brigid The Girl from County Clare
Gwenna The Welsh Confectioner
The Costumier's Gift

The Disenchanted Soldier

Available at
www.amazon.com/vickyadin   www.vickyadin.co.nz

Please consider leaving a customer review.

I'd be delighted if you would sign up for
my newsletter on my website.

Other Books by Vicky Adin

THE ART OF SECRETS SERIES

Emma's willingness to help others discover the mysteries of their past sometimes puts her in harm's way. Yet curiosity spurs her to solve the riddles of her clients' family trees – even the ones where she is threatened and everything she cares about is put in jeopardy.

Emma, the journalist in *The Art of Secrets* (**Book 1**) is a broken-hearted young woman who finally comes to terms with the painful truth about herself, thanks to her adversary, Charlotte Day.

Some years later, in her role as family historian and biographer of other people's family histories, a friend asks Emma to find an ancestor, *Elinor* (**Book 2**).

In *Lucy* (**Book 3**) Emma pursues her passion for revealing secrets, which tests her loyalty to her family and friends while she unravels Paige's intriguing past.

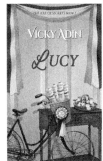

THE NEW ZEALAND IMMIGRANT COLLECTION

If you enjoy multi-generational family sagas, inspired by immigrant stories to a foreign land, then you will love these stand-alone stories set in New Zealand.

Become engrossed in this collection of suspenseful family saga fiction about overcoming the odds.

Journey alongside one of the immigrants as they cross the oceans for a better life, or follow their heirs as they uncover the secrets of bygone days in stories that bring the past alive. You won't be disappointed.

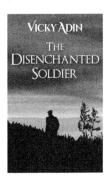
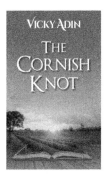
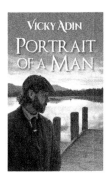

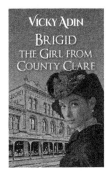
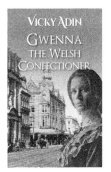

All available at
www.amazon.com/vickyadin   www.vickyadin.co.nz

Author's Notes

Women's Suffrage in New Zealand was attained in September 1893, the first country in the world to grant universal suffrage without barriers or discrimination.

Since the mid-1860s, feminists and social reformers – the likes of Mary Ann Colclough (Polly Plum) (1836–1885) and Mary Ann Müller (1820–1901) – had advocated for women's rights. To be treated as equals. In the late 1870s, and again in 1887, Sir Robert Stout and Sir Julius Vogel submitted bills and amendments extending the vote to female ratepayers only – for them to narrowly fail to pass in Parliament.

By the 1890s, a new generation of suffragists led the charge. (Note the use of the word *suffragists*, who used peaceful methods, rather than *suffragettes*, especially their British and American counterparts, who became more militant, and committed unlawful and violent acts.) The first petitions containing some 9,000 signatures were sent to Parliament in 1891 to again be defeated.

In 1892, women increased their efforts and submitted close to 20,000 signatures. That, too, failed to pass. In 1893, after gathering signatures from nearly a quarter of the adult female European population at that time, a monster petition of over 270 metres in length containing some 32,000 signatures was presented to Parliament by Sir John Hall. It passed by a mere two votes.

The New Zealand ten-dollar banknote is emblazoned with the image of Kate Sheppard (1848–1934) in recognition of her immense efforts to organise and promote the cause of women's franchise through the Women's Christian Temperance Union (WCTU). But she was not the only campaigner at that time.

The article referenced in the storyline, from the *Auckland Star* of 5 July 1892, says Mrs W C (Amey) Daldy presided over the meeting to establish the Auckland Branch of the Women's Franchise League of New Zealand (WFLNZ). (Reporters inevitably referred to women by their husband's initials.) Other speakers putting forward motions and seconding the resolutions included several prominent women such as Mrs William (Lizzie) Rattray, Mrs Kerr-Taylor, Mrs (Annie) Schnackenberg, Miss (Harriet) Morison, Mrs (Elizabeth) Caradus and six more.

Of the men supporters, Sir John Hall was considered their greatest advocate in Parliament, and in attendance were Bishop Dr Cowie, Rev. J Berry and Sir George Grey speaking up for them alongside William Fox and Premier John Ballance, amongst others.

A hundred years later, in September 1993, a memorial was unveiled to honour Sheppard and the other women who fought for the franchise. The bronze bas-relief sculpture stands 2.1 metres high against a five-metre wall in the gardens alongside the Avon River in Christchurch.

Included in the life-size figures are five of the most prominent campaigners: Helen Nicol of Dunedin (WCTU), Kate Sheppard (WCTU Christchurch), Ada Wells (educator), Harriet Morison (WFLNZ Dunedin) and Meri Te Tai Mangakāhia, the first woman to address the Kotahitanga Parliament. Meri asked for women to be given the vote and to sit in the Māori Parliament.

Last but not least, Amey Daldy, Auckland's leading suffragist.

In Auckland, in Te Hā o Hine Place, as Emma described, is a memorial consisting of over 2,000 handcrafted tiles honouring nine of the leading suffragists, including: Amey Daldy, President of the AWFL; Anne Ward (WCTU); Lizzie Rattray, journalist (AWFL); Elizabeth Yates, first female mayor of Onehunga; and Annie Schnackenberg (WCTU). Also mentioned are Elizabeth Caradus (AWFL) and Meri Te Tai Mangakāhia, along with Fanny Brown and Matilda Allsop, two of the first women who enrolled to vote.

The National Council of Women was founded in April 1896 to replace the Women's Franchise League of New Zealand. Its first office holders were heavyweights of the suffrage movement: Kate Sheppard was president; Marion Hatton, Annie Schnackenberg, Margaret Sievwright and Anna Stout were vice presidents; Ada Wells was secretary; and Wilhelmina Sherriff Bain was treasurer.

Many of the league members became NCW members to continue their work in making the lives of women better. We should never forget their names, or their determination. We should continue to honour them and fight for equality and protect women's rights throughout the world.

The Society for the Protection of Women and Children (**SPWC**) was established by Henry Wilding on 25 April 1893, spurred on by issues of child neglect and cruelty. He presided over it until his death in 1916.

The society aimed to help women and children who were the victims of violence and abuse, and to give aid to unmarried mothers and women who had been abandoned by their husbands. It took court proceedings on their behalf and lobbied for changes to the law to give women and children greater protection.

The first 'lady visitor', Elizabeth Porter, was appointed in 1894 to interview complainants, investigate the accusation and keep a register. Some licence has been taken with dates and personnel to include Lucy in the workings of the society and what they achieved.

Today, the society still operates as The New Zealand Federation of Home and Family Societies.

The Suffrage Petition – the 'Monster Petition' – was presented to Parliament in 1893 and is on display at the exhibition, He Tohu, at the National Library of New Zealand, Wellington. It is searchable by surname, town and region, through the New Zealand History website. Maybe your ancestor signed it. Do you know?

Myalgic encephalomyelitis/chronic fatigue syndrome (ME/CFS) – I would like to acknowledge the sufferers of ME/CFS and, in particular, Lee who told me her story about the daily struggle to live with this serious and long-term illness that affects many body systems. People with ME/CFS are often not able to do their usual activities and suffer from severe fatigue and sleep problems, which may confine them to bed.

Emma was lucky. Her illness did not develop into ME/CFS, but there are studies showing that long Covid is possibly linked, and after six months, sufferers risk becoming permanently disabled. Studies also show that people with severe depression can develop psychosis and feel sad and hopeless for most of the day, practically every day, and getting through it feels almost impossible.

Typical symptoms of depression may include: fatigue (exhaustion), disturbed sleep, changes in appetite, feeling worthless and guilty, and being unable to concentrate or being indecisive. Hence Emma's feelings of being a burden and her decision to leave her family.

Genealogy Research – For the uninitiated, genealogy is akin to sleuthing, being a detective, seeking the tiniest details to put together a complete picture. It can be fun, it's certainly addictive and involves a great deal of determination – and snooping. Visiting cemeteries, especially old ones, can reveal a lot of information and is a well-known pastime for many genealogists. There is even a name for them – tombstone tourists, or taphophiles.

I rely on Papers Past, the archived newspapers through the National Library, for a great deal of my information on events, history and sometimes people. Detailed reports on weddings, including the names of all the attendants and guests, and funerals, provide great insight into the workings of society at the time. It's fun to put in an ancestor's name and see if they show up. There are similar options around the world. Trove

(National Library of Australia) is one that is still free; others are paid services.

For history resources, I begin with the New Zealand History website but any genealogist and historian will tell you that three sets of evidence of the same story are needed before you can consider it might be fact.

My genealogy journey began in earnest in the 1990s on a visit to England. I've loved it ever since and continue to discover new and exciting facts along the way. I am currently writing a blog about some of my discoveries on my website www.vickyadin.co.nz.

About the Author

Vicky Adin is a family historian in love with the past. Like the characters in her stories, she too is an immigrant to New Zealand, arriving a century after her first protagonists, and ready to start a new life.

Born in Wales, she grew up in Cornwall until aged 12. Her family emigrated to New Zealand, a country she would call home. Vicky draws on her affinity for these places, in her writing. Fast forward a few years, and she marries a fourth-generation Kiwi bloke with Irish, Scottish and English ancestors and her passion for genealogy flourishes.

The further she digs into the past, the more she wants to record the lives of the people who were the foundations of her new country. Not just her own ancestors, but all those who braved the oceans and became pioneers in a raw new land. Her research into life as it was for those immigrants in the mid-to-late 1800s and early 1900s gave her enough material to write for many years about the land left behind and the birth of a new nation.

Her first book, *The Disenchanted Soldier,* is the most biographical of all her books, inspired by her husband's great-grandfather. For the rest, while the history of the time is accurate, the characters are fictionalised to fit with the events and happenings as they occurred.

Vicky holds an MA(Hons) in English, is a lover of art, antiques, gardens, good food and red wine. She and her husband travel throughout New Zealand in their caravan and travel the world when they can. She hopes younger generations get as much enjoyment learning about the past through her stories, as she did when writing about it.

Acknowledgements

I'm delighted when I can write a contemporary story set against a historical background. We can learn so much from our forebears about resilience, endurance and gratitude. To ensure the history of the period is accurate, I am always thankful for our easily accessible websites such as New Zealand History, and Te Ara: The Encyclopedia of New Zealand, but to find out about the people and how they lived, I turn to the newspaper archives at Papers Past at the National Library of New Zealand, my favourite source of social history.

However, no book comes to fruition without the assistance of many people – editors, designers, readers, library staff, historians, friends, and my family. I am certain that in naming individuals I will miss out some I should have included, so please take it as given – if you have contributed any information, advice, guidance or support, I am deeply grateful.

I would like to especially thank my team of beta readers and critics: fellow authors John Reynolds, who offers a different perspective; Jenny Harrison, my toughest of critics, and my husband Bruce, who knows New Zealand's history better than me. I could not have completed this book without your honesty and insightful suggestions.

I also offer my eternal thanks to my editor, Adrienne Charlton, of AM Publishing New Zealand, for her sharp eye, and her willingness to check and correct every detail to her complete satisfaction. Any errors remaining are mine and mine alone.

My thanks, too, go to Bev Robitai, photographer, for helping me put together vague and disparate ideas for the wonderful cover design, and to Adrienne Charlton for adding her flair.

Printed in Great Britain
by Amazon